I0721656

EASY, SCHMEASY!

BECCA SEYMOUR

RAINBOW TREE PUBLISHING

EASY, SCHMEASY!

FAST BREAK
BOOK 4

BECCA SEYMOUR

RAINBOW TREE PUBLISHING

Zone Defense

No Take Backs | No More Secrets | No Wrong Moves
| No Backing Down

Fast Break

Rules, Schmules! | Facts, Smacts! | Regular Smegular!
| Easy, Schmeasy!

True-Blue

Let Me Show You | I've Got You | Becoming Us |
Thinking It Over | Always For You | It's Not You |
Our First & Last | Next For Us

Outback Boys

Stumble | Bounce | Wobble

Fangs & Felons

Thicker Than Water | Weaker Than Instinct |
Brighter Than Fear | Stronger Than Fate

Stand-Alone Contemporary

Not Used To Cute | High Alert | Realigned |
Amalgamated | Under the Blazing Stars | Best Kind of
Awkward

Ream Short Stories

Shakes & Kisses | Cupcake Crushes

Easy, Schmeasy! © 2024 by Becca Seymour

All rights reserved. No part of this book may be used or reproduced in any written, electronic, recorded, or photocopied format without the express permission from the author or publisher as allowed under the terms and conditions with which it was purchased or as strictly permitted by applicable copyright law. Any unauthorized distribution, circulation or use of this text may be a direct infringement of the author's rights, and those responsible may be liable in law accordingly. Thank you for respecting the work of this author.

Easy, Schmeasy! is a work of fiction. All names, characters, events and places found therein are either from the author's imagination or used fictitiously. Any similarity to persons alive or dead, actual events, locations, or organizations is entirely coincidental and not intended by the author.

For information, contact the author: HELLO@BECCASEYMOUR.COM

EDITING: Hot Tree Editing

COVER DESIGNER: BookSmith Design

PUBLISHER: Rainbow Tree Publishing

E-BOOK ISBN: 978-1-922679-96-3

PAPERBACK ISBN: 978-1-922679-97-0

ALTERNATE PAPERBACK ISBN: 978-1-922679-95-6

AUTHOR'S NOTE

Easy, Schmeasy! is set in Georgia and uses both fictional and real locations and references. Some of the timeline runs alongside the same period as Ty's book, *Facts, Smacts!*, and Leon's book, *Regular, Smegular!* The basketball league in both the Zone Defense and Fast Break world is called the League, not the NBA. While I loosely followed the NBA structure, I created my own league and team names, my own competition names, and took liberties to make my fun, low-angst world work.

TRIGGER WARNINGS: RECOLLECTION OF PHYSICAL ATTACK, HOMOPHOBIC ABUSE BY A PARENT, SPORTS INJURY

THEN...
JUNIOR YEAR

CHAPTER 1
BENTLEY

It burns.

Don't throw up. Don't throw up.

I swallow as I grab my beer. I gulp the contents until the taste of whatever rancid shit Sammy put in the shot disappears.

"Best one yet, huh?" Grinning big, Sammy is the picture of a self-satisfied drunkard.

He looks so damn happy with himself that it's impossible not to shake my head and smile back. That I don't think my stomach will revolt has a lot to do with the smirk.

"It tastes like a coyote took a shit in a dumpster and invited a bunch of skunks along for the ride," I challenge, loving the dramatic parting of his lips and the incredulous gasp he shoots me a little too much.

Sammy is always the heart and soul of every party, but he makes the meanest, most toxic shot combinations. It's as funny as it is endearing, especially since he legit thinks he's the master of his creations.

"Screw you." There's zero heat in his tone. Instead, he thrusts a different shot my way. "Try this one."

I eye the off-green contents. The liquid looks vile.

It's time to retreat.

But Sammy knows my moves. My tells.

Being best friends since the first day of training, when he persuaded me and the other freshmen on the team to join him for a party that same night, has made the past three years interesting and admittedly epic.

He's why college has been the most incredible experience ever and why our team is so close. Our starting five crew especially.

That's all down to Sammy pulling us together and getting us involved.

He's also why I'm already dreading next year being our final one at Brixham U.

And with only a month until the end of the school year, I don't want the shot he's encouraging me to drink.

The last thing I want is to miss a thing by passing out from the radiation poisoning in a glass he's hovering in front of me.

"Nuh-uh."

With a gleam still in his eyes, he steps into my space and wraps an arm around my shoulders. I hold back the shudder of awareness—something that's been building for the past year, truth be told. He follows up with a smacking kiss on my temple and squeezes my shoulder, and fuck if I wouldn't mind being wrapped up in him all night.

It's his "Come on, sweetheart" that catches my breath.

My gaze snaps to his. He's so close, I can see the touch of gray in his startling green irises even in the low lighting of the party. When our eyes make contact, I first see his surprise. Yeah, the "sweetheart" is something new for us.

The arm he puts around me and the regular touches aren't so unusual.

Though they tend to be only for me.

It's a wayward, dangerous thought and should be confusing, since I've never given a guy a sideways glance. Not ever.

Until Sammy.

But he's an asshole, and I'm sure his mission—

whether he's aware of it or not—is to be as many of my firsts as possible.

Not that that's what I think is happening here. But fuck if the way we're standing so close that our breaths are exchanging doesn't make me wonder if I'm wrong.

"What the hell is that?"

Leon's question makes us jump. The contents in the shot glass spill over the edge, coating Sammy's hand.

Sammy's quick to respond. "Jerkoff, look what you've made me do."

With his arm still around my back, he angles to look at me, demanding my attention. I give it willingly—hell, automatically. It's like he's the damn sun: where he goes, I'm hot on his tail, desperate to be pulled into his orbit like he's living, breathing gravity.

His eyebrow arches high, and a smirk slips over his lips as he looks at me. "What do you think, Bentley?"

I don't need further clarification. Not with Sammy.

"Oh, absolutely. A request if ever I heard one." I grin, my heart hammering when Sammy's gaze dips briefly to my lips. It's the barest of movements and doesn't linger, but it takes strength to calm my reaction.

"Here." Sammy thrusts the glass at Leon. "You drink that and manage to tell me the correct ingredients, and I'll do your kitchen duties next week."

Predictably, Leon takes the glass. He hates kitchen duty and is regularly trying to exchange that chore with literally anything else. "Done."

A moment later, we're laughing our asses off as Leon coughs up a lung and fails spectacularly at guessing the contents. We're still giggling like schoolboys when we collapse onto the couch. Kieran has already commandeered one of the armchairs and Tyron another.

My ass has barely touched the cushion before Sammy's stretched out, his head on my lap, as he starts talking to Kieran about his summer work plans.

I'm half paying attention, hyperaware of Sammy being close to my dick. Close? I hold back a snort. Who am I kidding? His head's settled on it, and from how my arm instinctively drapes over him, hand landing on his chest, it's in agreement that it's where it belongs.

And I suppose it is.

Not a single person in our group bats an eye. There's no double take. No raised eyebrow.

Why would there be when this is how Sammy and I are together? We always have been.

If only they knew how much more significant these moments feel to me. How I wish for more.

"Huh?" I all but splutter when I hear my name.

Sammy's head rubs against my cock as he maneuvers to stare up at me. At the sensation, my breath hitches involuntarily.

A moment passes between us when we make eye contact. It's frozen. Our not-so-simple gazes connecting and wide-eyed awareness made even more palpable when my chubbing cock nudges Sammy's head.

A thick swallow from Sammy drags my attention to his bobbing Adam's apple. I wonder what his skin would taste like. If I kissed the column of his neck and sucked lightly, would he like it?

How hard would I need to suck for his dark skin to show a love bite?

He shifts again, and my eyes snap to his. "Kieran wanted to know if we're ready to leave. I'm feeling pretty wasted." Focus unwavering, he turns his head to rub against my dick in a deliberate move if I've ever seen one.

I can't breathe. Can barely think. I certainly can't speak.

Instead, I nod, swallowing loudly enough to capture Sammy's attention once again.

And then I lose his gaze as he peers at the guys, letting them know we're good to leave.

I'm mildly surprised to see Dean sitting on the arm of the other couch. When did he arrive?

To be honest, I shouldn't be all that shocked that he didn't go a whole night without finding his boyfriend, Kieran. Not that anyone beyond our housemates knows the real relationship between our Bears captain and our mascot.

I use my wandering thoughts to distract myself—or, specifically, to calm my hard-on. By the time we're all moving and head outside, my dick's only half hard. Not ideal, but at least a small adjustment conceals it well enough.

With plenty of street lighting around, it makes for an easy walk home. It's still warm despite being late. Summer's just around the corner, and the Georgia air is giving us just a hint of what's to come.

"You good?" Sammy's arm brushes mine as we head down the street. I can already see our off-campus rental.

"Yeah," I say. "Tired, and that last shot is kicking my ass."

I'm sort of telling the truth. I am tired. While basketball season is over, we're still training regularly. It's also close to finals, so I'm studying my ass off.

Sammy's last concoction also made my head spin.

Not that I'm really feeling it anymore.

Between the "sweetheart," the zap of awareness between us, and Sammy knowing he made my dick hard, I'm practically sober. The fuzziness in my head is gone. It's the boldness refusing to leave my bloodstream that's slightly disconcerting. It's making me think about a whole range of impossible things.

Mainly, if I kiss Sammy, what will he do?

I'm not even freaking out. Okay, I know when to call bull. I am a little overwhelmed, but not by the kissing-a-guy thing. Common sense tells me I probably should be. But intellectually, I know damn well that sexuality is nowhere near as clear-cut as far-righters proclaim.

The Kinsey Scale may be old as fuck, but there's a whole lot of relevance and truth to it.

"Thank Christ there's no training tomorrow." Sammy chuckles. "Coach would take one look at us and make us do his hangover regimen."

My lips twitch because Sammy is totally right. Coach may be epic, but he can be sadistic as hell. "You got plans beyond studying tomorrow?"

"Nah. I have an assignment due Tuesday. I need to get a move on with it."

I nod, a fresh tingle traveling along my skin when our arms brush for the hundredth time.

Kieran's walking ahead and reaches the door first. He unlocks it and lets Dean in before him. As soon as they're across the threshold, Kieran's hauling Dean close and kissing the shit out of him.

My stomach tightens in envy.

I glance away, letting Sammy in ahead of me and working hard not to lean into him to capture his scent one last time before I head to bed. Tyron goes to the kitchen, while Leon stumbles up the stairs.

As the last one in, I turn and lock the door.

I need a moment to pull myself together.

Sammy's my best friend. He also presents as straight. Maybe it's all in my head, this spark between us. Perhaps this awareness is just one-sided.

Dean's and Kieran's footsteps are gone, the sudden hush punctuated only by the closing of a bedroom door. Tyron's moving something in the kitchen, and I suspect Leon's collapsed on his bed. Probably fully clothed.

The hallway turns quiet.

With a shaky exhale, I press my forehead to the locked front door. What the hell am I going to do about all these trapped feelings? I rub my chest.

I don't want to lose Sammy. I can't. It's cliché as fuck, but the man means the world to me.

What I need to do is suck it up and get my ass to bed. When alcohol isn't flowing through my veins, my emotions will be easier to manage. A good night's sleep will help with that.

I turn, and the hallway is truly empty.

Sammy's not here, but what did I expect—for him to be standing behind me, ready to capture me in his arms and finally press his mouth to mine? *Jesus.* I release a self-deprecating snort.

I push away from the door, kick off my shoes, and leave them in the pile next to the overflowing shoe rack. I walk up the staircase, keeping my tread light. So, what, Sammy didn't say good night? I'm such a sucker for his attention, but that's on me.

I make a pit stop at the bathroom. I can't be bothered to shower, but I relieve myself, then brush my teeth and wash my face and pits. I leave the light on in the upstairs hallway, since Tyron is still up, and go into my bedroom.

The bedside lamp's on. Confusion pulls my brows low. I don't remember—

My heart jackhammers as the door closes with a quiet snick, and my gaze lands on Sammy. He's here. Next to my desk. He's ramrod straight and not moving. Well, his chest is heaving. His gaze locks with mine, and his lips part before he presses them together and swallows deeply.

Holy fucking shit.

Words escape me. The hell am I meant to do? How do I react?

What the fuck is going on?

Hope blooms in my chest, but I'm too terrified to give it room and space to grow.

Sammy being in my bedroom isn't new. We're together more than we're apart. The two of us falling asleep and sharing a bed isn't the most unusual thing ever.

But this is different. I know it is.

The air crackles, that gravitational pull between us sparking to life.

I swear, the way he looks at me, it's as if he can see right through to my soul.

His presence fills the room, dominating the space in the way only Sammy can manage. But where there's usually laughter between us, now it's all tension. It's palpable and thickening as each breath saws out of me.

I can't tear my gaze away from him. I should speak, right? Say something? Ask if he's okay?

But I don't get a chance. He's moving, one slow step in front of another.

My breath catches when our chests touch, and then he steals it from me as his mouth captures mine. And I'm floating, adrift on tongues and lips and overwhelming sensation as I willingly fall into the kiss.

As our lips mold together, time seems to halt. Every nerve in my body ignites and burns with an intensity that threatens to consume me. If that's the case, I'll go willingly and surrender completely.

What wouldn't I do to have Sammy like this?

CHAPTER 2

SAMMY

PANIC CONSUMES ME.

I'm covered in our combined cum, my lips are kiss swollen, and while I should be resting in sated bliss, my brain is screaming at me.

Get out. Get out. Protect Bentley.

He knows it too—that I'm freaking out.

As soon as my muscles stiffen, his hand stops stroking lazy patterns over my back. Sensibly, he doesn't say anything. Doesn't call me out.

How the hell am I going to get out of his room and away?

I don't think I'm going to be spotted by anyone, as the house is silent, and I suspect everyone is fast asleep. Though that's not my real concern. I wish it was.

There's only one thing to do, and even as I formulate my plan, my heart becomes leaden—so heavy that it's a struggle to move and take action.

But I have to. For both our sakes.

"Holy shit, the room's spinning." I add an exaggerated slur for good measure. "I'm gonna throw up."

I'm not completely lying. The thought of what I've allowed to happen means I'm close to spewing.

I push away and stumble once I'm standing, tugging up my jeans that are tucked under my ass. Mrs. Jacobs, my sixth-grade drama teacher, would be embarrassed for me. To be clear, for my shit acting skills rather than my exposed dick. I grab my T-shirt and yank it on, not giving a shit that it'll soak up our cum.

"You okay?"

I wince at the concern in Bentley's voice.

"You need help getting to the bathroom?"

I shake my head, refusing to look at him. I'm a coward, but he doesn't know what could happen.

"Sammy."

Fuck.

I turn to look at him. He's done up his pants, which I'm grateful for. I have no right to see him so vulnerable. Questions fill his gaze, but it's no good. I need to do this. For him.

He might not fully understand it, but he knows some of my family history. He knows my biological dad, Trevin, is still serving time for nearly beating a teenager to death. The court called it a hate crime. And it was, no question.

Bentley's the only person at school who knows Trevin was sent away for beating a sixteen-year-old within an inch of their life because they're gay. And from the look of worry in his gaze, I suspect he's beginning to understand why I'm freaking.

"I'm good. Just drunk. I need to wash up and crash. See you in the morning, yeah?" I don't glance away—he at least deserves eye contact.

A second later, he nods, and I exhale and finally smile. It's not totally fake. I'm relieved as fuck that he's letting me escape.

And escape I do.

I hightail it out of his room and head straight for the shower. In no time at all, I'm under the hot spray and desperately trying not to think about the weight of his cock in my palm. How good and right it felt.

When he'd touched me, taken me in his large hand, and pumped my dick in long, slow strokes, my eyes had rolled back in my head. Somehow, I'd held on for dear life, kissing him with all the pent-up need and desire I've been holding back since freshman year.

Yeah, *that's* how long I've been fantasizing about and falling for my best friend.

I've been able to bottle it up too.

A humorless snort escapes me as I duck under the water. This is so fucked-up.

Bentley means everything to me. He's hard-working and funny and quiet and gentle. The man's never encountered a day of violence or had to call the cops on his dad.

He's also strong and so fucking kind. And he gets me, as in *really* gets me.

It's why he let me walk.

I pour shower gel into my palms and soap off the cum sticking to the hairs on my stomach and my pubes.

It was a few months back that I first noticed Bentley started to look at me differently. Having his attention is heady, and honestly, I'm amazed I've been able to restrain myself for so long.

But tonight… hell if tonight that all went flying out the window. How could it not when I felt his thickening cock under my head?

I should regret being with him, but I don't. Not really. What I *do* regret is how I'm going to hurt him, as now that I've had a taste—a legit forbidden fruit dilemma—I don't think I can stay away.

And I should.

A flash of a bloody face made unrecognizable from multiple blows tries to creep into my mind. I squeeze my eyes closed, not wanting the memory to invade. Not now.

I hadn't known where to touch Jamaal as he'd lain unconscious on the blood-soaked ground. Every inch of his black skin had been stained red. His lips, which were wrapped around me when Trevin found us together, had been maimed.

I'd come off lucky.

I took a beating, but one thing to be said for my old man, he knew I was looking at a basketball scholarship. No way would he mess with a potential payday.

As soon as the court hearing was over—Trevin being sentenced to ten years—Jamaal had moved to another state with his parents. The last I heard, he was at college somewhere out east, but that was after a year of extensive physical therapy, and he definitely wouldn't be playing basketball again.

"Fuck." I clench my fists and consider pounding them into the tiled wall. Only thoughts of what Trevin did stop me.

I'll never be like him. Not ever.

I have Mom and my stepdad to thank for that.

With a heavy exhale, I press my forehead against the shower tiles.

Life is so fucked-up at times. I hate that it is. Resent it. I want to grab onto happiness with Bentley, but what if it happens again? If not by Trevin when he's released and finds out, then by some other homophobic asshole.

It'll be my fault. Completely. Wholly.

"I've got to do this." Maybe speaking aloud will make me believe it—that this is how it's got to be.

Pushing away from the wall, I scrub my palm over my face. It was a onetime thing, and I can control my urges. I have to.

All I need to do is focus on school and continue being Bentley's best friend.

I've got this.

I'M FULL OF SHIT.

How quickly I forget and break my promises, but Bentley is so easy to fall for, to be with.

Another night out, but this time, it's not a wild party, rather a team get-together, complete with some added friends. We're all too busy studying to make the most of the unapproved extracurriculars this year.

But still, I've had a couple of beers, and I can't take my eyes off him.

Do I need the drinks to take my fill? That's a hard no, as every time he makes a move, I'm always viscerally aware of him. What the alcohol does is lower my inhibitions—dangerously so. It makes me question why I'm holding back.

That night last week was hands down the hottest experience I've ever had. The two of us came so hard that the memory is never far from my mind. The thing is, I know he liked it just as much as I did. I've also seen his covert looks when he thinks no one is watching, but since I always am, it's not surprising that our gazes connect more than is wise.

Unable to stay away from where Bentley's talking to Leon, I swipe another beer from the kitchen counter and, in a few strides, reach his side.

His smile is immediate, genuine. I relax in his presence, my heart not sure how to react. It wants to punch hard while I bask and settle in the comfort I feel being close to Bentley. My heart's reaction seems an accurate summary of how I'm failing at figuring out what I can have, because I absolutely know what —or who—I want.

But actually exploring this thing between us fucking terrifies me.

Leon's talking about the upcoming League draft. He gives me an up-nod and eyes my palms.

I chuckle and show him I have nothing but a beer as he continues talking. No shots tonight, as it's not that kind of party.

The thought pulls me up short.

How the hell can I blame booze for falling into Bentley's arms if I've only had a couple of beers? The short answer is, I can't. There's a long-ass answer and argument to that as well, but I'm ignoring it.

"Actually, my creative juices are flowing. I think I should concoct something a little special," I say, interrupting Leon. "I'll be back."

I bounce my brows and turn away from Leon's "Not for me" and Bentley's "Fuck no."

I flip them off as I go, though I'm more than okay with their decision, especially since I'm a lying liar who lies, as I have no intention of making anything.

Pathetic, I know, but at this point, with my pulse beating faster just thinking about Bentley, and since we've already established that I'm full of shit, I'm willing to do almost anything for a chance to press my lips to his.

Even if nothing else happens, that's okay.

I hang out in the kitchen, avoiding eye contact with anyone. The last thing I want is to get trapped, and when I see Holly heading my way, I know it's time to leave and return to Bentley.

Our gazes connect instantly as soon as I leave the kitchen. Bentley's smile is swift, and I wonder if he's struggling not to sweep a look over my body, 'cause I certainly am finding it difficult.

"Where's Leon?" I ask when I reach his side, adding a little wobble for good measure.

"He saw you coming and thought you may have a shot glass with you."

I chuckle and shake my head. "There's no accounting for taste."

"True that."

A loud cheer erupts from the kitchen, catching our attention. Before I get the chance to peer back at Bentley, Holly's there, her gaze set on me.

Fuck it all to hell. She's a nice enough girl, but she's been looking to hook up for a while now. For obvious reasons, I'm just not interested.

"You wanna head outside?" Bentley asks, coming to my rescue. I have little doubt he's seen Holly too.

I bob my head and follow him, as he's already making the move to leave.

As we step out into the backyard, we silently head over to the furniture. It's battered but feels stable enough as I ease onto the seat.

"Holly's still interested, huh?"

I cast Bentley a scrunched-face look and shrug. "Either way, I'm not interested, and she can do better."

A frown appears on his face. "Better how, exactly?"

My frown matches his as I shrug again. "Not sure why I said that."

But it doesn't mean it's not true.

I'm not looking for sympathy or reassurance from Bentley. If anything, he's the last person who should be coming to my defense, considering how I left him with our combined cum drying on his belly last week.

His tone is firm, taking on a gruffness that sends a shiver down my spine as he says, "You know that's bullshit, right?"

"I was kidding," I lie, wanting to move away from my flippant comment. "I'm just buried with my exam schedule." I knock my shoulder into his and change the subject. "Three weeks. Then we can finally breathe again."

I really am a liar this evening. In three weeks, I'll go the whole summer without seeing Bentley. That'll mean the opposite of breathing for me. Sure, I won't be stressed by finals, but he offers a calming, quiet presence like no one else.

While he nods, he eyes me in a way that lets me

know he's not buying whatever bull I'm selling. As always, because he's a better guy than me, he doesn't call me out.

"How's your final design coming along?" I ask.

It's dark outside. While there's light spilling out of one of the windows, there are no outdoor lights on. We're lucky to have the tiny yard to ourselves. It probably means Troy, who lives here, didn't want the small party spilling out. It's not like we're raging out here. We're not even fucking. Though the thought has merit, that's one hell of a dangerous move I'm not bold enough to risk.

But it's nice out here, just the two of us.

The darkness eases something in my chest. Probably because I can stare at him without anyone seeing me do it.

"Good," he says with a nod, and I smile.

The landscape design he's been working on is fucking awesome. The last time he showed me, I'd been impressed. Sure, I don't know anything about outside spaces or trees or flowers or any of that stuff, but it doesn't mean I can't respect his talent.

And even though this project's for make-believe clients, it doesn't stop his joy.

"You know the winding path I incorporated with all the vibrant flowers?"

I nod, and he's quick to continue, "Well, it now

leads to cozy seating under a canopy of trees. I've researched natural materials for seating, but I wanted to include some sort of cushion that's not going to get moldy." He gestures excitedly with his hands, and his eyes sparkle with enthusiasm.

It's hard not to lean in and kiss his smiling lips, but that's not what this is about. Not now, right as he's describing his final project.

"It's the perfect space where the employees of the firm can escape the hustle and bustle of everyday life, you know? And specifically their manic workdays."

My heart flutters as Bentley paints a vivid picture, and I honestly can't wait to see the developments he's introduced.

His passion for his project is infectious, and fuck if I don't hang on to his every word.

"The sustainability of the garden has been the trickiest but most interesting part."

"And you think that's what you'd like to focus on still, when we're out of here?" He's mentioned it before, but a lot can change as new projects are assigned.

"For sure." He bobs his head and smiles. "I don't expect it'll happen straightaway. Even though I'll leave with a degree, it's likely I'll still take a job with someone like Grady. I know that's the physical side of landscaping, but it's still on-the-ground experience. I'm hoping Grady will be interested in giving me a chance to work with clients who want real design projects, but I won't be knocking down a job."

"You'll get your chance," I say with complete confidence. "And if someone won't give it to you, you'll make it happen yourself."

It'll take collateral to start his own business, but that doesn't mean it's impossible.

Hell, I could work every hour and save enough—

I cut my thoughts off and swallow hard.

Planning a future when I'm not truly living in the present doesn't scream *good idea*.

I shove the frustrating thoughts aside. Bentley's still grinning, and I don't want to be the reason his smile disappears.

"One day, maybe. I just need to figure out where I want to be to do that."

Surprise has me frowning. "You don't want to head back home?" That's where Grady, the owner of the landscaping company he's worked for the past two summers, is based. It's not far from his parents' house.

He shrugs, and while he meets my eyes, his expression shutters a little. "I'm not completely tied to San Antonio."

I don't know what to say. This is the first time he's

indicated his plan isn't solidly formed. I settle on "Okay. There's plenty of time to figure things out."

His gaze flicks around my face before settling on my lips, but then he glances away into the darkness. "Yeah. A lot can happen in a year."

The sound of smashing glass startles us both.

"You think we need to check that out?" Bentley seems reluctant to leave our bubble. I feel the same.

"Maybe it's time we make our escape. Those shots hit me pretty hard."

Fuck it all to hell, as that's where I'm going to end up.

Sure, I sipped at something toxic in the kitchen to at least get the scent of potent booze on my breath, but still….

"Come on." I stand, as does Bentley. "You wanna shoot the guys a text or go inside to—"

His shaking head cuts me off. The movement shouldn't be filled with anything other than an obvious response, but the air practically sparks between us. My breathing turns choppy, and we seriously do need to leave.

As we escape through the side gate, Bentley sends a message to our group text. I ignore the notification alert in my pocket and focus on putting one foot in front of the other.

What I should do is lock myself in my room alone

when we get back, but Bentley's knuckles brush mine, and goose bumps dance across my skin.

I can't make this thing between us real. I can't acknowledge it. But maybe it'll be okay. Bentley's on board—or at least from the way he hovers at his bedroom door once we're inside and silently urges me into his room, I think he's more than okay with what's happening.

CHAPTER 3
BENTLEY

END OF JUNIOR YEAR

Tomorrow, at the ass crack of dawn, I'm heading home for the summer.

Finals ended two days ago, and as keen to catch up with my folks as I am, the thought of not seeing Sammy for a couple of months hurts my gut.

The last four weeks have turned my world on its head in the absolute best way possible. Well, almost the best way.

Before Sammy gives in to this craving between us, he's always knocking back shots and downing beer like there's a hops shortage. I don't think it helps that this summer, he's been coerced into visiting his bio dad.

At least his mom and stepdad have his back.

Sammy's already told me they don't want him to visit the prison, but he's going regardless. It's Trevin and the shit he pulled in the attack against Sammy's high school friend because of his sexuality that weighs Sammy down. Christ only knows how he's really coping by hooking up with me. And I wish I did know, but he refuses to talk about it.

Not that I've pushed.

I won't do that to him.

It might also be self-preservation guiding me. I don't want Sammy to bolt or to call this thing between us off. I crave the nights he comes to me. Hell, I'm the first to agree to a night out, knowing it's the only way Sammy will allow us to get together. Not that he's ever truly drunk or seriously impaired.

Still, it's seriously shit, but I'm whipped.

I shake my head at myself as I stuff my dirty laundry into a trash bag. Whipped? It's a lot more than that.

My heart no longer lives in my chest. I pulled it out and gift wrapped it before handing it over to Sammy. I did so a long time ago.

Before our first kiss. Long before the first time the chemistry fizzed between us like Mentos in cola.

Honestly, it's likely that I gave it to him the first time I heard him laugh. I just didn't know it at the time.

"You about done?"

As always, my breath catches. Sammy's leaning against the frame of my open doorway. He peers around the room with a look on his face I'm struggling to decipher.

"What's wrong?" Sure, I may not ever talk about the nights of stolen kisses and cum with Sammy, but I don't hold back anywhere else.

"Just already wishing this summer was over."

Not for the first time, I say, "It's still not too late to change your mind and head home with me. Grady would let you work the same hours as me. He's always looking for extra hands with landscaping projects." The pay for laboring as a casual employee isn't all that great, but it's likely the same as he'll get busing tables at the diner he works at every summer break.

Stepping fully into my room, he searches for an empty place to sit. Since the place is a mess while I'm trying to get myself organized, he makes a beeline for my bed. It's all I can do to stay put as he picks up my training jersey and falls back onto my mattress with a huff.

He did something similar four nights ago, fueled by booze and high from my kisses.

"Don't tempt me."

But what if I want to?

I keep a tight grip on my thoughts and offer a smile. "If you change your mind, you can always head on over. Open-door policy, remember?" My parents think he's awesome and know we're thick as thieves.

"Thanks, man. You know how it is back home." His shrug is carefully casual, which means I'm not buying it. "Denzel messed up a couple of weeks back. Mom wants me to spend some time with him."

I bob my head and stuff the last pair of dirty sweatpants into the trash bag before I move onto my bed. Settling with my back against the headboard, I don't even bother to hold back my smirk when Sammy eyes me before shuffling over to sit at my side.

His heat against my arm, against my legs, settles some of the need inside me.

I swear, I wasn't this needy for human contact growing up. This is all Sammy. And I love every time we touch and hug. It's something we've always done. Sammy gives affection freely.

After seeing him with his family the first time when we were freshmen, I understand why. The whole family is super close, even with Leroy, their stepdad. Which makes sense, since I think he's been their dad since Sammy was, like, five or six or something.

His mom has this whole hug-and-hold-tight thing she does, and Sammy and his siblings throw around "love yous" alongside driving each other to distraction unlike any family I've ever known.

Hell, I love my folks, but that's so not us.

And until Sammy came along, I didn't realize how nice it is to be wrapped up in so much affection.

"Denzel will be fine. He's a good kid. We all mess up. It's the whole beauty of being young—having room to screw up every now and then." I follow up with a nudge, which earns me a smile. "And you know," I start, sure my parents will be fine with me offering, "if you want to visit, bring Denzel with you. It might do him good."

Sammy angles toward me so he can see my face. Fuck, he's beautiful.

"You wouldn't mind? Or your folks?"

I shake my head. "'Course I wouldn't mind. And you know my parents love you."

His grin is back. "I did warn my mom that they'd be up for adopting me."

"I'm surprised she hasn't called mine and tried to get the paperwork set up."

Sammy snorts. "She considered it. Thought it would be great for me to be out from beneath her feet. Already started to plan out what she can do with my bedroom."

I shake my head. He's so full of shit. Not only does he share a bedroom with Denzel, but his mom is the ultimate protective mother.

"You mind if I think about it? See what Denzel's really been up to? I know for a fact that he hasn't been telling me everything. Taking him away with us and putting him to work laboring may be the kick in the ass he needs."

"Absolutely." I glance around my room. It really looks like a tornado's been through here. How the hell I'm going to get this done and be ready to head to tonight's party is beyond me.

"Come on. Ass up."

I clamp my lips together, stopping myself from offering myself up to him. Hell, it's not even as though I like the thought of bottoming. But for Sammy, I'd try it.

"Let's get your room sorted." As he hauls himself off my mattress, Sammy studies my room. His gaze lands on me before he latches on to my arm and tugs me to stand. "I have no idea how you've accumulated so much shit this past year."

I snicker. "Me either." Though I'm something of a hoarder, so honestly, I'm not all that surprised.

"You go through your designs and all those magazines. I know better than to try to throw something away." He focuses on my desk. "You're taking your Mac, right?"

"Yeah." I enjoy designing landscapes too much to be without my computer.

"Cool. I'll get that packed up for you."

"Thanks," I say as I head to the pile of sketches in the corner of my room. We're seriously lucky the landlord lets us keep this place over the summer for a fraction of the price. Not having to pack up and move out completely is one hell of a relief.

Together, we organize my room, shooting the shit while Sammy regales me with some of the things he and his two kid brothers got up to over the years.

By the time we're done, we're exhausted. The last thing I want is to head out tonight, especially as the plan is to be on the road by six in the morning.

I wipe my dirty hands on my sweatpants. They're already filthy, so a bit more isn't going to hurt any.

Sammy's chuckle catches my attention. His focus is on me, his gaze roaming my face. "You look like you stepped out of *Mary Poppins* or something."

My brows shoot high, and amusement settles in my chest. "Are you comparing me to a chimney sweep?"

Admittedly, the pack of charcoal pencils under my bed broke free, so I kinda made a mess.

"Well, it would need to be one wide-ass chimney to fit your—"

I launch a pillow at him.

"What? I was talking about your shoulders." Glee fills his gaze, brightening his eyes.

I shake my head. "Whatever, asshat. I could question how often you sit by yourself watching *Mary Poppins*." I don't say anything about how I know there's a chimney sweep in the movie.

"Have you met my mom?" he sasses. "If death by watching too many musicals was a thing, she'd have an empty nest by now. She made us watch every singing, dancing movie going. Saves up every year to go see one at the theater at Christmas. I'd complain, except it makes it so damn easy to buy gifts for her."

My heart melts a little at the affection in his voice when he talks about his mom.

"Next time I see her, I'm going to ask for the photos of the performances you were in as a kid." I grin, wondering why I haven't pestered his mom for them before now.

"Like fuck you are. Those images will be deleted or burned."

"That just makes me want to see them more."

Sammy shakes his head at me as he makes his way to the door. "The guys want to head out in an hour." He peers back at me, shoulders relaxed and smile carefree. "You need to shower."

I roll my eyes. "So do you." There's a smudge of dust on his cheek. Before, I would have wiped it away, but with everything that's been happening between us, I'm hyperaware of every single time we touch.

Fortunately, Sammy's not so shy and is just as tactile as always. It's a relief he hasn't pulled away.

A yawn escapes, and I rub a hand over my face, no doubt smearing the dust I suspect is littering my skin.

"None of that."

"Urgh." I flop back on my mattress. It's so comfortable and even more tempting to stay here for the rest of the night. But I don't want that unless Sammy's at my side.

Okay, that's bull. It'll be the perfect way to end the school year if he's under me, but no way is that going to happen unless I go out.

Lifting my head to check if Sammy's still here, as he hasn't said a thing in the past minute, I see him in front of the closed door. His lids are low, and there's definite jaw clenching going on.

Holy shit, his gaze is on my stomach. My tee's ridden up, revealing an expanse of skin that he trailed his tongue over for the first time ever last week.

I dare not speak, unwilling to spook him, but it doesn't matter. His expression shutters, any hint of lust disappearing before I fully blink. Instead, his usual carefree smile is back as our gazes connect.

"No falling asleep. It's the last night we can all be together for a couple of months."

Us. From the look he quickly covered, that's what he really means, right? *Us and not the whole household?*

Even though my heart's beating erratically, and I know I'm likely getting way ahead of myself for wishing for a time we can be open about what's happening between us, I roll my eyes and collapse once more onto my back.

"An hour. I got it." I wave him away, needing some time to regroup even though I hate to see him go.

Two months is a long-ass time to not see each other. It always is.

But this time, it's different.

This time, I'm afraid that when we see each other again, there are going to be no more secret rendezvous. Sure, my heart aches a little, but hooking up with Sammy is a high I never want to come down from.

I reach for the clothes on my bed, wanting to tidy them away. I move a couple of items and frown.

My training jersey is missing.

With a heavy thud from my heart, my head snaps to the door where Sammy just left. My gut tightens before it fizzes and a smile splits my lips.

Sammy took my jersey.

I collapse back onto my mattress with a sigh that is all swoons. This is one of a hundred reasons why it's impossible to let Sammy go and why I so desperately want more with him.

A sappy grin remains on my face as I finally get to work finishing off my room. I wonder if he'll wear it over the summer. Hell, maybe he'll sleep with the thing. My heart flips over a little wildly.

Maybe I should sneak into his room and see if I can steal a shirt of his.

CHAPTER 4

SAMMY

SUMMER BREAK

THE ACHE IN MY MUSCLES FEELS SURPRISINGLY GOOD.

God, I needed this.

I stand straight and arch my back, wiping the sweat off my brow. The sun is fierce and high in the sky. It means it's close to lunch. A quick glance in Bentley's direction, and I forget to breathe.

At some point this morning, he took off his shirt. Usually, I'd grumble at him for not wearing sunscreen, but he's in a large shaded area, planting a flower bed. His hands are covered in soil, and as he pats down some earth, he turns to my brother and laughs at whatever Denzel is saying to him.

Bentley's so good at this—settling Denzel and making sure he feels involved. No one would think he's an only child. But maybe that's the reason why he's so good with my brother. He has a patience I sometimes struggle with. Plus, he's super calm and has that quiet confidence that seems to put everyone at ease.

"Lunch," Mateo, the site manager, calls out.

Perfect timing, too, as I was caught up in watching the way Bentley's biceps flexed.

I take off my leather gloves and stuff them into my back pocket before doing a quick sweep of the area to make sure I haven't left any tools lying around. Confident I haven't missed anything, I wait for Bentley and Denzel as they head my way.

I make sure to smile at my brother, happy he's smiling despite the smudges of dirt on his skin and how soiled his clothes are. Back home, he wouldn't be caught dead like this. He's all about image, and while I get it, I really hope that by having some space away from his friends and from school in general this summer, he'll start to gain some perspective.

It was a no-brainer, taking Bentley up on his offer to come and stay awhile. Terry at the diner was a bit annoyed at me, but he's a good guy and knows my mom well, so he didn't kick up too much fuss when I explained I was heading to Texas for three weeks with Denzel.

Denzel grins back before he tugs out his phone.

My attention shifts to Bentley, still shirtless and looking sinfully sexy as fuck. His muscles are cut and a fair bit bigger than mine. And fuck if I don't love it when his weight is pressed against me.

Not that we've done any of that over the ten days I've been here.

While my dick's constantly hard for him, being around him is enough. It was before hooking up, and it is now, especially after the initial two weeks of not seeing him.

I'll appreciate Bentley in every way imaginable. While at his parents' house with my brother playing a fifteen-year-old chaperone, it means we're best friends. Period.

"You coping okay?" He tilts his head and does a cursory sweep over my body before making eye contact.

While I feel the heat of his gaze as it licks over my skin, I know he's checking for injuries.

Seriously, I don't think anyone on the crew believes I'm a kick-ass athlete, not with the number of mishaps I've had.

Just yesterday I fell into a rosebush. I have the scratches to prove it. It hurt like a fucker, but Bentley going into nurse mode and cleaning and applying ointment to my scratches made it worth it.

Two shifts before that, we were finishing packing

up, and I went ass over head when pushing the wheelbarrow up a ramp. The manure I fell into made Denzel laugh his head off at me as he hosed me down before I was allowed in the work truck to head to the main depot.

"I'm good." I roll my eyes and shake my head. I won't tell him about the close call I had with the shears. Not that it would have been my fault. Bentley is a constant distraction. Every time I hear his deep laughter, it's impossible to not seek him out.

"Let's keep it that way this afternoon too." He nudges my shoulder with his as we walk together toward the parked truck where our cooler is.

Rather than answer him, I check on Denzel, who's walked ahead to catch up with his new friend. Mateo's son Hector is working on his dad's crew this summer and is the same age as Denzel. He also seems like a really good kid.

Tomorrow, we're going to spend the day at the water park, and Hector is going to come with us. I have everything crossed that Denzel will get into the headspace that smoking joints and hanging out at the abandoned factory a few miles from home isn't all that. The kid is growing up too damn fast and has stopped finding fun in legit things to be doing when hanging out with his friends.

It's not even like he doesn't have a great group.

But apparently, a new kid joined his grade a few months back, and Denzel started to get it into his head that skateboarding at the park or spending time at the arcade was no longer cool enough. Or whatever word fifteen-year-old kids use these days.

And fuck if I don't feel old just thinking that.

Hell, when my mom and stepdad came home from the hospital with Denzel, it was the first time I'd felt even an ounce of responsibility. I remember all too clearly thinking how lucky he was to have two awesome parents. Sure, I call Leroy Dad, but Trevin left a blemish that's been impossible to scrub clean. And back then, when I was seven, I promised myself that I wouldn't let my brother go anywhere near assholes like Trevin.

Me being here is one way I can keep that promise.

"How's Denzel doing?" I ask, slowing my steps till I pause and face Bentley. I don't want my brother to hear me checking up on him.

"Great. No grumbling or complaining. He's looking forward to the water park tomorrow."

Warmth fills my chest. Thank fuck. He was a surly asshole the first couple of shifts until Hector started talking to him about football. I hadn't even sneered over the fact that they were almost creaming over the upcoming season rather than salivating over the Basketball League draft. I was just glad the kids had something in common and Denzel seemed happier for it.

"Excellent. We still meeting up with some of your high school buddies tonight?" My stomach flips. I don't especially want to be sharing Bentley with anyone. I'm a selfish fucker. But a couple of beers and sneaking into his room tonight? My dick twinges and my pulse picks up speed, liking the possibility more than I should.

Sure, spending any time with him is incredible, but we're only here for a little while longer, and having one taste could tide me over.

That makes it sound like a future with me being all up in his business next year. I swallow hard as the familiar lump of frustration forms in my throat.

Focusing on the present needs to be all I'm concerned about. Otherwise, I can't stand looking at myself in the mirror.

"Yeah, at eight. We won't go too crazy, not with the water park tomorrow."

I nod. "Makes sense. Slides and heights with a hangover sounds like a pile of shit."

Bentley chuckles, and we finally make it to the truck. Denzel's already inhaling a sandwich and looks to have almost finished the potato chips. There's also an empty candy wrapper next to him.

"Hell, kid. Grab an apple too. Geez."

Denzel flips me off, rolls his eyes at me, and angles back toward Hector and whatever he's watching on his phone.

"He told you." Bentley passes me a sandwich with a smirk and indicates he's heading toward one of the large trees offering shade. I have no clue what type of tree it is. Bentley did tell me, but retaining tree names isn't easy.

Hell, add in Latin names and it's even more confusing.

I bob my head, swipe a couple of bottles of water, and settle next to him, my ass landing on the soft grass.

"It's always entertaining when I hear you offering nutritional advice." Bentley smirks before taking a large bite of his sandwich. A groan of satisfaction spills out of him, and I take too much delight not only in the sound but that I made the chicken salad sandwiches this morning.

"You need me to leave you alone with that sandwich?" I tease.

His gaze snaps to mine, a soft pink appearing in his cheeks. A chuckle follows before he shrugs. "Hey, it's a good sandwich, and I'm seriously hungry." His eyes all but twinkle as he arches a brow at me.

I hold back my remark that I'll make him all the sandwiches he wants if he continues to make that noise. Instead, I focus on his teasing me about my adventurous palate.

Adventurous palate. I barely hold back my snort of amusement. Truth is, half the weird combos I try are for shits and giggles. It's just luck that some of them taste fucking delicious. "I swear, there'll be a day when you'll mourn the loss of my cooking. You'll be pleading with me to never leave your kitchen."

Bentley chuckles even as the red on his skin deepens. I ignore the reason why that may be and focus on the sound of his laugh. It's a good laugh. Deep and quiet, it manages to soothe any trace of heaviness that may be sitting on my chest. It does every damn time.

"Peanut butter and pickles." His lips twitch. "I can safely say I'm not going to be chaining you to my kitchen if that's on the menu."

I cringe at the mention of that combination. It absolutely did not work. "That was an unfortunate sandwich, I'll admit. However, I've been thinking of something new that'll blow your mind."

Bentley raises his brow skeptically even as curiosity and amusement gleam in his eyes. "All right, I'll bite. Hit me with it."

Grinning triumphantly, I tug my cell out and open it. The recipe, a legit one with instructions, is one I stumbled upon when looking for things to do in San Antonio. How I ended up on the blog, I have no idea. I bookmarked the shit out of the page, though.

"Banana and bacon delight." I hold my phone out so we can both stare down at the photo. To be fair, the lighting isn't great, and it looks like a lot of mush, but I like both bacon and bananas, so why the hell wouldn't it taste awesome?

His smirk falters, a look of mild horror quickly replacing it. "Banana and bacon? Are you serious?" He doesn't wait for me to respond as he shakes his head and says, "Hell no."

Undeterred, I nod. "Trust me on this. Apparently, it's a 'flavor sensation unlike anything you've ever tasted.'"

Bentley sighs, and I know I've got him as he takes another bite of his sandwich before gesturing for me to continue.

"Okay, so we fry up bacon and make it extra crispy." Just the thought makes me salivate. "Then we slice up the banana and—"

"Please don't tell me you fry the banana in bacon fat."

"Nope. Fresh out of the skin. You see? Nutritious. You simply stack the bacon and banana. The blog suggests drizzling it with maple syrup."

His expression shifts from horror to mild curiosity. I so have him hooked, and he'll definitely try it.

"Maple syrup?"

I nod.

"Okay, that doesn't sound so bad." He narrows his gaze as he unscrews the lid of his water bottle. "If I try it and it's as godawful as the ranch dressing on watermelon, I'm not responsible for the consequences."

That is not the threat he thinks it is. A thrill shoots through me instead. Rather than respond and the possible shake in my voice give me away, I simply laugh before finishing my food.

We've still got an afternoon of work to get through before we can kick back with a few beers. You never know, at the end of the night, I might see if I can sweet-talk him with banana and bacon and steal a kiss.

CHAPTER 5

BENTLEY

Drinks in hand, I return to the table and place Sammy's bottle in front of him.

He angles his head, gaze catching mine as he smiles. "Thanks."

I nod and sit beside him, taking a moment to listen to the conversation so I can catch up.

"… had to try and smuggle him into the house, but we failed miserably. Mrs. Sandford caught us on the first step and threatened to call our parents." Richie tosses a look my way. "What was your punishment again?"

Richie knows exactly what my punishment was. Asshole. He just finds it hilarious is all.

"Ooh, punishment. Please tell me it was something good." Sammy claps his hands together, and it's impossible to not smile at his enthusiasm.

Since meeting up with my high school friends, Sammy's fit right in. Not that I'm surprised. He's everyone's friend. Hell, that saying about strangers being friends you just haven't met yet, or however it goes? That's totally Sammy.

"Urgh." I shake my head at the memory. "It was the vomit that was the problem."

Sammy's snort is all amusement. "You threw up in the house?"

I wince at the memory. "The first step. It's why we got caught."

"Subtle, man. How old were you?"

"Fifteen. It was Dave's birthday party." I shoot Dave, who's also home from college this summer, the stink eye.

"Hey, it wasn't my idea to ask Leanne's brother to buy the tequila," he answers with a smirk.

"As I live and breathe," Sammy says with a dramatic flair. "Bentley Sandford being a bad influence." Mirth dances in his gaze as he peers at me. "I need all the stories of you getting up to no good, but first, what was your punishment?"

"Mom woke me up at the crack of dawn with a bucket of soapy water and a scrubbing brush. I had to clean the whole staircase and hallway. After that, she sat me down, put a plate of bacon and eggs in front of me, and handed me a shot of tequila."

Sammy's laughter is loud and abrupt. "Priceless. Hell, I didn't know Mrs. Sandford had it in her. Mad respect."

I roll my eyes at him while shuddering a little at the memory of Mom seriously teaching me a lesson. Obviously, I didn't drink the shot. Instead, I vomited in the soapy bucket, but still, it worked.

It put me off tequila for life.

Well, straight tequila. Sammy's made more than his fair share of cocktails with the potent liquor in them.

"Holy shit. Incoming." Richie's brows jump high as he shoots me a look that's all amusement and a little alarm.

Dave's snort opposite me doesn't do a thing to settle my fast-beating pulse. Nor does it make me want to turn around. Sammy does, though. At my side, he half turns and angles back. I tilt my head slightly, focusing on his reaction.

His brow quirks, and his gaze dips down and up before turning to me. "A friend of yours?"

From the guys' reactions, it can only mean—

"Benny, baby."

Fuck. My eye twitches at the same time I form a sardonic grin.

I don't want to turn around, but I have no choice.

A slow turn in my chair, and there's Carlie. With

low-slung jeans and an exposed midriff, she looks good. She always does. For the two years we dated, she was nothing but sweet and kind. As far as I'm aware, that hasn't changed.

The problem? She struggled with our breakup, and every time I'm home, she tries to convince me we were good together.

She's not exactly wrong. We were.

But since starting college, I've always turned her down. It would be easy, falling for a girl like Carlie. When we split, it was because I didn't want long distance, and she understood that. I also know the casual hookups she promises would mean a lot more to her than they would me. I don't want to do that to her.

Plus, each and every time, my heart just wasn't in it.

Her gaze travels to Sammy, and my pulse races.

Sammy.

Holy shit.

The two of them in the same room together is like a final puzzle piece slipping into place.

All this time, he's been at the forefront of my mind—since my first visit home from college.

Fuck. Has it really always been him? Has there always been a part of me that's been pining for him, attracted to him?

Is he the reason why my party hookups have been mediocre at best over the past three years?

I swallow hard. What am I to do with this epiphany? More to the point, how am I to keep going the way things have been when Sammy refuses to acknowledge that anything's changed?

"Sammy." He reaches out and shakes Carlie's hand.

Shit, I'm being rude. I'm also having a minor meltdown, and now is neither the time nor the place.

"Sorry," I say quickly. "Sammy, this is Carlie."

His gaze snaps to mine. He knows her name. As he's my best friend, there's been little I've held back.

He nods and offers Carlie a smile. It's bright, but it doesn't reach his eyes.

Is he jealous? My pulse jumps and accelerates. If that's the case, I get it and can totally relate. Every time I see Sammy flirting, my gut twists.

Not that he does anything about it, despite the regular offers he gets.

"Hey," Carlie says, then turns her attention to me.

I stand and move away so I can accept her hug. Her flowery perfume tickles my nose, a scent I used to love. Now? I move out of her hold and take a step back, effectively standing with Sammy at my side. I feel him angle to peer at me, but I dare not glance his way. Heat crawls across my chest and up my neck.

Fuck, is it hot in here?

Carlie's staring at me, wide-eyed and smiling so big and genuine that discomfort slivers across my skin.

"I can't believe this is the first time I've seen you since you've been home. I called you a couple of times." She blinks at me, some of her smile slipping.

"Right, yeah. I've been working all the hours. Then Sammy headed over to spend some time."

Carlie bobs her head and flashes a smile at Sammy. "You guys are on the same team, right?"

"Sure are." He stands, his arm brushing mine. "We also share a house."

"Awesome. I hope Bentley no longer hoards magazines like he used to." Friendliness fills her tone as she reaches out and shoves me super gently on my arm.

The ground opening up right now would be incredible.

Sammy chuckles. It's a little tighter than usual, but his shoulders are relaxed. I glance at his expression and exhale. He's taking this in stride. It's rare that Sammy is a dick, but he has it in him. I wouldn't want him to be that way with Carlie, since she's done nothing wrong.

Interest sparks in his gaze when he looks at her. There's nothing malicious, just genuine curiosity.

"Oh, he does. They've just moved on from architecture to landscaping." He glances behind her, and I follow his line of sight. Tanya and Sarah, Carlie's friends, are at the bar, looking this way. "You and your friends want to join us?"

"Yeah, sure, that would be great." Carlie bobs her head. "Let me just go tell the girls."

As she turns away, Sammy squeezes my arm. "You good?"

"Yeah." I nod. "You didn't need to invite her to stay."

Sammy searches my expression, saying, "I know. But she's your friend, right?"

A soft sigh escapes before I nod. "Yeah. I just always feel like shit after seeing her, you know?" And he does know. I've told him how things are with her, our history. Obviously, without sharing the realization that since meeting him, hooking up with anyone hasn't been on my radar.

Or barely. I'm not a complete angel.

"It'll be fine." He indicates for us to sit, so I do. Immediately, my friends' gazes are on me, brows so high, they're almost touching their hairlines.

"They coming over?" Dave asks.

"Yeah. Looks that way."

"So, does this mean you're going to finally give in

and give her another chance?" His voice is filled with curiosity more than anything else.

"Nah, it was right to end it. Hell, it's been three years. It would be good for her to move on. Be happy." I mean every word.

It's not like when I'm away, I spend much time at all thinking about life before college or my ex. I've moved on in every way imaginable. But it's awkward when she hits on me and I turn her down, especially when I don't want to be an asshole. It's not like she's forceful or pushy or even in my face either. It would be easier to tell her to fuck off if that were the case.

"Interesting."

"What's interesting?" I ask Richie.

"It sounds like you're a taken man. You've met someone?"

Heat slams into me, and I turn rigid. It's so tempting to cast a glance at Sammy. Instead, I force a chuckle and shake my head. "Nah, man. It's not like that."

The lie tastes sour.

But is it really a lie when hooking up with my best friend is a secret? Geez, it feels like it's a secret from the two of us as well, since we've not discussed a single thing.

I'm just as responsible as Sammy is for that.

Do I even wish things were different? Kind of. Maybe? Yes. I think.

This is still so new to me. I've already admitted to myself that I've been drawn to Sammy from the moment I met him, but it's only been recently that I've felt something more. Fuck, I didn't even know I was bi. Is that even what I am? Sammy's the only guy I've even considered doing anything with. The only man I've ever been attracted to.

"I call bullshit," Richie says with a laugh. "What do you say, Sammy? Is our boy here lying out of his ass and is actually dating a hot chick?"

Sammy shifts at my side and shakes his head. A light chuckle follows—though it's not as carefree as usual. "There's no hot chick that I'm aware of."

My gaze latches on to his, and I swallow the lump in my throat at the fire I see in his eyes.

Fuck me.

The look alone is enough to get my dick interested and have me wishing I could drag him out of here. The blood in my veins heats for a whole other reason than mortification at Richie's questions.

"Hey." Carlie's back, and if she wouldn't take it the wrong way, I'd kiss her for the distraction.

Without her asking, we reshuffle our table. Standing up, Sammy glances around, and then he's off and collecting a couple of chairs.

Once the girls sit, there are two chairs left. They're next to each other with one beside Carlie, the other beside Dave. Before I can speak or even move, Sammy takes the chair next to Carlie.

As soon as his ass touches the seat, he glances at me with an arched brow. My lips twitch, and I quickly look away as I sit beside him.

It's a tight squeeze, and without even trying, our thighs press against each other. I sigh at the contact, some of the weird tension disappearing that's been sitting on my chest since Carlie entered and was then exacerbated by Richie's line of questioning.

Sammy's "Just over a week" catches my attention. He's answering Carlie.

"And you're working with Benny?"

I wince at the nickname. I've always hated it but never pulled Carlie up on it.

"With *Bentley*, yeah," Sammy says pointedly, and my heart flips. "I brought my kid brother with me."

"Oh, that's great. How old is he?"

"Fifteen going on twenty-five." Sammy chuckles as he picks up his bottle. He takes a sip while Carlie smiles at him, then peers around him to look at me.

"We should get together one night." She flicks her gaze briefly to Sammy. "I'm sure one of the girls would like to come, too, so your friend can come."

A knot forms in my stomach. I hate to let her down, but I more resent that she keeps pushing and putting me in this situation. It doesn't help that our parents are best friends. Talk about awkward. I'm grateful my folks don't put me under any pressure, though.

They're pretty supportive of all my decisions. Splitting with Carlie to avoid a long-distance relationship, they understood. Changing my degree… they sat me down and talked everything through before encouraging me.

I'm lucky for sure.

Sammy's quick to say, "I don't think we're going to have time for that. The two of us being out tonight was a one-off."

I sit a little straighter when he answers for us.

"We promised my brother we'd spend time with him. Thanks, though."

Wide-eyed, I glance at Sammy. It takes barely a couple of seconds for him to make eye contact with me. The asshole winks. *Winks.* Who the hell does that? I barely contain my laugh, but damn do I want to kiss him for shutting Carlie down.

"Oh, right, of course." Her smile's a little forced. Confusion plays out on her face, but she's too polite to call me out. That doesn't stop her from peering back at me and trying a different tack by saying,

"Well, maybe when your friend's gone, we can get together? Maybe talk?"

Why is it so hard to say no? We've got a lot of history, and I hate how turning her down makes me feel rude and like the bad guy. But fucking hell, that might just be what I finally need to—

"He can't," Sammy cuts in. "I'm stealing Bentley away."

He is?

My heartbeat spikes, the pace quickening.

With a furrowed brow, Carlie asks, "You are? Mom didn't say anything."

Think, Bentley. Think. I'm so not cut out for thinking on my feet, not when my pulse is racing because I'm lying out of my ass. "Uhm… yeah. We've only just decided."

Sammy steps in. "Yeah," he confirms. "Mom asked for me to talk him into heading home with me. She wants help with landscaping our backyard. Thought she'd get the opinion of the rising star in all things landscaping."

Jesus, he's good. The man was born with a gift, for sure.

Carlie's attention flitters between the two of us before a smile settles on her lips. "That sounds wonderful. You seem really happy with your new major, Benn—tley." With a tilt of her head, her smile becomes more genuine. "To think how much has changed. I suppose it just goes to show when we're kids, we really don't know shit."

I laugh and shake my head, lifting my beer bottle. "That's something I can definitely agree with." I clink my bottle with hers and then Sammy's, meeting his gaze and holding it for a beat before taking a swig.

Eighteen-year-old me really didn't know anything. In a couple of months, I'm going to be twenty-two, and so much has changed. My younger self wouldn't recognize me.

My heart warms, and I smile and nod at whatever Dave is saying. Because this is *me*—the here, the now, the present version of myself. I think over these past couple of months, I've finally become the man I'm supposed to be.

CHAPTER 6
SAMMY

Bentley didn't end up coming home with me. He needed to stay and work. Plus, his grandparents were having a big wedding anniversary party the week after I left. It all sucks, but I understand.

It doesn't mean I don't miss him like crazy.

Especially now when I could really do with him by my side, even though this is the last place I'd ever want him to be.

I never want him to come face-to-face with my old man. Not ever.

The buzzer sounds. The slamming of a door echoes around the soulless waiting area.

I don't want to be here. Both Mom and my stepdad tried one last-ditch attempt to talk me out of coming, reminding me that I don't owe Trevin anything.

They're right. Of course they are.

What they don't know is that he caught me and Jamaal. They don't know I'm responsible for Trevin attacking him. If we hadn't been together, Trevin would have just walked on by.

Sure, he would have had a few choice words to say about Jamaal—like several people had about the only out player on our high school team—but he wouldn't have almost killed him.

And that Jamaal never outed me, nor Trevin—and fuck, I never outed myself, absolutely not telling the whole truth in my video testimonial for the trial— well, this is my penance.

I always come at the same time of year like clock-work, courtesy of a deal I struck with Trevin.

Being a coward and feeling like shit is something I wear daily, and fuck, I'm exhausted—and scared. So fucking scared, and not even for myself.

Another buzzer sounds, and the green light turns on.

I take a deep breath, steadying my nerves before I follow the other visitors. Heading to window five in the sterile room, I exhale slowly and try to regulate my racing heart. Just twenty minutes and I can get out of here. Twenty minutes and I can go a whole year without seeing his face and being reminded of the nightmare.

The plastic chair creaks as soon as I sit, and I wait beneath the cold fluorescent lighting that casts shadows on the linoleum floor.

Hurry up. Hurry up.

A kid screams somewhere to my right, and a man is talking loudly, but I try to tune them out.

The door opens, and I sit upright, putting on my armor.

He's the fourth inmate through the door and is easy to spot, as he towers over the men before him, his presence commanding attention.

As he approaches, his gaze doesn't stray from me. We have the same strong jawline, the same deep-set eyes. But where I can sense uncertainty and a shit-load of apprehension in mine, his are hardened. We make eye contact, and for the briefest of moments, I'm sure there's a hint of emotion there, but it's quickly replaced by indifference.

He takes a seat across from me, and even through the thick walls and plexiglass, I hear the metal chair creaking. We stare at each other, and with an impressively steady hand, I reach for the phone. He does the same but doesn't speak.

Neither do I.

The silence between us is heavy, suffocating. But I have nothing to say to him.

Before I take another breath, he speaks, his voice low and gravelly.

"Hey, kiddo." His tone is brusque, but that's nothing new. It's the "kiddo" that rattles me. It's the first time he's called me that in years. Certainly long before he was sentenced. It catches me off guard.

"Hey," I reply, my voice strong. That's the thing with Trevin—you can't show fear or weakness. He's like a circling shark just waiting for the first drop of blood.

He doesn't respond immediately, so I study his face, the lines etched into his skin. They're faint. Truth is, he looks good, even here. He was just nineteen when Mom got pregnant, something I still struggle to wrap my head around. While I know the story of how they got together, how she left him when I was a toddler, it's difficult to imagine them as a couple.

"You won the championship," he states, a nod of approval following. "Good. What's the plan for next year and entering the draft?"

My heart sinks. Of course he's asking about that. I shake my head. "I'm not."

I see it. The transition. The sneer forms in almost an instant.

"The fuck do you mean?"

"I've no interest." I keep my voice steady while

my heart hammers. Don't get me wrong, if I thought I was in for a real shot, I'd enter, but while I'm good on the court, I'm not fucking phenomenal.

"That's fucking ridiculous. I fucking sacrificed everything so you'd have a shot at joining the League."

The fuck?

"Sacrificed?" I shake my head, hating the wobble in my voice. "What have you ever sacrificed for me?" White-hot anger sparks to life in my chest.

"You fucking know what. Do you think for a second that you'd be where you are now if everyone knew what I caught you doing?" Disgust laces his words, and lead solidifies in my stomach.

This is the first time he's ever mentioned what happened.

I grit my teeth, my back molars grinding. *Don't bite. Don't bite.* There's no point—not with someone like Trevin.

"What the fuck do you think everyone would say, knowing you're the reason why your old man's in prison? The reason why that cocksucker got the shit kicked out of him?" A menacing smirk plays on his lips. "You won't feel so precious then. You'll be left in the cold like I am."

Jesus.

I shake my head. Not a chance I'm putting up with this bullshit.

I pull the phone from my ear and go to stand. The bang on the plexiglass has me pausing.

With a sigh, I put the phone back to my ear.

Trevin's shoulders relax. "So, you got a job lined up, then? What are you doing with your fancy fucking business degree?"

I shrug. "I'm not sure yet. I'll start looking in the new year."

He nods, acting like his outburst from a few moments ago never happened.

"I need you to do something for me."

Here we go. This is much more standard.

"What?"

"Have you seen Calvin or Caleb?"

Surprise flitters through me that he's asking about his brothers. "No." It's not like I'm at school in the same state. As far as I'm aware, they still live in Shelby, where I was born, which is a good three-hour drive from where I grew up with my parents and siblings.

"I need you to get in touch with them for me."

I dip my brows. "Why?" Though I suspect I know the answer. While I have nothing to do with Trevin's side of the family, the last I heard, neither does Trevin. He smashed too many bridges over the years.

"I've applied for an early parole hearing. It'll be in January. Good behavior." He snorts as though this is all a joke, making the ice of dread already slithering through my veins drop a few degrees cooler.

Early parole? No fucking way.

"They'll be talking to you, I suspect, so don't you let me down." There's no disguising the threat in his tone. "I need Calvin and Caleb to vouch for me. They've always had steady jobs. Upstanding citizens and all that bullshit. Need one of them to get me on the payroll too."

Words freeze in my throat, held hostage by panic.

Almost four years. That's how long I should have left with him locked behind bars. The thought of him being released early turns my blood to acid.

He leans forward, closer to the plexiglass. "You hear me, boy?"

Numbly, I nod.

"Good." He settles back and swipes his thumb over his bottom lip, revealing his scarred hand complete with fresh cuts.

Good fucking behavior? What a joke.

"Stop on the way out and put some money in my commissary. And make sure you get looking for a job. And get my brothers to visit me." He stares at me hard, waiting for me to nod. I do so before he places the phone back on the cradle and stands.

Fuck.

I need to get out of here.

The next few minutes are a blur as I escape the confines of the correctional facility. It's all I can do to get in my car, start the ignition, and remember how to drive. Everything is on autopilot as I start the three-hour trip home.

What I don't do is put money in his commissary. Nor do I have any intention of calling his brothers or talking to anyone who might want to speak to me about his early release.

There's no way a board would agree to that, right? Jesus, he nearly killed a kid and battered me in the process. Six and a half years isn't long enough.

The heavy thud against my ribs hurts. I rub at the area, though it's going to take more than that for my panic to dissipate.

What the fuck am I going to do?

The first thing I should do is warn Jamaal. I have no idea if he still has the same number, but my friend Booker's still in touch with him, I think. Giving him a heads-up is the least I can do.

Fuck.

I slam my hand against the wheel. The sting helps me catch my breath.

I need to tell my parents. Bentley.

Fuck, Bentley.

I trust him more than I've trusted anyone. He'll understand, right?

Dread sends a shiver down my spine. Not telling him—who am I kidding? Not telling *anyone*—is unforgivable.

I glance in the rearview mirror when my stomach churns. Seeing nothing behind me, I pull over, open my door, and throw up.

The acid from my empty stomach burns.

I take a couple of deep breaths, my forehead pressed against my car door.

At some point, all this shit is going to catch up to me. Trevin will make sure of that—well, if it's in his best interest to. I also know the last thing he'll ever want to admit is having a gay son.

What I should be doing is telling the people I love the truth. And I will. The threat of my world blowing up isn't exactly a motivator, but at some point soon, I need to. And before Trevin's hearing.

My cell rings, making me jolt. I glance at the screen, my heart leaping. Bentley.

I pick up immediately. "Hey," I say.

"Hey." His voice is soft, and in that one word alone, I hear his worry. "You've picked up, so I'm assuming you're on your way home?"

"Yeah. Been on the road for maybe fifteen

minutes." Rather than sitting back, I exit my car and lean against the warm metal of the back door.

"It's quiet."

A humorless laugh stumbles out of me. How the hell is he so observant?

"Yeah. I needed to pull over."

"Shit. So it didn't go well, then?"

"Not exactly. He's going to apply for early parole."

"Fuck, seriously?"

The sound of a door closing reaches me. I can visualize him leaving whatever room he was in for privacy. That or he's grabbing a beer. God, I could do with one right now.

"As a heart attack." I sigh. "He said something about good behavior, but I don't buy it for a second." It's not like Trevin was ever a gangbanger or deeply into drugs or anything. But he was a drunk and constantly in and out of jobs. He also hit my mom. It was the second time he hit her that Mom packed our things and left.

She was so damn brave. Still is. Yet here I am, sitting on all this shit. Shame makes it difficult to breathe.

"Hey, Sammy. Sammy? It'll be okay. Even if he does get out, you're away at college, and he won't be allowed to leave the state, right? It'll be okay."

I tune in to his words, the familiar cadence registering and easing the weight of my panic.

How he does that should boggle my brain, but it's a skill he's always had.

"Fuck, I miss you." My words escape before I can stop them. I should want to take them back, but I don't have it in me. He's my best friend, the man who I can't get out of my head. I miss him all the damn time. I'm finding it more and more difficult to breathe when he's not by my side. "I don't deserve you, you know that?"

"Sammy." There's a roughness to his voice that wasn't there a moment ago. "I miss you too. Of course I do. Not long now and we'll be back at Brixham, and everything will be as it should be."

I close my eyes, grasping on to his words like a promise.

"Yeah, I know." I shake my head and clear my throat, pulling myself back together. "Sorry, you know I'm like this every year after I visit."

He doesn't call me out, even though I'm not usually so "woe is me."

"You're still heading to school a few days early, right?" I ask.

"Yeah, for sure."

A smile forms on my lips. I can't wait to hang out and talk shit late into the night.

Who am I kidding? I can talk shit at any time of the day. And for some reason, Bentley likes this about me.

"You really are going to be okay, you hear me?"

He ignored me earlier, but I really don't deserve him. "Thanks, Bentley. I'd best get back on the road."

"Sure. Let me know when you're home, yeah?"

"Will do." I can't help but smile again. "You have a good afternoon. Don't get scraping up those hands. It'll be practice again before you know it, and Coach will kick your ass if you can't dribble 'cause your hands are fucked-up."

Bentley snorts. "I'll keep my gloves on. Drive safely, and don't forget to text or call me later."

After hitting End, I get back in the car and start the engine. A wave of relief washes over me, a soothing balm to the panic scratching at me.

Strength… I swear, I don't know how he does it. Our exchanges are simple. There are rarely any moving speeches or anything like that, but honestly, he gives me so much strength that I feel centered and able to tackle the world.

At some point, I'll need it to take on Trevin. If not this year, then likely at the end of his ten years.

I just hope that by the time I have the courage to tell Bentley everything, he's still willing to keep lending it to me.

NOW...
SENIOR YEAR

CHAPTER 7
SAMMY

The fraternity house is heaving, which is usually my jam. I fucking love parties and hanging out, socializing. There's even a decently stocked liquor table for me to make my specialty shots.

But I'm not feeling it.

It doesn't dim the smile on my face. Nor does it impact the volume of my laugh at something Jeremy, one of the team's sophomores, says. And Stacey, who's flirting with me? I flirt back, because of course I do.

The latter stops me from seeking out my friends. *Bentley.* Yeah, there's no lying to myself, as much as I might try.

But this is what I'm supposed to do. Flirt, be the life and soul of the party.

Be looking to hook up with the hottest girl in the room.

The beer in my Solo cup is flat and warm. I've been nursing it for so long, it could be used as a prop in a documentary about tepid beverages or some shit. If not that, maybe a "what not to do" series about falling for your best friend when you had every intention of playing the straight card and burying deep down inside the fact that you're gay.

The series would be a hit.

It would lay out my woes and shine the spotlight on what a prick I am. I could dazzle the producers with my guide about how I'm the worst best friend in the world by stuffing all my feelings for Bentley so far into the closet that we've started a support group for lost socks.

It stands to reason that I'm the president.

I may not have my ducks in a row—in truth, the ducks are synchronized swimming in a lake of chaos, each quack perfectly timed to the sound of my "good friend" awards splashing into the water—but I'm the king of pretending everything is fine.

Yeah, nothing to see here, folks.

"You can always come back to my dorm." Stacey does a weird finger walk up my arm. Goose bumps burst to life beneath her touch, but think classic *Alien* reaction rather than sexy awareness.

If Bentley's looking this way, he'll know my smile is faker than a Liberty Haven Lions player claiming he never committed a foul. But I dare not check.

Is it because I'm a pussy and don't want to see his hurt expression? Abso-fucking-lutely.

I don't play this game to make him jealous or get his attention. I'm not that much of a shithead.

"Sammy."

I startle when Stacey says my name. The tone suggests she's said it a couple of times. Spacing out has made her drop her hand, at least. Thankfully.

"Sorry, Stace. I have to be in the gym by five in the morning," I lie. "You're a sweetheart for asking." Like the gentleman I am, I kiss her cheek. It's not her fault that I'm a prick and Bentley is the only person I'm interested in.

Interested. Ha.

Yeah, right. If "interested" means I'm full-blown gone for the man and so fucking in love, I could spout poetry or some equally romantic shit, then yeah, I'm "interested."

The narrowing of her eyes lessens a little after my peck on her cheek. "I get it. Another time, maybe?"

The hopeful lilt in her tone has me fixing my smile in place. "Sure, another time."

She nods, seemingly happy with that, but it's my time to retreat.

Keeping up the charade is exhausting. Especially sober—though it's a damn sight easier not getting shitfaced and forgetting I can't eye-fuck Bentley from across the room.

I could, though.

I can't think about *that* possibility. Instead, I search for my housemates. They've likely taken over a quiet spot somewhere.

Dean's laughter catches my attention. With his arm around Kieran's waist, whose arm is draped over his boyfriend's shoulders, Dean's looking at Kieran like he hung the damn moon.

Envy twists my gut.

I could have that.

I clench my jaw. Those thoughts are so fucking dangerous.

What's the worst that could happen? It's not like I'm fifteen anymore.

I can't handle the scenarios that try to encroach on my brain. They consume me too easily, and now is not the time or the place to lapse into a pity party for one.

What I can't do is hold back anymore.

I search him out, my pulse spiking as I look for gray eyes the exact shade of storm clouds. Though, to be fair, the shade is more of a sage when the sun's out and high in the sky.

Whatever the color, whenever he captures my gaze, I'm lost, adrift in the sea, absolutely without an anchor.

Bentley would be my anchor. If I let him.

Fuck my reckless thoughts all to hell.

My stomach dips when I don't find him.

"Where's Bentley?" I say by way of greeting, drawing the group's attention to me.

Tyron, leaning against a wall, his arm around Logan's chest in a hold that's completely claiming, answers, "He left."

Our gazes connect, and my heart flips at the intensity directed my way. Sure, Tyron often wears a mask of either indifference or impermeable stoicism, effectively telling everyone not in our close group to stay the fuck away. Neither of those are the emotions he's firing at me right now. But no way am I engaging with anything Tyron, with his big brain and terrifying ability to read people, wants to say to me— whether silently or verbally.

The fucker *knows* things.

I cannot be scrutinized by our resident FBI agent wannabe.

If interrogated, I wouldn't last more than ten minutes—and that's being generous.

I focus on Tyron's words instead of what he's not saying, then turn to Kieran, our team captain. He's more levelheaded than the rest of us. Though, when it comes to his protectiveness of Dean, maybe not so much. But Dean is a firecracker, and I don't think he will ever need anyone to protect him. "When did he leave?"

"About thirty minutes ago. Leon and Tiller went with him. We want to head out too. Just wanted to see what you were up to. You hooking up with Stacey tonight?"

As casually as I can manage—which is tricky, as my pulse skyrockets and guilt presses down on me—I shrug and shake my head at Kieran. "Nah. Not feeling it. Too much to drink as well."

When none of them call bullshit, even though I only passed around a single shot to our group, I'm home free.

"I'm good to head back," I continue. Bentley leaving sours my gut. What's worse is that I'm not even surprised.

Bentley's been hit on so many times. Hell, all the damn time when we're out. He's fucking hot and an even better guy. And apparently, chicks dig the whole tall, handsome, and quiet man vibe.

Not that he's shy.

He's actually super confident. He's also intelligent and so fucking good with his hands.

My dick twitches when I think about just how

good he is. But his skill is with landscaping. From design to creation, he's freaking amazing. The muscles that flex and move, holding strength and so much power, are not all made in the gym.

But back to me being jealous as fuck, because that's absolutely the point I was trying to make. When he's being hit on, and he's all smiles and sweet blushes—for real, he does not comprehend just how fucking sexy he is—I turn an unattractive shade of green and become a grumpy fucker.

And that's without him flirting back. Because, of course, he *wouldn't* flirt back. Not when he's with me, even though there's technically no "we." That would require discussions and opening my heart, and we've already established that I'm a chickenshit.

What I should do is stay true to Bentley and stick with being his best friend. We've done it so well—the whole best-friends relationship—and for so many years already.

But somewhere along the line, our signals got crossed. My heart and my dick were challenged, fucking changed irrevocably, and, honestly, brought to life by Bentley's kindness, his compassion, his… everything.

Once we're outside, starting the short trek to our rented house, I tune out the conversation between the couples around me. The wind is biting, a cold front having swept into Georgia a little earlier than usual. The cool air is refreshing. If I were drunk, it would definitely help sober me up.

I wonder if the cool breeze can make my uncertainty fly away. Maybe it can shake my core and help uproot the fear keeping me grounded.

I want nothing more than to be true to Bentley and myself.

I want to be ready. Want to give him everything he deserves.

Not that he's ever asked for a single thing from me. He's never asked for my faithfulness. However, I've absolutely stayed true. He's never forced me to discuss what we do when I stumble into his room pretending to be drunk so I can take what I want.

Instead, he gives willingly, without question.

It makes pulling away impossible. How the fuck do I walk away from someone like Bentley?

The truth is, I can't.

I won't.

CHAPTER 8

BENTLEY

Two things jolt me awake.

The hand on my dick and the scent of beer on Sammy's breath.

"Fuck." I jerk my hips upward, chasing his hand.

"Did I wake you?" the asshole says with a chuckle. His voice is an octave deeper than usual, and like always when he wakes me like this—or when we stumble into a room with a locked door together—his words start to unravel me.

There's no playing it cool when I push into his firm grip, a shaky exhale escaping me. "Uhm… nope?"

Sammy can wake me this way anytime he wants.

It's a problem, and I'm a glutton for punishment. But as heat whips around my body as he licks a wet trail up my neck, not stopping his attention to my cock, I don't want to be anywhere else.

I angle my head and am rewarded with his soft lips meeting mine. It's like I can finally breathe, something I've struggled to do all night. With his lips sloping against mine, I sigh into the connection, chasing his tongue.

I don't even care that Sammy can no longer do two things at once—too lost in the kiss. His lips on mine are worth the neglect of my dick.

It's been seven long, frustrating, painful days of not being together like this. Seven days of not partying. After losing the game against Doncaster, Coach has been riding our asses. That's meant no wild nights out—or in. No drinking.

His body presses against me. Naked flesh, hard muscles, and the perfect weight that just does it for me.

Wrapping my arms around him, I groan.

Fuck, I love it when he's like this. Horny and hard, rocking against me. With his velvety steel cock brushing against mine just so, I'm already leaking and close to blowing my load.

But it's his "I missed you" that he presses against my mouth that has my heart aching.

But I'll play his game. I always will.

"Just climb up here and feed me."

Because fuck yes, I want his cock in my mouth. Want to swallow him down. Hear his cries. His desperate pleas.

And thank fuck for soundproof rooms. I have no idea why the previous tenant locked this room down tight, but it's times like these, I'm hella glad they did.

I need him to unravel, and even though we'll pretend this never happened tomorrow, I need him to share this with me.

Sammy smiles against my lips but doesn't move straightaway. Instead, he laps at my mouth, gently fucking me with his tongue. It's slow and languid, almost decadent.

And I'm here for it, holding him close and letting him set the pace.

Our bodies gyrate as our lips mold together, a slow dance that makes it hard not to overthink. But Sammy like this, not racing to the finish line, not attacking my mouth with a speed and ferocity that usually has me blowing in ten minutes, means he's dealing with some sort of feels. And while I wish those special feels were about me, I know he took a call from his dad today.

It explains why he talked the guys into attending a party, even though we have training tomorrow.

His soft groan against my lips sends fresh sparks

of lust through me, pulling my focus to the familiar hard body grinding against me.

"You going to let me fuck your throat?" he pants against my lips.

With a nod, I move my hands to his tight ass, squeezing, eager for him to do just that.

Whether Sammy knows it or not, I'll give him everything he wants and needs. Always. Without conditions. Without negotiations or the need for him to beg.

He leans up, and I can finally take him in, my eyes fully adjusting to the small night-light I may or may not always have on for situations like this: when Sammy stumbles into my room at whatever o'clock it may be.

"But don't blow." His eyes are wide and full of heat as he speaks. "I want you to wait until you've swallowed my load so you can come on my tongue."

"Fuck." A bolt of desire zaps me in the balls. It's as painful as it sounds, but fuck if it doesn't get me going.

I dig my fingers into his hips and practically drag him up my body. His balls scrape up my chest, and with the way a soft groan spills past Sammy's lips, he's eager for every touch.

Once he's straddling my shoulders, I adjust my pillow and angle my head back. I want him to fuck my throat raw. The rasp when I wake will be the reminder that tonight really happened. And as much as Sammy may act like nothing's changed, I know damn well, every time he hears my gravelly voice, his dick will chub.

I wet my lips. "Feed it to me." My gaze is connected to his rather than on his cock that's a lick away from my mouth.

With blown pupils and a stuttering breath, Sammy palms his dick before lifting a little and painting my lips with his precum.

Fuck, I love this part.

Sticky and tangy, his precum hardens my dick even more. The taste has become one of my favorites over the past seven months—because yeah, that's how long this has been going on.

Seven months of what started as the both of us being shitfaced and sort of falling into each other. First, our mouths collided, and then our hands and tongues roamed. Now sucking and then finger- and tonguefucking are what keep me awake at night, desperately hoping Sammy will seek me out.

It's been a long time since I've needed booze. Honestly, after the first time, I stopped getting drunk, not wanting to miss out on a single memory of us being together.

"You're so fucking hot, your lips glistening like

this, sweetheart." Sammy bites down on his bottom lip, eyes flaring as he finally feeds me his dick.

I open my mouth wide, letting him dip inside. The underside of his cock strokes my tongue. He's heavy, weighted just right.

I wait until he's dipped in and out two, three times, his lips parting with soft groans and his eyes never straying from my face. Like this, he's open, letting me see how eager he is for me. Desperate even.

I slowly reach for the lube stuffed under my pillow—for reasons—and withdraw it. The move is deliberate, giving Sammy enough time to say no if he wants. When his eyelids lower even farther and he rises a little more, his ass an offering, I make quick work of opening the cap and slicking my fingers.

The whole time, Sammy gently slides in and out of my mouth. He doesn't press too far in, not while I'm doing this. He knows the drill. Just like the fact that I'm a fucking whiz at doing all this without a single glance.

Burying my fingers in his ass is another of my favorite things. My tongue a little ahead of that.

I dream of it being my cock buried deep inside him, but we've yet to cross that boundary, and as I angle my fingers around and dip into the crease of his ass, I don't want to think about the possibility of Sammy never being ready.

This is enough. It has to be.

My fingertip breaches his hole. Sammy's chin drops to his chest, his dick jerking in my mouth. His soft sigh is all contentment, and his leaning back, pulling out of my mouth until just the tip remains as he sinks onto my digit, is all acceptance.

My dick throbs, enjoying every single thing about Sammy letting go.

Not a chance I'll come, though. The visual of my jizz on his tongue while I have the taste of him in my mouth is too perfect to miss out on. Plus, from experience, it's hot as fuck.

I slide in a second finger, filling him. He's snug and tight and oh so hot. It's also what he needs to start fucking my mouth in earnest while I bury my fingers in his channel, matching his speed.

Each gasp that passes his lips is one I capture. Savor. *That* I'll absolutely keep for spank-bank material. I relax my throat and push deep, urging him to take what he wants.

His moan is feral. A garble of pleas, a litany of "Fuck… so good… your mouth… fuck… more" falls from his lips. And as his cock finally catches the back of my throat, a tingle at the base of my spine lets me know this is close to being over.

It's all so easy, so perfect. So fucking right.

I swallow around his dick, wanting him to lose his mind and release. I fucking crave it. Am desperate for the way I can make him unravel.

I pull back, needing air, my vision blurring. But I'm far from done.

Tugging my fingers out of him, I get far too much joy at his whimper. It's one of loss.

He fucking loves this.

I reward him with a third finger, pushing all three inside him as far as they can go at this angle. This time, I search out his prostate, that perfect spot that I've been avoiding, knowing he likes me working up to it and leaving it till the very last second.

And since my balls are tight and sparks are dancing in my eyes—from the lack of oxygen as well as being turned on—I need him to come.

I suck and bob and fingerfuck him. A slight crook of my fingers, and he jolts.

A long, sinful moan pours out of him. An erratic push of his hips follows before he turns rigid.

Sammy throws his head back and releases into my mouth. As he spills into my throat, I manage to swallow before easing him away, my fingers still inside him.

I suck him gently, teasing out the last of his spurts. I lick and caress, savoring his taste and the moment, committing the way his channel pulses around my fingers to memory.

"Fuck, Bentley."

My name is a croaked gasp. Another favorite. I have so many—everything in my life is becoming more and more Sammy-centric.

I don't want it any other way.

"Let me taste you."

I groan and ease out of him as he removes his softening cock from my aching mouth.

He shifts down, hand immediately going to my rock-hard dick. My moan is instant. And when I lose his hand for a second, I hold my breath, knowing what he's doing and wishing I could see.

His slick palm connects with my dick.

Why the fuck is that so hot?

With the lube from his ass all over my cock, I greet his mouth with a desperate kiss.

He chases his cum, just like I knew he would.

This kiss is hot and dirty, all tongue and teeth, Sammy's hand unrelenting as he jerks me off.

I'm close. So fucking close.

Thrusting my hips in time with his movements, I cup the back of his head, not wanting this kiss, this hand job, or this night to end. But with my head buzzing and desire skating across my skin at the speed of a basketball soaring across a court, this is going to be over far too soon.

Just one more minute.

Our tongues tangle, our lips pressing and nipping, mouths working seamlessly as though we've spent forever doing this.

Fuck, Sammy is everything.

He's sin and sex and light and joy.

"Oh fuck." I gasp the words against his mouth.

His grin is immediate, and even though I lose his lips, it's worth it when, in barely a second, he clamps his mouth around my cock, sucks once, and I spiral, shooting my load while I skyrocket into the stratosphere.

I come long and hard, and Sammy, I'll give it to him—not only my cum but my respect—he doesn't shy away. He's anything but selfish when it comes to getting off.

Every single time, we're left sated and wrung out.

A final shudder ripples through me. After seven months of doing this, Sammy can read every nuance of my body, so he pulls away, but not before dotting a kiss on the inside of my thigh.

I close my eyes at the contact. At the tenderness.

Try as I might not to wish it was like this all the time, emotion rushes to the surface.

But I can't let it spill over.

"That was fucking epic."

He's sober. All pretend slurs have gone. The only thing in his gaze is sated lust.

We both know it, but tomorrow, we'll pretend otherwise.

"The best way to be woken up." I mean every word, but my tone is teasing.

Sammy is my best friend, but he's not ready to hear the truth. I don't know if he ever will be. If he'll ever be able to reconcile his fear to accept us.

I want to be okay with that. Need to be.

I don't want to lose this, but even more, I don't want to lose my best friend.

I can't.

He's too important, but fuck if this isn't getting harder to take.

And right on cue: "Fuck, I'm drunk. I need to get my ass in bed before I pass out."

Since he's not looking at me, I pull my lips in between my teeth, swallowing my disappointment. He doesn't need to see it. I know what this is. What this means. Expecting more and bringing feelings into the equation was never part of the deal.

Have we talked about any of this and made an actual deal? That's a big fat no.

But Sammy's my guy. My best friend since the first day of basketball training at Brixham U.

For over three years, we've had countless discussions without saying a single word. It's a gift and a curse.

As Sammy eases off the bed, I school my features and give a fake-as-fuck yawn.

Keep playing the game.

It's the only way to stop my chest from gaping wide open.

"Those last shots will do it." I smirk.

I did absolutely zero shots tonight. We both know it.

"The golden cream apples...." He bounces his eyebrows. "My best recipe yet." He tugs on a pair of his shorts that live by the door. And yes, by the end of tomorrow, they'll be sitting in the exact same place, just waiting for the next time he wants to make a quick exit without dressing in his jeans.

"You keep telling yourself that." I roll my eyes. Sammy really does have the worst shot-creation ideas. "Now get your ass to bed before you end up sleeping in my doorway." I give him the free pass—I always do—just like when we're on the court.

And like the good small forward he is, he takes it effortlessly, burps for good measure, then turns and waves at me from over his head.

The silent room is stifling. The scents of sex and longing seep into my pores.

Am I an idiot for inhaling it and wishing I could bottle it up to wear on the days Sammy is "just" my best friend?

Clenching my jaw, I punch my pillow, trying to get it comfortable while taking my frustration out on the feathers.

Yeah, I'm an idiot.

But I've made my peace with that, so in a few hours, I'll wake up, smile, joke, go to classes, and act like my heart doesn't beat for Sammy.

I've only myself to blame, and months ago, I decided to stay the course.

No way I'm backing away from him now.

CHAPTER 9
SAMMY

My grade glares at me from the screen, but no matter how long I try to stare it down, wishing it would magically change, it stays put.

"Can you believe this shit?" I'm talking to anyone who's willing to listen as I throw imaginary daggers at Brixham's online assessment page.

When no one bites, I huff and look around at my group of asshole friends. Obviously, they're only assholes because they're not tripping over themselves to lament about what a fucking boomer Professor Rice is.

Another huff, and I finally get Kieran's attention.

About freakin' time.

"What are you sulking about?"

I narrow my gaze at him, offended that he thinks I'm sulking. That's so not it. I'm... incredulous, dammit, and put out. I worked my ass off on that assignment.

Sort of.

I may have left it to the last minute, but life's apparently a balance that I'm shit at maintaining.

Between other assignments, basketball games, practice, hanging out, making my awesome alcoholic shots, and dealing with the bullshit from back home, honestly, I'm impressed I handed the damn thing to Professor Rice on time.

Let's ignore the fact that I'm missing something super important from that list and swiftly move on.

Back to the screen before me.

But my grade just isn't going to cut it. If I get another result this bad, it's going to impact my GPA.

Rather than argue with Kieran about how I am absolutely, nuh-uh, no way sulking, I instead focus on the real problem. "Professor Rice is a twatwaffle."

Dean, who's sitting between Kieran's legs, snorts. "Twatwaffle. Nice. It's been a day since I heard someone use that."

I give him an up-nod, happy he can appreciate where I'm coming from.

"And why is Rice a twatwaffle, exactly?" Kieran pushes, not giving me his full attention, since he's stroking Dean's hair like he's a pet or something.

Admittedly, Dean is kinda cute. He's also our

mascot and kicks ass doing dance-offs when dressed as Bryson Bear. But still, I'm the one having a dilemma. Complaint… whatever.

"She gave me a C-minus for my business start-up project."

Kieran arches a brow at me, and I can see the switch as he falls into team-captain mode. "Isn't that the one you had to stay up until, like, 4:00 a.m. or something to get finished, as you decided it was the perfect time to go to the Iota Sigma Delta party just two nights before the assignment was due?"

Fuck it. I totally called him slipping into mom—captain, whatever—mode. I just knew he was going to point that shit out to me.

It's not like it was my finest idea, since I did in fact know I had an assignment due, but seriously, my balls had been at the point of passing for a new Smurf character. And my dick had been close to chafing from all the attention my hand was giving it.

It may have also had something to do with me holding Bentley close and losing myself in the peace only he can offer.

Plus, there was the whole thing of my hand not being able to kiss me, making me unravel and lose my mind with each touch and moment we were together.

If my hand had the power to do that, life would be a whole lot less complicated.

But of course it isn't.

Instead, for the past seven months, as much as I've tried to resist, only one person has had the power to make me see stars.

My throat dries from the memory of two nights ago. If I could have gotten away with it, I wouldn't have brushed my teeth, hating that I had to wash away the taste of Bentley.

And fuck, now all I can think about is the next time I can take his mouth, lick his cock, fuck his—

I clear my throat. My dick hardening is a sure road to disaster.

Unable to resist, I glance around the room, acting as casual as possible. It's all bullshit. I'm totally checking out Bentley, wondering what he's doing, if he's list—

Our gazes connect, and for the briefest of moments, I take my fill. It's risky doing this. Dangerous as fuck. It tears to shreds all my "I was drunk and don't remember a thing" excuses I play in my head.

At least I don't have to lie to his face anymore.

Does that make me feel any better? Not especially.

Truth is, I hate what I've done to him. What I'll continue to do for as long as he'll let me.

Before I tasted him, I never thought I could be this selfish, this spectacularly awful, and the shittiest of friends.

Goes to show what I know.

His storm-gray eyes don't stray from mine. His light skin flushes, and fuck it, so does mine. I'm sure it's not obvious to anyone else but Bentley. But he's mapped out every inch of my dark skin. Every part of me that can flush, he's seen and been responsible for.

I still when an emotion crosses his features that has me catching my breath. Disappointment. It hits me square in the gut. I don't know why he's allowed this thing between us to carry on for so long, but there's something in the way he's looking at me that tells me he's wondering the same thing.

My stomach cramps at the thought of losing him. Like the pussy I am, I drag my eyes away, focusing on Kieran and pretending what I saw on Bentley's face isn't real.

"I still spent hours on the assignment. And you know how Coach has been riding our asses—no offense, Tiller." I scrunch my face in apology as I glance at Coach Maple's son, who's also recently become one of the assistant coaches.

Thankfully, he's a cool guy and not that much older than us. And he and Leon just work.

Envy stabs my gut, a pretty familiar sensation of late. Coach Maple accepted Tiller and Leon's relationship with only a little exasperation, which was actually nothing to do with his son's sexuality.

"None taken." Tiller salutes me with his tea. Yes, tea. Because that's what our senior household has become. A bunch of loved-up couples—with the exception of yours truly and Bentley, which we're absolutely not going to analyze or overthink—who drink tea and hot chocolate in the evening and have early nights unless we're studying.

"When's your next assignment for Rice due?" Tyron's deep voice pulls my attention to him.

I hesitate, glancing at Logan. He looks thoughtful as he sits quietly, watching the interaction. Tyron, the resident genius—as in legit huge-IQ brainiac—goes above and beyond all the damn time, truthfully.

His question is undoubtedly going to be the beginning of an offer to help me, but he's already stretched crazy thin. And from the look on Logan's face, it's clear he agrees.

I may not be as smart as most of my friends, but I'm pretty good at reading body language and situations. Growing up with a dad like mine, I kind of had to be.

"After Thanksgiving, so I've got time."

"I can help. Let me know what course numb—"

"Nah, man," I'm quick to say. "Thanks, but I'll study and get it done."

He nods at me. "Okay, but if you change your mind…."

"It's okay, Ty. Other than the trip back home over Thanksgiving and the fistful of games we have, I don't have anything going on. I'll make it work."

Because that's the truth of it all.

Kieran, as always, was right, calling me out on my shit about complaining.

My not-so-stellar grade is all on me and my screwed-up brain and out-of-control emotions.

Figuring it's best to change the subject, since no sympathy is coming my way anytime soon, I turn to Dean to ask him what he's set up for the Virginia game in a couple of days. But I slam my lips together.

Kieran's got his face pressed to Dean's neck, whispering, or licking, or whatever the hell he's doing. Envy is an ugly thing to have swirling in my gut, but it's a stubborn gremlin that seems to be my companion.

The worst thing is, I only have myself to blame.

The mountain of issues trapped inside me leaves no room for a snowball, let alone me actively dealing with anything.

I'll only admit it to myself, but I'm shit-scared of the avalanche that will 100 percent bury me if I do.

But fuck, do I want.

I want Bentley. Want to be able to hold him like the guys around me. To hold his hand whenever I wish.

You can.

I sigh, my attention snagging on Leon's quiet voice.

The asshole stands, hand in Tiller's as, with no stealth whatsoever, they leave the room.

Fucking hell.

The rest is inevitable.

The couples all but stumble out of the room, clutching their laptops and notepads and eye-fucking their respective partners.

Which leaves me alone with my best friend. With the only person to ever know me inside and out. The man who makes my heart stumble and wish for everything.

I don't know how long I can keep doing this to him. To me.

Before looking at him, I need to arm myself and relax into the "before we started fucking around and I realized how goddamn perfectly we fit in every imaginable way" version of me.

Still glancing away, I start speaking. It's easier this

way. If not, I'll get lost in staring at him and forget that I need to simply be his friend. "Are you still gathering notes for your field study?" I finally make eye contact, fighting hard to ignore the flush of awareness I always feel under his attention.

"I'm about finished." He closes his laptop and cracks his neck. Bentley's been working his ass off on his project. It's worth a lot of credits for his Bachelor of Landscape Architecture degree.

I try to ignore the stab of guilt for waking him up the other night. We've both got so much going on and need all the sleep we can get.

A real man would step up and stop being a pus—

I fight against the words drilled into me since I was old enough to open a bottle of beer for my dad. Which was five, in case you were wondering, because yeah, despite him being an asshole and Mom and I moving halfway across the state, he retained visitation rights. Sure, it wasn't very often that he saw me, and he pretty much stopped when I was ten, but it had a lasting effect.

Listening to poison will rot away my soul. My sense of self.

I know this and remind myself of it.

But still, there's a semblance of truth in my dad's scathing words. If I swap out "real man" for "honest" or "good," then I wouldn't be far off.

These days, I'm neither of those things, even though I desperately want to be.

"I can help you study." Bentley's soft words catch my attention, and once again, I realize I've drifted off. At least I wasn't ogling him and drooling.

I'll take it as a win.

"Only if you'll let me help you with your project."

His lips twitch, and I roll my eyes, shaking my head.

"What? I can handle a shovel and a stabby thing."

"Fork." Amusement colors his words, the sound rolling over me like a comfortable caress.

"Whatever. My guns will come in handy for more than shooting hoops." I bounce my brows and make a show of kissing my right bicep.

Bentley snorts and launches a pillow at me, because somehow during the past few months, we've apparently also become a house that has fucking throw pillows. "You've got a deal, but no touching plants or trees."

I'm all wide-eyed innocence. "Me?" I push out a heavy huff of fake bemusement. "You'll find it's Leon who killed those flowery things, thinking they were weeds. I was just an innocent bystander. Wrong-place, wrong-time scenario."

"Uh-huh. Still the story you're sticking with?"

"Until I'm in the grave," I say, not taking my eyes

off him as he stands, his white tee rising just so to reveal a sliver of skin that I've run my tongue over so many times, the memory of how it tastes pushes to the front of my mind.

By the time my gaze settles on his face, he's peering down at me.

Usually, Bentley takes it easy on me, giving me a free pass by playing my bullshit game. But that's absolutely not the case now as he stares at me, eyes all heat and lust. Awareness buzzes along my skin.

Would it be so bad if I just took what I want without playing the game?

Desire sparks in the air, so intense that I can almost see a soft glow arching between us, latching on and tethering us together.

Bentley breaks the spell, his voice gravel when he says, "You want me to help you study now?"

I want that so badly, the thought of not following him to his room makes me want to scream and tear my hair out.

He can see the war. The worst thing is, on some level, I know he understands it—or at least as well as an outsider with a non-fucked-up family can. He's the only person who does. The only person who knows the truth. Well, some of it, anyway.

"Sammy."

Fucking hell. My breath hitches.

I'm doomed. Honest-to-God dead.

"Please come to my room."

This is the first time he's asked me. Ever. He's always understood my reticence.

Whatever he sees in me that's shifted, I kind of hate him for.

Because the asshole is right.

I want to go to his room, the only thing clouding my mind being lust and the sugar from the killer hot chocolate Tiller made me.

I can't speak, afraid my voice will crack.

So I don't. I don't even have to nod as his lips lift just a fraction, and he leaves the room, not looking behind him. Knowing I'll follow.

Fucking Bentley and his mind-reading Obi-Wan powers.

I close his bedroom door behind me, the lock engaging and sounding loud despite the heavy pounding of my heart.

And as I stare at him, his back toward me as he busies himself with emptying his pockets, I think maybe for a while, I can pretend everything is okay and this is my real life.

I don't want to think about tomorrow.

CHAPTER 10

BENTLEY

My heart's in my throat, my cock's pulsating in time with its fast thudding, and at the sound of the door locking with a soft click, I'm close to losing my mind.

He followed me.

With my back to the door, it's hard to turn around. Am I worried that when I do, he's going to freak out and run? Fuck yes.

But I want to see his eyes. Want us to be here in the moment with not a lick of booze between us and no bullshit game forcing us to be indifferent.

I also need him to come to me.

Sure, Sammy is here at my silent plea, but I need him to make the first move. It's the only thing that'll stop me from spiraling.

Do I know what it'll mean to him? To us?

Likely not. But it's a start, right? Finally, the beginning of something, because I was on the verge of ending this for good. It doesn't matter how perfect and easy it is between us. If he's not willing to finally take what he wants and admit it to me, I'm going to have to walk away.

He's constantly in my thoughts. In my dreams. Hell, when we're together, I'm aware of every breath he takes. It's stalkery as hell, but this is what he's done to me. What we've done to each other.

And if he doesn't—

The creak of the floorboard catches my breath.

I dare not breathe. Move.

My lungs burn, my head at the point of spinning, waiting, just fucking *waiting* and wanting and needing and—

Sammy cups the back of my neck, the touch gentle as he strokes his thumb up and down the column.

I gasp for a breath as a tremble travels down my spine.

I turn, not fully losing his touch, when he adjusts his hold to press his palm to the side of my neck as our gazes connect. Wide-eyed, he looks close to jumping out of his skin.

Please don't bolt.

If he does….

I shake off the thought. He's still here, still stroking the pad of his thumb along my skin.

There's a slight shake of his hand as he does so, and I get it, live and breathe it.

Fear keeps me silent.

If I speak, will it break the spell? Will it sever this connection? Will it—

"If we're going to do this," he begins, startling the fuck out of me.

Do this? Is he finally saying—

"—we can't tell anyone. Not the team, not the guys." His eye twitches, his frustration riding him. "I know they'll understand and can keep a secret. Fuck, we kept Kieran's for three years, but—"

"I know why." I nod a little too eagerly, so desperate for this to happen.

Sammy Hardy is going to change my world. He's already begun. He did when he first stole a kiss and, soon after, my goddamn heart.

"So, just us?"

"Just us." My mouth is already on his when I speak.

Sammy sighs into the touch, the heaviness of the past few minutes disappearing into a blissful fog of heat and want. We kiss like it's the first time. Our lips brush, tongues caress like we can't get enough.

I know I can't. And from the way he wraps his

arms around me, his chest pressing against mine, he feels it too.

As our mouths connect, he steals my breath while giving me life.

I've wanted this for so long. Him. Us.

His denim-covered cock brushes mine, and while we both groan, dual hitches of breath escaping, the urgency to get in his pants isn't driving me forward.

This is different.

We're not racing to the finish line. Sammy's not trying to hurry this up so he can escape like a thief in the night.

A caress of my cheek gets my attention, and I ease back barely a fraction, not willing to fully part from him. His eyes are already on me when mine flutter open.

"You're still going to come home with me over Thanksgiving, right?"

It takes a second for my brain to catch up. My brow furrows. "Yeah, of course."

Something in his gaze has me moving back a little more, but I don't let him go.

"What's wrong? What's happened?"

I've been to his home a few times now, visiting his mom and stepdad. He's just a couple of hours' drive away, a lot closer than my home over in San Antonio.

"Nothing's wrong."

I want to call bullshit, but I don't want to push him. If he doesn't want to or isn't ready to tell me, all I can do is wait for him to change his mind.

His family is complicated.

That's the polite way to say there's a whole lot of fucked-up mixed with the love. With the complexities in mind, I need to check. "And that's still okay with you, yeah? You're okay for me to come?"

He's nodding before I finish, the action loosening something in my chest.

This all feels so heavy and serious. But I suppose that's what seven months of fooling around and living a lie will do to a relationship—because, holy shit, I think that's finally what this is.

My softening cock is on board and rethickens.

Sammy followed me here. He says he's ready to do this.

"Get undressed, Sammy."

Heat flashes in his eyes, the worry burning away, and in silence, we undress. Our gazes wander, the air between us building to a low sizzle.

He's so damn beautiful. His skin, the color of rich mahogany, slowly reveals itself to me. Each muscle, divot, dip, and angle is perfectly sculptured.

I lean in, sweeping my tongue over his taut nipple, a shade darker than his skin. He sighs on contact, holding me to him. I smile against him as I lick and tease. His sensitive nipples always get a rise out of him, and in no time at all, he's panting and trying to grind on me.

Easing back, I peer up and make eye contact. Yearning stares back down at me.

"You want to lie down and me to—"

The shake of his head cuts me off, and I stand upright. Wild-eyed and flushed, he's breathing hard, his chest moving up and down.

"I want you inside me."

I freeze, surprise and need making it hard to breathe, let alone process.

Vulnerability is stark in his expression, though his gaze doesn't lose mine.

Through trial and error more than actual verbal communication, it's always been clear that Sammy loves my fingers and tongue deep inside him. Full-on penetration, though… yeah, it's been a gaping void between us.

But honestly, as long as I can have him, if he's mine, I can cope without if that's what he wants.

With gravel in my voice, I have to be sure. "You want me to fuck you?"

"Yeah," he says breathily, a coyness to him that's so alien and not at all like the Sammy the rest of the world knows.

Except for me. I know this man. Know his tells, his insecurities.

"I want that. I want you to fuck me."

Heat pulses through my body with the speed of a grassfire, and I smile so goddamn big, I don't hide what his words mean to me. What this means for us.

"So, me inside you"—I step close so our bodies are flush—"means we're doing this?"

It has to, right? Do I feel like a goober for asking? A big fat yes. But for the first time, he's opened up about what's happening between us. Not a single drop of alcohol has passed his lips. So finally—fucking *finally*—we get to talk at least some of this shit out.

Not that I want to waste the time chatting when I could be balls deep and blowing his damn mind.

With a nod, he bites down on his plump bottom lip. "Yeah." His cock presses against mine, thick and long. Sticky precum paints my stomach, and while the thought of tasting him makes me salivate, to finally make love to him… I want that so badly.

It's on the tip of my tongue to tell him he can have anything he wants or needs. But those words aren't even close to the depth of my feelings. Instead, I lead him to the bed and ease him back onto the mattress, saying, "Let me take care of you."

Emotion flickers in his eyes. I don't need him to

voice his feelings. I know what my words mean to him.

Naked and spread out, Sammy looks edible. And I absolutely want a taste.

I make my way between his spread legs; my roaming gaze slows as I take in every inch of skin. While we've been in this position before, it's always been about tongues and fingers.

My cock throbs, and I shiver as a pearl of precum drips over the head.

"You want me to use a condom?"

His headshake is instant. "No. What I want is your cum in my ass and dripping out me so you don't want to ever see your jizz anywhere else."

I grip my dick and groan at the visual. It's dirty and hot as fuck.

Sammy smirks, his gaze dipping to where I'm strangling my cock so I don't blow.

"Maybe another time, you can get me off first and use my cum as lube."

All control disappears. "Fuck." I capture his mouth and shut him up before he really does make me explode.

He kisses me with familiar ease. Claiming me. Possessing me.

And fuck if I don't light up for him.

Lips, tongues, and all fucking passion as we grind against each other.

This is what he does to me. Sammy Hardy owns me body and soul.

He's close to devouring me as our kiss turns almost frantic. A raspy moan spills out of him. I capture it, drinking the sound down.

He angles his head a little abruptly to capture my gaze. The tender desperation I see there is almost my undoing, but it's his "Fuck me, sweetheart. Please" that has my heart constricting.

"Anything for you, Sammy."

A smile lifts his kiss-swollen lips, and my heart stutters.

"You're so fucking beautiful."

I cut off any argument he may have with a swift kiss before I pull away and gather the lube from my bedside table.

Back between his legs and my gaze wholly on him, I trail my fingers up his thighs. "You okay on your back like this?"

I've imagined this moment a million times and every single way possible. But for this moment, I want him just like this. To see his face when I sink into him, to watch his expression when I make him mine.

Because unequivocally, that's what he is. We both know it.

He replies with a breathy "Yeah" as he holds on to the underside of his thighs, revealing himself to me.

"Fuck, Sammy."

He's perfect.

His skin is flushed a deep red, but there's not a lick of embarrassment. It's all desire and desperation. And fuck if I don't love this about him.

When Sammy commits, he seriously fucking commits.

I stare at his hole. It's puckered and begging for attention.

"Bentley, sweetheart, you're killing me here."

My gaze snaps back to his face. "You need me inside you?" I keep my voice steady as I slick my fingers, even though I'm barely holding on to my restraint. But this is what he needs: to escape, to let go, to relinquish control.

"So fucking badly that I think I'm going to blow the moment you sink in."

I smile down at him, pretty sure I'll be the one shooting my load the moment I breach him.

Stroking my cock once, twice, I control my breathing. A tremble works through his body, but it's when Sammy widens his legs even more, somehow exposing himself more fully, that I know he really is on the edge.

My slick fingers circle Sammy's hole before I dip one digit in. I push deeper, and a heavy exhale that's all relief bursts out of him. His searing gaze is on mine, unflinching as he silently encourages me to give him everything.

Two fingers, then three. We've done this before—my fingers exploring—but not so openly, not with me staring down at him, everything in my heart sure as hell painted on my face.

"You're going to take me so good," I murmur, my gaze dancing between my fingers working his ass and his expression.

"Damn fucking straight I am."

I huff out a laugh but don't stop diving my fingers in and out.

This—everything about it—makes the past few months worth it. The frustration, the unknown, and the secrecy.

"I'm ready," he pants.

I quirk my gaze, not so convinced. In response, Sammy latches on to my wrist in a firm grip and starts to fuck my fingers in earnest.

"You're so impatient." I don't take my eyes off his face, crooking my finger as he bears down, wanting to catch the moment—

A deep, loud groan punches from his chest. Since I forgot to hit Play on my phone to connect to my speakers, I hope to God that the soundproofing is really as effective as it appears to be.

Another groan, and the last thing I'm thinking about is anyone hearing.

Sammy's coming apart at the seams.

What I want is for him to be coming around my cock.

Pulling my fingers out, I reach for more lube, Sammy's needy moan echoing around the room.

"Bentley…."

A shiver ripples through me as I slick my dick and peer down at him. "I know. I said I'll take care of you."

Those words do it. It's not the first time I've noticed the effect on him. His body relaxes. Hell, he practically melts into my mattress, his lids dipping a little, his eyes settling at half-mast.

With my cock lubed, I turn my attention back to his hole. It's a little looser. I swallow hard as I push more lube into him. Yeah, looser for sure, but he's still so incredibly tight. I'm going to bust a nut so damn fast.

But I can't worry about that.

"I want to make this so good for you," I whisper as he pulls his knees back up and toward his chest.

He nods. It's a little wild and frantic, but the smirk I love plays on his lips. "Seven months of fore-play.… It's going to make this fucking amazing."

I need to kiss him, so I do. With my head spinning and desperation urging me forward, I capture his mouth. Desire pulses in my veins, but I kiss him slowly, a gentle press of our lips, a slide of my tongue against his. It's so at odds with the pulse of desire making my cock throb.

But fuck if it isn't right for this moment.

Our kiss softens while my dick hardens, and Sammy arches up, our cocks brushing against each other. I ease back when a shudder racks his body, take hold of my dick, and position myself at his entrance.

With a lick of his lips, his gaze intensifies as I nudge his opening.

His nod is all I need to push forward.

Mine, mine, mine is the chant in my head as I breach the first tight ring.

"More. You're not going to hurt me."

The words never crossed my lips, but he knows my fear anyway.

He *knows* me.

I push farther inside him, my legs shaking as I fight to hold back. Sammy's grip on my cock is stran-gling, perfect. The way he grips my ass, though, tells me everything. He wants me to fuck him and blow his goddamn mind.

The slow pump of my hips picks up the pace a little, the tight ring giving way completely. Sammy closes his eyes, his brow furrowing until a deep, guttural moan flies from his lips.

I still. I'm so deep inside him, his cheeks to my groin, it's all I can do to remember how to breathe. My hands shake, my balls tightening. Fuck no can I come. Not yet.

Beneath me, Sammy's breaths saw out of him. A sheen of sweat paints his skin, and when his eyes fly open, my heart soars.

What I see in their depths has me moving. Making this good for him drives me forward. It's likely that I'll be blowing far too soon, but not without him covering us with his cum.

Pleasure spears my gut as I thrust into him. "Fuck, Sammy." Another thrust, and his lips part. "You feel so incredible."

At my words, he clenches like a vise around my hard-as-steel cock. His grip on my ass also tightens.

He doesn't urge me on, but his hold is firm; it's another way to connect us.

"You're taking me so fucking good." I slam into him. "I knew you would."

My breath stutters out of me. He feels so incredible. How are we going to survive not having this every day?

Not a chance am I willing to let a whole week pass us by without him being in my arms. Not again.

"Your ass is mine, Sammy."

His eyes flare, and he reaches for me, hauling me down for a kiss.

I go willingly, tasting, taking, and possessing until I can barely breathe or remember a time before Sammy came into my world and made me his.

I break the kiss and peer down at him, sinking as deeply inside him as I can go until I still.

His lips part, likely to ask what the hell I'm doing. But whatever he sees in my expression has him stopping.

"*You're* mine, Sammy." I search his gaze, desperately wanting him to understand.

At his whispered "Fucking always," my world tilts. Lust, desire, need, and love battle it out for domination. But there's no need. Love, every single time, will win.

"That makes me yours too."

A small smile pulls at his lips. My heart leaps at the hint of arrogance in that one movement, and a full-on grin forms on my mouth.

I kiss him again, this time sucking his tongue. His hips jerk when I do.

With fresh need and feeling a little more in control, I pull away, getting onto my knees and scooping his legs over my forearms so I can fuck him like he needs me to.

I snap my hips, our combined grunts sexy and downright dirty.

Somehow, his gaze doesn't waver. The way I'm his whole focus settles a deep longing in my gut. He's in this for real. He really is all in.

My cock throbs each time I sink inside him. The new angle of my thrusts earns fresh grunts and groans. His words are almost incoherent, and fuck if my chest doesn't puff out.

I've done this to him. I'm the reason Sammy's losing his mind and speaking in tongues.

And still, he looks at me like I have all the answers and am his whole world or something.

I want to be that and so much more.

"Are you mine, Sammy?" I slam into him harder. It doesn't matter that I'm repeating myself; this is what he needs to hear.

"Fuck yes," he pants.

The glowing embers already sparking in me burn brighter.

"Tell me," I demand.

"I'm yours. All fucking yours."

White light, hot and blinding, shoots into me.

Fuck, I'm going to blow.

I pick up my pace, my movements on the perfect side of punishing as my hips snap, my glutes tightening with each thrust.

"Fuck your hand." I want to do it myself, touch him, have his cum all over me, but seeing white cream paint his dark brown skin will be even more perfect.

Immediately, Sammy grips himself, his hand moving fast and in time with my thrusts.

His whole body flushes, and sweat peppers his skin. "Nnghh." His hand stutters, hips pausing from fucking against me. "There… fucking there, baby."

God, what that word does to me. Melts me every damn time.

Another hard thrust followed by another, and Sammy is all I can see. All I can hear.

I want his orgasm. Want his needy cries and moans.

Want us to be this way forever.

Gripping his legs, his thigh muscles quivering, I tighten my hold, fucking him deep and hard. Heat spreads through my body, settling at the base of my spine and my balls. "Sammy." Desperation clings to his name as my balls tighten. "Fucking come, baby. I need you to let go."

His hand shuttles across his dick, fast, then slow, until his whole body is a quivering mess of groans.

And finally, fucking finally: "Bentley."

My name on his lips is the sweetest sound, followed by his cry of relief as cum shoots across his abdomen, painting his hand and his delicious skin.

The sight sends me flying. His name spills from my lips as I soar so high that only the connection between us can stop me from floating away for an eternity.

Wave after wave of pleasure rolls through me, the intensity settling with each jerk of my hips as I whisper his name like he's a damn deity.

His "Baby" reaches me at the same time his strong hands do. He tugs me down, accepting my weight like a familiar blanket.

I'm shaking as he wraps his arms around me. Pressing my face next to his neck, I breathe him in, committing his scent to memory.

Silently, he caresses my back, long strokes up and down over my pebbling skin. I'm pretty sure I should be taking care of him in this moment—you know, checking his ass, offering to clean him up—but fuck, being in his arms like this is so right and comforting.

So perfect, it'll be hard to leave.

CHAPTER 11

SAMMY

I wake up alone and in my own bed. For a beat, my heart feels hollow. Until I remember how good he loved me last night.

I tense my glutes, the action squeezing my hole. It's tender but not painful. I clench again, this time embracing the slight ache. A smile pulls at my lips.

Last night was incredible. Everything we shared, each touch and kiss, the way Bentley felt inside me, how perfectly he fit—it was fucking magic. I'm not even embarrassed that I'm gushing.

Bentley Sandford legit rocked my world.

I made the right decision, going to him like that. I've been battling for so long that it was the panic holding me hostage. But we can do this.

Seeing his expression was the breaking point. Though, I don't know if it truly was one single thing.

Maybe it was the days apart without touching intimately. Maybe it was knowing he walked away from the party a few nights ago and me hating his hurt. I suspect it's a combination.

That and being around all the couples last night, longing most definitely had punched me in the gut.

But I'm here.

After last night, I *want* to do this. And not just because he fucked me so good that for a moment there, I forgot my own name.

Okay, maybe it's a little of that too.

Bentley reminds me that there's good in the world. When he's touching me, it's possible to escape and feel free. While I know I can't live with his dick up my ass—not that I couldn't totally handle it— knowing he's mine takes the sharp edges off life. He helps to chase away the bullshit and the darkness.

Cliché, maybe, but who gives a damn? I certainly don't. Not if it means we can actually make this work.

Needing to see him and steal a morning kiss before anyone wakes, I scramble out of bed. I've got classes this morning and strength training this afternoon, so it's going to be a busy day surrounded by people. There's also the studying that I need to make a start on.

But first, kisses.

There's already movement in the house, so I need to be stealthy, especially as all the guys stayed here last night. I need a pit stop to the bathroom, though.

It's free, which is a win. I freshen up, making sure my breath is nice and minty, then leave. From the bathroom, there's Leon's door between me and Bentley. But that's okay. Me going to his room is nothing new. Hell, Bentley's my best friend, and over the past three and a half years, we've rarely not been attached at the hip.

I've got this. *Nothing to see here, folks.*

While I think it, I still keep my footsteps light. I pass by Leon's door and hear quiet voices. He and Tiller are awake, which means I need to be super vigilant.

By the time my hand's on Bentley's door handle, my pulse is racing, and a smile is curling my lips. The wood I'm sporting isn't ideal—not if Leon or Tiller leaves the room—but just the thought of kissing Bentley, all pretenses gone, and after what we shared, is making it impossible not to chub.

I turn the handle, grinning even wider when I find it unlocked, and step inside. Brightness fills his tidy room. Bentley's bed is made, the curtains are open, and the man who makes my heart flip is on the bed, pulling on his socks.

His gaze snaps up, a smile fast forming when he

sees my grinning face. "Morning." He searches my expression, but I don't let guilt crush my high.

I'm here. That's what matters.

In three strides, I'm before him and between his legs. He clasps my waist and peers up at me. His smile stretches even farther, and his bright eyes are more green than gray this morning.

"Morning, sweetheart," I manage before I bend down and meet his lips.

I sigh at the connection, rightness settling on my shoulders. Our mouths brush slowly, tenderly. We don't have time to start anything deeper.

When I pull away, Bentley's eyelids open. Pink stains his cheeks, and even though our lips only brushed for a few seconds, his are a shade darker than normal. My gaze eats him up, landing on his chin and the stubble rash.

"Should I say sorry for that?" I gently sweep my fingertips over the sensitive skin.

"No." He shakes his head and eases me back a little with firm hands on my hips so he can stand. "Shaving rash." He winks.

I chuckle, my heart feeling full to the point where I'm practically swooning. But processing this shift is messing with my mind. I just want to capture his mouth again, then hold his hand and walk on out of here.

The worst thing is, I could. I know he would let me. There'd be no grand announcement about our status or our sexuality. We'd just be us.

I'm the fucking idiot holding us back, which means I need to get on and suck it up.

"Are you good this morning?"

I nod, understanding what he really wants to know. That doesn't mean I'm going to take it easy on him, and while I shouldn't play with fire… "If I tell you I still feel you, that I'm pretty sure I'm still stretched, what—"

His mouth is on mine, tongue probing, lips unrelenting as he kisses me. Heat licks up my skin and travels to my pulsing cock.

I hold on to him, snaking a hand under his T-shirt. The warm skin against my palm is centering but does nothing to calm me down. I want Bentley so desperately, so completely—

The sound of thundering feet jerks us apart.

The house is officially awake and up.

Bentley groans and presses his forehead to mine. "You can't say shit like that to me."

I smirk, even though getting rid of this hard-on is going to be a nightmare. "So it's not something that'll help you get through the day?" I'm a teasing asshole at the best of times, but now that I can *tease* him with my *actual* asshole? Hell yes, I'm going to have some fun with this.

"Only if you plan to ride my cock at multiple points throughout the day."

Fuuuuck.

Okay, that backfired. My dick pulses behind my jeans. "You'd want that?" My voice is breathy and doesn't sound like my own.

What this man does to me.

I'm also fishing and woke up needy, apparently. I know exactly how much he wants me. Bentley has never played games with me.

"Every damn day of forever."

My eyebrows dart high in surprise, and while pink covers every inch of visible skin on Bentley's neck and face, he follows up with a "well, what are you going to do?" shrug.

The asshole may not play games, but he knows how to tease and make me his fucking bitch.

My admiration for the guy flares to life.

There's no doubt Bentley lets me lead outside the bedroom, but he has the skill to unravel me impressively fast.

Talented fucker.

Another round of loud footsteps on the staircase, and our time here is done.

"Later?"

"To pick up this conversation or for me to be bur—"

I press a kiss to his mouth to shut him up. He grins against my lips, and I pull back.

"I've created a fucking monster."

Bentley snorts, pecks my lips, then swipes his Nikes off the floor.

But I'm deadly serious. Okay, only slightly serious. He's always been bolder and louder when we're alone, even before this started. I think it's an only-child thing, maybe. For a kick-ass basketball player who's in the starting five so regularly, he has plenty of attention as well as camera time, but he doesn't lap that shit up.

Unlike me. I can showboat the hell out of the spotlight.

Honestly, no one would believe the Bentley I know exists.

My heart flutters as we head downstairs. He gives me this side of him and chose me to be the one to know the real him.

I angle back to look at him and find his attention already on me. I smile and look forward once more. Going to him last night and making the split-second decision to take something for myself is either going to be my making or my destruction.

I vote for the first one.

The kitchen is full of bodies when we arrive. This house is not big enough for eight men, six of whom are well over six feet. Somehow, we make it work.

"Morning, sexy mofos." I grin at my friends, making my way toward the fridge to tug out the container of yogurt.

There are a few grunts and smiles around the room as everyone is fixing up their breakfast. Tyron eyes me, his gaze flashing to Bentley, who's breaking a couple of bananas off the huge bunch sitting in the fruit bowl. When his attention moves back to me, he gives me an up-nod before he turns back to Logan and peers at something on his boyfriend's phone.

Who the hell knows what he's contemplating. It's easier to let Tyron just be himself and not question everything he's mulling over.

Having put the yogurt on the countertop, I grab a couple of bowls. Bentley moves to my side to cut up the banana, dropping the pieces inside while I scoop out the mango yogurt. He follows up with some muesli.

With our concoction created, I pass him a spoon, my focus lingering a little longer than usual. It's an effort not to lean in and kiss the smile from his lips.

"You forgot your honey." Bentley's moving before he finishes speaking.

This time, it's impossible to tear my eyes away.

The honey's at the back of the cupboard under the countertop, which means he's bent over, peachy ass just there for the viewing.

I want to bite into it, grind against him.

When my cock twitches, I look away quickly. Getting a hard-on in the kitchen isn't my idea of a good time.

A glance around before I drop my focus to my breakfast lets me know that no one's paying me or Bentley any attention.

I need to be cool. Act natural. I just have no idea how to do that anymore, which is ridiculous. I've managed it pretty spectacularly over the past few months. So what that he's taken my ass, finally given me what I've been craving but have been too fucking terrified to take.

"Here you go." Bentley squeezes in a blob of honey, catching my gaze.

"Thanks." I dip my head, ignoring the rush of heat in my chest at the sweet intensity in his stare.

It's official. I'm a fucking goober. I can't even look at the man without flushing or remembering how good he dicked me.

"I'm heading out." Tiller cleans off his plate and dumps it into the dishwasher. "See you all later at practice."

Leon's on his heels as Tiller walks out, saying

goodbye. We wave him off while I make quick work of my breakfast.

"Hungry?"

My attention snaps to Bentley's. The asshole quirks his brow as I shove the last spoonful into my mouth.

"All these calories I keep burning," I throw back.

Pink unfurls up his neck, and he clears his throat but doesn't tear his gaze from mine.

"Aren't you eating enough?"

Somehow, I don't jump at Kieran's question, but I do ask an articulate "Huh?"

His eyebrows are dipped as he looks at me, then my empty bowl. "Food. Aren't you packing away enough calories?"

It takes me a second for my brain to come back online. If I keep burning the extra calories with intense sessions like last night, I'm definitely going to be under my intake.

Not that I'm going to tell him anything about my hopefully nightly extracurriculars.

"I'm good. Just feeling hungry this morning."

Kieran's in full captain mode as he eyes me. My wink has him rolling his eyes before he turns back to Dean.

"You need something else to eat?" Bentley asks quietly.

Fuck, he's sexy, especially with concern in his expression and the way his assessing gaze roams over me.

"I'll get an extra-big portion at lunch. I'm good."

The look in his eyes lets me know he doesn't believe me. I should just grab a protein drink, but those things are expensive as fuck, so I need to stick to my meal plan.

Thankfully, the rest of the guys clearing up saves me from answering. A glance at the time lets me know I need to haul ass too. Larkin, the lecturer who I have first up this morning, is a stickler for punctuality.

The household gets moving. We all have early classes today.

We tidy up, which takes no time at all, since Kieran's trained us well over the years. Not that I don't grumble about it sometimes, but not living in a shitheap is good.

In no time at all, we're heading out and walking the short distance to campus. Bentley's at my side, standing just close enough that every now and then, our shoulders rub. It doesn't get a raised brow or a secondary glance from anyone, but my heart hammers in my chest anyway.

"Meet me in the library in a couple of hours?" he asks.

I nod without question. "Sure thing." Yesterday, he was serious about helping me study. Thank fuck. It's nothing new that I can struggle to sit still for long enough to properly study. Having Bentley by my side may add a layer of distraction, but he also helps rein me in. "See you in a couple of hours."

Kieran and Dean have already kissed and said their goodbyes as they head in opposite directions. Leon's gone to his lecture, and Tyron's backed Logan up against a wall.

Something green and ugly forms in my gut. I look away and stare at Bentley. He's already looking at me, his lips curled up slightly. It loosens the ball forming in my stomach.

He knows. He feels this.

"Make notes, and I'll see you soon." He turns to walk away.

"Bentley."

Stopping immediately, he turns back to me.

I swallow back words I have no plan to share, even though they're eager to fall off my tongue. But what I can do….

"Find a quiet alcove on the second floor."

His brow shoots high.

Making out in the library is obviously something we've never done before. It would have been hard to pretend I'd been day drinking for that to happen.

Since I no longer need to pretend, and I'm already desperate to kiss the fuck out of him, the library sounds like an awesome idea.

"Two hours." I back away, my steps feeling lighter, the smile on my face so fucking wide that he narrows his gaze at me. I bounce my brows before turning. I really can't be late.

But I do catch the shaky breath Bentley releases before I haul ass to my lecture.

CHAPTER 12

BENTLEY

Strength training always kicks my butt, but the burn is addictive. Even though my arms feel like Jell-O and my legs are shaking, my grin comes easily.

Sammy's giving Leon shit about bench presses, and the whole team is laughing, including Leon. Like this, Sammy's in his element. He loves being the joker and entertaining. His gorgeous eyes are bright with amusement, and the smile curving his full lips is genuine.

I'm catching my breath after doing squats, a towel draped over my shoulders, when Sammy wraps his arm around Leon.

A full-on smirk is on his handsome face. "Are you lifting those weights or just showing them the view?"

Rolling his eyes, Leon snorts out a laugh. "Unlike

you, I'm not auditioning for the next superhero movie."

Fresh laughter breaks out. Sammy may be the shortest guy on our team and probably parties the hardest, but he takes his fitness seriously.

"Hey, someone's gotta save the day. Might as well be me and my guns." He kisses his sweaty bicep, and I swipe my tongue over my bottom lip, jealous that I can't just walk up to him and trail it over him.

I school my reaction just in time as Leon shoots me a look, an arched brow that screams "how in the hell do you put up with this guy?"

If only he knew how perfectly I reined him in and silenced him last night when I shot my load deep inside him.

I manage a shrug, trying to block out my wayward thoughts.

Leon turns his attention back to Sammy. "A snack villain, maybe. The amount of weird shit you put in your body is likely a superpower."

"Right!" Kieran intervenes. "Who the fuck eats peanut butter and pickles on a sandwich?" A shudder follows while the team adds their agreement.

I agree. It's gross.

Smoothing his features into mock seriousness, Sammy nods solemnly. "It's a tough job, but someone's gotta do it. It takes something special to get these babies looking so fine." The asshole rubs his hand over his six-pack.

Because of course he's shirtless. I suspect he's trying to get me worked up, as I left him hanging, hard and needy, in the alcove earlier today.

Unable to resist, I follow the movement, my gaze tracing the contours of his sculpted abdomen. The chiseled lines draw my attention, a magnetic pull that's dangerous at the best of times, especially when we're in a room with our teammates.

But still, I watch, only pulling my attention away when Sammy shifts and our gazes clash.

The fucker smirks, knowing exactly what he's doing to me.

I shake my head, ignoring my flushed cheeks, hoping the pink blends in with the heat from my exertion.

"Jesus, whoever gets to handle your ass has their work cut out for them. It makes sense that Bentley's the only one able to deal."

I swallow hard at Leon's comment. As far as I'm concerned, I'll be the only person handling Sammy's ass. Ever, if possible.

Sammy bounces his brows. "It's understandable why you can't keep your eyes off my *assets*, Leon.

Glutes of steel are no joke. *Oomph*." A towel smacks him in the face, a good aim from Leon.

We're all snickering as Coach Maple steps into the gym. "It's not quitting time yet."

"Sure thing, Coach." Sammy salutes him, then sensibly moves to the bench press.

I head to the medicine ball, half my attention on Sammy. It's not like last night flipped a switch in me. Honestly, since the first time we hooked up, my attention is never far from him.

I'm borderline obsessed. Not something I'm exactly proud of, but I'm not running from it either. Especially not now. Not since he came to me yesterday.

I'm so focused on Sammy and the way his muscles are bunching and how the overhead lights make his sweat glisten over his dark brown skin that Tyron appearing at my side makes me fumble the medicine ball.

He quirks a brow at me, his lips twitching.

"You good?" I ask.

"Yeah."

Silence settles between us, but that's okay. I'm not much of a talker in general, and while Tyron can be almost as mouthy as Sammy, he also appreciates the quiet.

He moves opposite me and indicates for me to

throw him the heavy ball. I do so, and he catches it effortlessly before he passes it back.

After a few throws, he asks, "Are you still heading out to Sammy's this Thanksgiving?"

I bob my head. I spent last Thanksgiving with Sammy and his family too. "Sure am. Sammy said we're dropping you off at the airport on the way."

"And Logan."

My brows shoot high, and I smile. "No shit. Taking him home to meet your dads, huh?" His parents are pretty fucking cool. They try to watch a couple of games every year despite having to fly here.

"Yeah, thought it was about time."

It's been a few months—since the start of the school year—that they started seeing each other.

There's an uncomfortable stab in my gut. Will Sammy and I ever get the chance to do that?

Obviously, he's met my folks and me his mom and stepdad, but will the two of us together, as a couple, ever happen?

I finally land on "That's great," aware Tyron is studying me a little too closely. "I'm happy for you, man."

And I am. Truly.

Even though I believe those words, it doesn't stop envy trying to barrel its way into my gut.

Tyron nods at me, throwing the ball back. "And you're good helping Sammy study?"

Gratitude blooms in my chest. Tyron can be an intense asshole at times, but he cares a lot about his friends. That includes making sure we're doing okay in school.

"Absolutely. He'll be fine. He just gets in his head a little sometimes."

He sends another nod my way. Tyron is the most observant guy I know. While I don't think anyone else has a clue about all the shit Sammy holds close to his chest, Tyron clearly has a decent idea that Sammy is not as carefree as he pretends to be.

"And you?"

His question catches me off guard.

"Me what?"

That damn quirk of his brow is aimed at me, but at least he's not technically pushing. Seriously, Tyron can be a pushy bastard at times.

The arched brow and intense gaze he directs my way don't waver, but I can't fold. I won't betray Sammy. At all or ever.

After a beat and me offering the barest of shrugs, which isn't as carefree as I'd like it to be, Tyron simply nods and says, "Come on. Time to hit the showers."

It's a relief. Not only because my muscles are screaming at me but because Tyron is backing off.

"My arms are shot." I shake them out at my sides. They're going to kill tomorrow. It's a good thing there's no game till the day after next.

"Damn… there goes our arm-wrestling tournament tonight." Sammy brushes his arm against me as he appears at my side.

I shake my head and smile, ignoring the way my stomach flips at his proximity. The combination of sweat and body spray shouldn't be sexy, but it is. I suspect it has everything to do with the man who ties my stomach in knots.

I drop my voice as I say, "I think I could still take you."

He trips over his feet, head snapping my way at the gravel in my voice.

Tyron snorts and walks ahead of us, leaving me to stop and shoot an amused smile at Sammy.

"You doing okay there?"

"You're an asshole." His lips twitch even as he narrows his eyes at me.

The only thing I'm buying is the hitch in his breath. Now *that* I believe.

"Me?" I quirk my brow, 100 percent happy to tease him. Unraveling Sammy is a heady feeling. "You don't think I can take you?" Maybe I should add on "in an arm-wrestling match with weak arms," just in case anyone overhears us, but the heat in Sammy's gaze is addictive.

I'm playing with fire, but the promise in his expression as he stares me down is absolutely worth it.

I could totally bullshit myself and wonder what's gotten into me. Sure, I tease and can joke around with the guys, but I'm so much more reserved than anyone else on the team.

But I know exactly what's changed: Sammy showing up yesterday, saying he wants me and wants this thing between us to work.

If that's not an incentive to step up and make sure he knows exactly where I stand when it comes to him, then nothing short of a flashing neon sign could make things clearer.

"Or are you too sore for that?"

I'm going to hell, but fuck if the double entendres don't just keep coming. My dick twitches despite us being a few steps away from the locker room, and my basketball training shorts leave nothing to the imagination with a hard cock.

Sammy glances around. We're alone in the small corridor between the weights room and the locker room. The door of the latter swung closed a little while ago when Kieran stepped through.

As he takes a step toward me, Sammy enters my space, and I'm backing up against the wall. My heart pounds wildly, doubling down when he flicks his tongue out and dampens his bottom lip, his gaze raking over me.

I've never concealed what he does to me since this all started—even when I should have.

Need is a magnetic force, drawing us together with an irresistible pull. There's barely an inch between us. The air charges with an electric intensity that's sure to buckle my knees if I'm not careful.

"After last night," he says close to my ear, and I close my eyes, head pressing back to the wall at the sensation of his hot breath fanning over me, "I'll always be ready for you. Sore or not. It'll just make me feel you more intensely."

Breathing raggedly, I can barely focus on anything but Sammy's promise.

Last night was absolutely the best night of my life. While Sammy came his brains out, knowing he loved me being buried balls deep inside him that much is almost too much for my mind to digest.

Laughter coming from behind the closed locker room door has me wrenching my eyelids open. Sammy's still there, not bouncing away like usual.

For a beat, he stares at me, a smirk on his lips that

I love a little too much; then he edges back, turning away to take a step toward the door just as it opens.

It's Davey, one of the freshmen. His eyes dart up, pink touching his cheeks.

He's been super wary since the bullshit surrounding Tiller becoming our new assistant coach.

"Just forgot my headphones." He darts past us, and I watch him go, hoping Coach made the right call keeping him on the team.

While my eyes stay on Davey, I feel Sammy's unwavering gaze on me. As soon as the freshman disappears, I slowly angle my head to peer back at Sammy. Since he's just a couple of inches shorter, it's easy to be this close to him and take him in.

A playful twinkle dances in his eyes, something familiar and reassuring.

"Is your third leg under control?" A slow arch of his eyebrow joins his question.

My chest swells and almost puffs out. He thinks my cock is big? Fuck yes.

Sure, when he's been on his knees going to town on me, his gags are the hottest thing ever—as is his praise—but any and every conversation we have with no masks between us gets me going.

So, of course my cock chubs even further. I swear just the sound of his breath and the touch of his skin can make me hard in 0.3 seconds.

"I'll take that as a no." The asshole smirks. I want to kiss it off his face, but Davey's going to be heading back this way any second now.

"Can you blame me?" I challenge. He knows full well what he does to me.

Tilting his head to the side, Sammy does a lazy sweep of my body. "I think it's a miracle we've lasted all these months without me jumping you whenever I can. *Sweetheart.*"

Fuck. He knows what that word does to me.

Heat slams into me. The need to shove him hard against the wall and take what he's freely offering is a living, breathing ball of instinct threatening to override my restraint. I've never related to words more. I feel them deep in my gut.

His smile slips a little. I don't like whatever he's thinking that's doused the fire in his eyes.

"What is it?"

"I'm sorry for the shit I've pulled. That I'm still pulling."

A lead weight drops into my stomach. I'm not even surprised Sammy's saying this to me. It doesn't matter that no other fucker would believe he's capable of such raw honesty.

I know. That's all that matters.

What it doesn't mean is that I'm not afraid and insecure. "We're here and together now, right?"

"Yeah." His voice dips low, but a door closing has me pausing and taking a small step away. This conversation is way too personal for us to continue having in the corridor.

My dick's flagging, though, so that's something.

"Come on. Let's get showered and head home." I tug him away from the wall and risk putting my arm over his shoulder.

This is usually Sammy's move. The guy is the touchiest, feeliest person I know. Not just with me either, which is more than okay. It makes me draping an arm over him, like any friend of his might do without anyone taking a second look, possible.

"Any chance to wipe against my man sweat, you'll really take, huh?"

My muscles loosen at his sass. "Just what every guy dreams of," I fire back.

"I don't need any guy. Just you."

I almost stumble as he drops those words on me and then shuffles out of my hold as he steps away and through the door of the locker room.

What a fucker.

I grin wide.

I seriously need to find a way to spend a whole night with him uninterrupted and without the threat of someone bursting in on us.

CHAPTER 13

SAMMY

THE ONLY WAY TO KEEP MY LEG FROM BOUNCING IS TO do what I do best.

Talk shit.

It's not a long drive home, but I'm eager for the time alone with Bentley, so the sooner I drop Tyron and Logan off at the airport, the better.

As the car hums en route, Logan and Tyron are seated in the back. I've been chatting pretty much nonstop in my eagerness to help the time speed by.

"I swear, as soon as I'm home, I'm going to demolish a whole batch of Dad's Thanksgiving cookies." My mouth waters at the thought.

"Thanksgiving cookies?" Logan asks.

"Fuck yes. No idea what he adds to them, but they're the best thing I've ever had in my mouth."

As soon as the words leave me, there's movement at my side from the passenger seat. I flick my attention to Bentley, whose eyebrow is arched high as he stares at me. That look alone is 100 percent a silent "Really, the *best* thing you've had in your mouth?"

Fucker.

I can almost hear his follow-up: "That's not what you said last night."

And he'd be right.

I shift uncomfortably in my seat but don't admit anything for obvious reasons.

"So," I say quickly, trying to steer the conversation back on track, "have you guys ever tried deep-fried turkey? Heard it's a game-changer."

I catch Logan's gaze through the rearview mirror. Both his eyebrows are high. "Deep-fried turkey? Sounds dangerous, man. I'll stick to the classic roast, I think."

"You know," Tyron says, and I prepare myself for an awesome random fact he's about to share, "Benjamin Franklin once suggested the turkey should be the national bird of the USA. He said the bald eagle had 'bad moral character' and that the turkey was more respectable."

I snort. "Can you imagine a turkey on the Great Seal? Hell, maybe if 'gobble, gobble' had been used in the national anthem, there'd be more love when it came to blow jobs."

Logan snorts out a laugh, and I have a feeling Bentley's arching that damn sexy eyebrow my way again.

"Damn, Sammy," Tyron starts, "you're not getting blow-job love? That sounds tragic."

Heat touches my cheeks. I'm getting so much cock and ass love that my mind is never far away from the man who's a master of making me come my brains out. "Don't you worry about me and the attention given to my cock."

"Thinking about your cock is not on my to-do list now or ever," Tyron is quick to say. "You know, nearly one in five Gen-Zers identify as not straight."

The fuck?

Admittedly, I'm baffled. But also… one in five?

I'm tempted to side-eye Bentley.

I know he's never been with any other guy before me. My one and only experience is one I bury deep. As far as I'm concerned, Bentley's the only one. Ever, most likely. The thought should likely make me break out in a sweat, but instead, a thrill of awareness and possibility shoots through me.

One in five.

"Is that figure from that global survey a few years back?" Logan asks.

"Yeah. So, statistically speaking, our team is right on average."

I focus straight ahead as Tyron speaks, still stumbling over that figure.

I suppose it makes sense. In truth, it's not even that I'm into a guy that's an issue. Okay, on some level, it is, but I'm not ashamed of how I feel about Bentley. And taking it up the ass? Not a fucking chance I can ever be a hater of that. How I feel when Bentley's inside me is beyond anything I've ever experienced. It's right. *We're* right.

"I like to think we're better than an average team, though," Tyron says.

Usually I'd be pumping my fist in agreement, as he's absolutely right about that, but I'm still processing.

For almost eight months, the most I've admitted to Bentley is that obviously I'm into him, and that literally happened only this past month. Though, sucking his dick on the regular all this time was a dead giveaway.

I know I talk a lot of shit—and often—but *that* conversation makes everything real. And considering the shift in our relationship over the past few weeks, I suppose we should have it.

I should at least tell him the whole truth.

Maybe?

Fuck, is it even something that needs to be done?

"Not to say bromance isn't a thing."

My brow wrinkles at Tyron's words. I have no idea what the hell he's talking about now, or why he's even talking at all.

"Because it is, but let's look at Gale Sutton and Jayden Moore. Ultimate bromance goals right there."

Tyron's on a complete tangent. He does this even more than I do.

But fuck if his words don't pull me up short and make my brain screech to a halt. My heart, too, before it restarts and bounces all over the place.

Moore and Sutton.

Hell, two League players. Teammates and best friends for years. Everyone knows that.

The similarities smack into me.

That's fucking us, right? Me and Bentley?

Holy shit.

Sure, Sutton and Moore are pro, something Bentley and I have no real aspirations of being, but still…. They're also engaged.

Not that *we're* engaged, but we could be one day, right? Hell, we could get married. No fucker could split us up then.

Those guys have figured it out. I don't think Moore and Sutton even spoke up and said anything about their sexuality. It was literally a kiss on camera, then later an engagement announcement.

Tyron is still talking. I still have no idea why, but all these thoughts bouncing around my brain are making it difficult to concentrate—something I need to do so I don't crash and kill us all.

He continues, saying, "They were friends, inseparable, and I assume at some point secretly crushing on each other. Had a whole relationship on the down-low too. A hell of a thing to keep that a secret from the media so long, since they're in the spotlight."

There's movement from Bentley. His gaze is on me. I feel it like a gentle caress.

If I look at him, everything I feel for the man will be front and center. For as successful as I've been at keeping this thing between us contained, the past few weeks have made it increasingly difficult.

Is that because I wish like hell it didn't have to be like this? That's a hard yes.

"Were you going somewhere with your bromance and statistics speech?"

Thank fuck Logan asks.

"Don't I always have a point?"

I hear the smirk in Tyron's voice, and I kinda want to punch him right now. Or maybe hide his not-so-secret stash of candy.

Somehow, I find my voice. "No." I risk a glance in the mirror. Yeah, I definitely want to hide his candy. The weird, satisfied smirk he directs my way has alarm bells ringing.

Because the fucker is right. He does always have a point.

He's also an observant asshole.

"Well, in this instance, all I'm saying is that my own sexuality came as a surprise, and the whole team has been fucking awesome about it."

"Well, of course we have," I answer immediately and focus on the road.

My throat feels tight. He knows. My IQ is nothing like Tyron's, but it doesn't take a genius to figure out he's absolutely onto us.

"And there's been no 'why didn't you tell me before?' bullshit. Just complete acceptance," Tyron continues like a dog with a fucking bone.

Maybe I'll also eat all his damn candy too. Fuck hiding it.

I'm viscerally aware of every move Bentley makes, even though the number of thoughts bouncing around my brain is taking its toll. When he shifts and peers back at Tyron, I hold my breath.

"Did you surprise yourself as well?"

Jesus H. Christ. How is it that this whole weird-as-fuck conversation is shedding light on stuff I know we should have likely talked about at some point but never have? When Bentley and I kissed, it was a moment, the start of something I'm beginning to understand was years in the making.

Did I think he was hot the first time I met him? Absolutely. But like always with any attraction I felt for any man, I pushed it deep, the memory and threat from my dad a living nightmare.

"I figured out I saw sex and attraction differently when I was about fifteen. I put it down to the way my brain worked and didn't think any more about it, honestly."

"Seriously?" I shoot my gaze to Tyron, not hiding my surprise. "You didn't go into research mode?"

"I didn't feel the need to. That I wasn't interested in anyone, I accepted as being my normal. Told Dad that I didn't want to date anyone, and he was ridiculously happy that I was focusing on studying rather than risking getting a girl knocked up."

I side-eye Bentley when he moves again. Color sits high on his cheeks. "And you've hooked up with a girl before, right?"

I'm so focused on the flush, thinking about how ridiculously sexy he is, that I miss their next words. We might not be at my home for long, but there's a lot more privacy there than in our college house. I plan to make good use of that time. The basement bedroom has super-thick walls.

I tune back in when Bentley says, "So, you didn't know you were interested in men before Logan?"

My breath catches at his words, my sexy thoughts screeching to a halt.

Bentley flicks me a glance, and our gazes connect for the briefest of moments before I stare at the road ahead. This trip has taken a gazillion years. Why the hell aren't we at the drop-off zone already?

It's when Tyron mentions OnlyFans that my brain short-circuits completely.

"You… what… you do?" I splutter, struggling to get my brain around Tyron subscribing to a guy jacking off.

"Hell yes. I'll send you the link."

A heavy thump punches against my ribcage. "That's not what I—" I start, but Tyron cuts me off.

I only half listen, sitting up a little straighter when I see the sign for the airport.

Halle-fucking-lujah.

"Friends who fuck is a thing, and I'm sure it can be fun."

I snap my attention to Tyron through the mirror. I'm not just going to eat his candy. I'm going to leave the empty wrappers all over his bed as a big fuck you.

That's not what this thing between me and Bentley is. Not anymore.

A flash of a sign catches my attention, and my shoulders practically sag in relief. I throw on the blinker like it's the lever to my survival. I need Tyron out of the car.

There are too many thoughts stacking on top of each other in my head. There's also a loop as I reluctantly mull over everything Tyron said. The things I keep circling back to are that he doesn't know my situation, so he can't possibly understand, and the whole social media coverage of Sutton and Moore is on replay.

"But it's inevitable that one person is going to get hurt, and the friendship's likely going to be ruined."

Tyron is still talking, but there's buzzing in my ears.

Like fuck anyone is going to get hurt. My eye twitches. I hate it, only because I know for a fact how I previously handled my relationship with Bentley was fucked-up and that I did hurt him.

But that was then.

I pop the trunk of my car as Tyron steps out, Logan following closely.

As they say goodbye, my brain is stuck on how to

make sure I don't hurt Bentley again. It's the last thing I want to do.

Everything I've done has been to protect Bentley and myself. He knows that. It doesn't matter what Tyron says or what he thinks; he doesn't have any idea of why it's necessary to protect Bentley.

"You okay?"

Bentley's quiet question is enough to cut through the loud noise in my head.

I turn to him as much as my seat belt will allow. The blinker is still on, the engine still running, but all I hear is my racing, thundering heart.

Concern etches his features, and I know he wants to reach out and comfort me. I hate that he hesitates, even though I appreciate it.

But for the moment, he can comfort me. Here, in our little bubble alone, Tyron and Logan long gone, and before reality smacks me in the face when we arrive at my folks' house, I can do this for him. For us.

"I love you, Bentley." Despite the dryness in my throat, I push on. "Somewhere between you being my best friend and the person I trust the most in the world, I fell so fucking hard for you. I want to give you everything you deserve, and I promise someday I'll make that happen."

I've surprised the hell out of him.

He clutches my hand, wide-eyed and breathing heavily. The flush in his cheeks is back.

Outside, a car horn honks—likely at me, since I should have pulled out straightaway. But Bentley demands my whole attention. Even if that's not his intention, he has it anyway.

Thoughts continue to circle, almost at the point of spiraling until they land on what I need to do.

Fuck that, what I *want* to do.

But to do that, I need to burst this bubble we're in before I ask him the question that's desperate to erupt.

I need to tell him the truth.

"What's wrong? Your expression's changed." He drops his gaze and peers at our joined hands. "You're shaking. What's going on?" Worry makes his words tremble.

My mouth turns Sahara dry, but I can't put this off. If I really want to do this with Bentley, he needs to know the truth. "It's about what happened to Jamaal, and my—Trevin. What he did."

A furrow appears between his brows. Usually, I'd smooth it out, but I can't get distracted.

"O-kay?"

I swallow hard, the click loud in the car. "I'm gay."

Bentley startles, his brows shooting high even as

confusion sweeps over his features. Honestly, I wasn't expecting to say those words either. Fuck, it's the first time I have.

He doesn't respond with words. Instead, he squeezes my hand, and a sweet smile settles on his lips.

"I've known I was gay since puberty. Jamaal and I were going at it in the storage closet in the gym." Heat slams into me as I speak, and I can't believe I'm finally sharing this with him. "Uhm… he was blowing me when Trevin burst into the room." I wince at the memory, and Bentley squeezes my hand tighter.

I shake my head as the moment flashes in my mind. "I didn't even know Trevin was in town. We had a game that night, and he was never around. Jamaal and I had told Coach we'd sort the storage room and make sure it was locked up. The only person who should have been on-site was the janitor. Fuck."

"Hey." Quiet and calm, Bentley's voice washes over me. "You don't have to tell me any more. I know the outcome, right?"

Mutely, I nod. I'd told him about the attack—so technically the outcome. Not in graphic detail, but why would I share that with anyone? Even the police didn't need much confirmation. The iron bar covered in blood and hair with Trevin's fingerprints on it had been more than enough evidence.

"It wasn't your fault." He leans into my space and tugs me into an awkward hold, grasping me so tightly, I'll be feeling his touch long after he's let me go. "I know you, Sammy. And I'm telling you now, this was not your fault. What you were doing wasn't wrong. Trevin is completely responsible."

I go to pull away, denial on the tip of my tongue. If we hadn't been there… if Jamaal hadn't been sucking me off—

"No." He holds on, refusing to let me ease out of his hold. "You were fifteen, and what you and Jamaal went through, no one should ever have to go through. Nothing about what happened is okay or right or fair, nor is any of it your fault."

Fuck. A tear slips down my cheek, and I burrow my head into his neck. "But I didn't tell anyone what Jamaal and I were doing. He was out, and Trevin admitted he attacked him because he didn't want his son corrupted. I never corrected him. Neither did Jamaal. Fuck, Trevin never told anyone that I was getting blown by a guy. Who the fuck does that? Keeps their mouth shut like that? I'm a fucking cowa—"

"No. Fuck no." Holding on to my shoulders, Bentley eases away and looks me in the eyes. My vision is blurry, and I can only imagine what a mess I look like. "You were fucking fifteen. In no situation ever should you be forced to come out. Jamaal was protecting you. He chose not to tell the whole truth. Did you ask him not to? Force him?"

My face scrunches in horror. "Of course fucking not."

"So that was his choice." A tender smile forms on his lips as he wipes away my tears. "I love you, Sammy. So fucking much. Thank you for trusting me with the truth."

A shuddery breath escapes me, and I struggle to get my thoughts together, let alone my emotions.

"You don't hate me?" God, I hate how pitiful I sound, but I need to know, even if I don't understand it.

"I could never hate you, Sammy. Not ever."

Our gazes remain connected. There's no hesitation, no shying away. He's letting me see what's in his heart.

I still need to talk about Trevin and my fears. But first, I need to say this, ask this, fucking do this before the words explode out of me.

"Marry me."

Bentley parts his lips, his brows darting so high, it should be comical. But I'm deadly serious about this. About him.

"Now. Today. Before we go home. Bentley, I love you so fucking much, and what I'm asking of you, to keep everything quiet, is shit and harsh, but I promise it won't be forever. I just…." I trail off, my words catching in my throat at the tears welling in his eyes. *Fuck.* "I love you so fucking much. Will you marry me?"

CHAPTER 14
BENTLEY

Surprise has my mouth gaping like a fish struggling for oxygen. Between the genuine need to take a breath and the loud, fast pumping of my heart, it's a struggle to think, let alone function like a normal adult.

"What?"

I can't have heard him right.

That Sammy, the man who's been burying his head in the proverbial sand about his feelings for me, feels what now?

He parts his lips to speak, but I rush out first with "You love me that much?"

And it's fucking crazy that I'm asking that after everything he shared with me. Plus, I told him the same thing literal minutes ago. But still, those are the words that decided to spill out.

Emotion slams into me for a second time. Everything looks hazy through my eyes. Shit, I'm going to cry. The fuck is that about? I've only just wiped away his tears, yet it looks like it's my turn.

His "More than anything" hits the mark, and fuck it all to hell, I feel dampness on my cheeks.

The last time I cried was when I was legit devastated by loss when my grammy died. But crying from happiness? Is that even a thing? Hell, when we won the championship, I'd been so ecstatic, though not tears-of-joy happy.

But he loves me more than anything.

Nerves dance across his features, but Sammy, my Sammy who can be a dick and a fool, has never looked more earnest. And with his story, his pain between us, fresh in the air, my heart feels full to the point of needing to spill over.

He touches my cheeks, wiping away my tears with a tenderness that doesn't help my emotions one damn bit.

A fresh one rolls down my cheek even as he swipes them away.

Fuck me dead. Fuck me more that I can't find my words.

He loves me. Like really fucking loves me. Loves me enough that he wants to marry me.

Like, holy fucking marriage with rings and vows and a promise of forever.

"Marry me, Bentley."

Holy fucking Jesus and all the big-dicked unicorns.

It's real. He's really asking.

Words lodge in my throat, even though my heart is trying its hardest to force them out.

The click of his swallow catches my attention, piercing the overwhelming reaction of my emotions.

"I just…."

For the first time, he loses the shine from his eyes, his certainty wavering at my hesitation.

I match his swallow, clearing the emotions tightening my throat, and finally say, "I love you too. More than anything."

Of course I do. Fuck, before we even kissed all those months ago, how I felt had come close to unraveling me. That'll happen to a guy who's thrown a double whammy of "what the fuck" when he starts wanting things not only with another man for the first time ever but also with his best friend.

"Oh thank fuck."

His relief is so visceral that it pulls a laugh from me. Hell, maybe the first time I said it, the words never registered. Not that I blame him, since he was in the middle of pouring his heart out.

He matches my grin, happiness shining brightly in his gaze. It's instant and looks so perfect on him.

My brows shoot high when he all but launches himself at me, sweeping me up in a spine-tingling kiss.

I close my eyes, sinking into the connection.

All I focus on is Sammy's touch, the warmth and honesty of his promise.

"Yes," I gasp, pulling away from him. *Fucking hell….* "Yes," I repeat. "Let's get married."

An honest-to-god gasp escapes Sammy. My heart is galloping. A buzz vibrates in my brain, nudging at me, quite possibly urging me to think more clearly about this, but screw being sensible or over-thinking.

"I want to marry you."

I don't think I've spoken more genuine words. Before this moment, I may have had fleeting thoughts about marriage, but it seemed so far in the future—if it ever happened at all.

"You do?" Sammy's wide-eyed and smiling so big, and his voice… it's full of tenderness and a hint of disbelief.

I nod, even as my stomach does somersaults.

"And we'll tell people once my old man doesn't make parole, yeah, and once we've moved?"

The ache for Sammy and all the crap that must be

regularly bouncing around in his head hits me hard and squeezes my chest.

I don't want to know the answer to the possibility of what his bio dad making parole and being released early will mean for us. How can I when Sammy's staring at me with such openness that's all hope and love?

I'm nodding, ignoring everything but the adrenaline pumping through my veins and how fucking crazy and amazing this is.

"Let's do it." My words are breathy but so certain. This is madness. But when have Sammy and I ever played by the rules or done anything that would make sense to anyone else?

"Fuck yeah." He unbuckles his seat belt and hauls me to him.

Our mouths connect with a softness that leaves me breathless. It's at complete odds with the speed of my racing pulse and the nervous excitement swirling in my gut.

When Sammy pulls away, he opens his eyes, and our gazes collide with an intensity that I hope will always be between us. "Find the address of the closest probate court so we can get a license."

Fuck, we're doing this.

With my heart in my throat, I tug out my phone. My hands tremble. I want this so badly, I want to be there right now. I don't care about anything but making this happen. It'll make the secrecy, the longing, the painful months worth it because Sammy is worth everything.

The next three hours are a blur.

It only took a couple of hours to fill in the wedding license paperwork and for us to leave the probate court with shaky hands, matching grins, and a license. We headed straight to the closest courthouse, relieved it's not a public holiday until tomorrow for the long weekend.

It's been just thirty minutes of sitting here, shooting the shit while Sammy hasn't removed his hand from mine. It's distracting in the best way. Our joined palms and the gentle stroke of his thumb over my skin keep me grounded and stop me from freaking out.

"Seventeen."

It's our number.

Hand in hand, we stand and peer over at the man dressed in a cheap suit who's clutching a pile of paperwork. His attention flicks to us, and I see it, the recognition in his gaze.

The slight widening of his eyes makes my heart

stumble, and I tense. Is Sammy going to realize and freak the fuck out? This whole thing needs to be kept secret.

"Come on." Sammy tugs my hand, and I exhale, matching his stride as we make our way toward the man who I assume is the judge's clerk or something.

"Do you have your paperwork?" The clerk holds out his hand and offers us a friendly smile. It relaxes me immediately.

"We sure do." Sammy hasn't let the paper go since we picked it up. It's hella sweet. He grins widely as he passes it over, squeezing my hand as he does so.

"Great." The man takes it. "Do you have witnesses with you?"

I shake my head. "No."

"Not a problem. If you'll follow me." We do as he says. "I'm Carlos, and I'll act as one of your witnesses today. Mary, another court administrator, will join us. Once we've completed a little more paperwork, I'll take you in to meet Judge Jeffries. She'll officiate the ceremony."

We nod in the right places as he leads us into a small office.

After making copies of our IDs and completing some paperwork, he hands everything back to us.

"Ready?" Carlos's eyes are bright, his smile even more so. His enthusiasm settles me that much more.

For a fact, I know my parents are going to kick my ass when it comes time to tell them about this. Not that they know Sammy and I are a thing, obviously. As far as they're aware, I'm straight as an arrow. But since Sammy and I are attached at the hip, it won't be that much of a shock, right?

I'm likely kidding myself about the shock factor, but what I'm certain about is their acceptance.

My uncle John married his longtime boyfriend as soon as same-sex marriage was legalized in San Francisco. Mom stood by his side as a witness, and I'm pretty sure if given the opportunity, she'll become the president of her local PFLAG chapter.

Sammy angles toward me, capturing my gaze. "So fucking ready."

My heart is getting a serious workout as, once again, it somersaults. But it's when he leans in and presses his lips to mine, here, in front of someone, that I know I'm where I should be—marrying my best friend.

Breathless, I pull away and eagerly follow Carlos into the judge's chambers.

It reminds me a little of Dean Cartwright's office at school with the oak paneling and almost regal look to it. But unlike Dean Cartwright, who comes across as a surly asshole at times, Judge Jeffries is nothing but smiles.

She stands from her large desk, her teeth gleaming against her dark skin. "Mr. Hardy," she says, shaking Sammy's hand. "And Mr. Sandford," she follows up and shakes my hand, her gaze assessing though her pleasantness doesn't dim.

"Judge Jeffries," we both greet.

"I have to admit, your names on the paperwork made me do a double take."

It's probably a good thing she's just come right out and said something. Our faces are on sports channels often enough that college basketball fans will know who we are.

What I also know and had read out to Sammy en route here was their privacy disclaimer. Unless we're unfortunate enough to get photographed on the way out of here, we should be safe. It's not like we have paps following us around or anything. We're not League players, but still, news of what's happening here would definitely blow up social media pages, at least.

Sammy, his hand still in mine, finally answers, his small smile still present. "When you know, you know."

My gaze is immediately on him. Not hearing an ounce of bullshit, I want to see his expression.

As the judge says, "Well, that's definitely how love works for some people," Sammy turns his head.

His intense green eyes connect with mine. He lets me see his nerves. But that's not the only emotion playing out on his face.

Excitement and determination are front and center.

"It's how love works for us." Sammy squeezes my hand, and I'm close to dropping to my knees to ask him to marry me. Pointless and ridiculous maybe, but it doesn't stop the rush of emotions from overwhelming me. It does make me wish I could have asked him first so he knows just how much I want him to be mine forever.

"If I can take that paperwork from you, we can get started."

Her words snap me out of staring at Sammy, and for the next ten minutes, we go through the motions until we're standing before Judge Jeffries, my left hand gripping Sammy's right while she's saying words I've heard hundreds of times on TV and in movies.

But this is so real, even though it feels like I'm in a dream. Everything is a little fuzzy around the edges of my vision, and my heart feels close to exploding. It's surreal as fuck, but there's nowhere I'd rather be.

Not now. Not ever.

The judge had previously asked if we'd prepared words. While we said no, Sammy is keen to say something, so we're going to do so on the fly. Sammy was born with the gift of speaking his mind and having no qualms about anything that passes his lips.

Me not so much.

But for Sammy, I'll do it.

"Sammy," the judge says with a smile, "do you have words you'd like to share with Bentley?"

My stomach tumbles with relief that he's going first. I still have no idea what to say.

"Yeah, thanks, Judge Jeffries." Sammy's smile is so damn wide as he turns toward me, taking both of my hands.

Jesus. Sincerity pours from him. I've never seen him look so intent and earnest.

"Bentley," he begins, a sheen in his eyes that constricts my heart, "when this started, all I understood with certainty was that my best friend knew yet another part of me that no one else did or ever could."

I squeeze his hands. At the tingling in my nose, I press my lips together. I hope I keep myself together.

"You're patient and kind and a kick-ass center." My lips twitch, and I hear our witnesses chuckle. "There's no one else I want to go on this journey with. I know this is fast and that we keep making this sh—stuff up as we go, but you're it for me, Bentley. We just work. It's so easy with you, so right, and loving you is the easiest thing I've ever done."

Damn this man.

A traitorous tear spills down my cheek. His palm is on my skin in the next second, and he wipes the tear away. I lean into his touch, finding strength in the heat and connection.

"Bentley."

I flick my gaze to the judge, who smiles kindly at me and gives me a nod of encouragement.

I bob my head and swallow down the emotion clinging to my throat.

Keep your shit together.

"Sammy." A fresh smirk appears on his handsome face as soon as I say his name. It does the trick of calming my galloping heart. "I've had a million firsts since we met."

The asshole's smile turns salacious, and it takes everything inside me to keep going and not snort out a laugh.

"There's nothing I want more than to turn some of those into lasts… with you. Wherever we end up, whatever happens today, tomorrow, or twenty years from now, as long as you remain my always, then I know we'll figure it out."

By the time I've finished, Sammy's gaze is soft.

We both know that acting rashly like this will possibly have consequences, but that we're doing it anyway, fighting for our future together, means everything.

Have we half-assed it?

Of course.

But beyond basketball training, half-assing it rings pretty damn true about every other aspect of our lives. Admittedly, I have a career and a goal, but those weren't my original plans when I started college.

I trusted my gut then—changed my major—and I trust Sammy implicitly.

We'll work this out together.

Holy shit….

Sammy slips the cheap band that we picked up from a store a couple of blocks away onto my finger, and I do the same to him.

"By the power vested in me by the state of Georgia, I have great pleasure in announcing you married."

We're married.

As Judge Jeffries's words echo around the room, disbelief washes over me. A swift rush of exhilaration mixed with absolute joy follows.

It's real. We're really married.

My heart pounds as I glance at Sammy, his eyes

damn near sparkling with the same disbelief and happiness that's zipping around me.

The weight of the moment hits me, and it's impossible to keep these feelings down. A grin splits my lips as I pull Sammy close, unable to resist the urge any longer.

Our lips meet in a fiery kiss, igniting a spark that electrifies the air. Passion, gratitude, and a huge-ass promise pass between us as our lips glide against each other, and the tiniest touch of tongues has me holding him closer.

Breathless and flushed with emotion, we pull apart. I meet Sammy's gaze. He's feeling this too. I have no idea how we're going to drive to his parents', not with the need that's burning with an intensity I've never experienced before between us.

I don't even know how I'm going to let go of his hand.

This is wild. My emotions, the way I feel like I can't be without him.

"Are you ready?" Sammy asks, his voice all gravel.

Wordlessly, I nod.

With Sammy by my side, I'll be ready for anything.

CHAPTER 15

SAMMY

There's nothing more that I want than to ditch the plan to head home today, but there's no way I can let Mom down. Staying in a cheap motel with my husband is absolutely the only thing I want to do.

Husband.

A grin stretches my lips, and I pull Bentley's hand to my mouth and press a kiss there. As soon as I drop our joined hands back onto my thigh, I side-eye him. Unsurprisingly, Bentley's stare is already on me.

"You just thought it again, huh?" While he's smirking and teasing, it's obvious how much he loves that I can't keep my emotions in check.

"You know it." I angle toward him, keeping half an eye on the road, making it crystal clear that I want his lips on mine.

He leans into me with a soft chuckle, pressing his mouth to mine before easing away.

Contentment washes over me like a gentle breeze on a warm Georgia day as we draw closer to my parents' house. I can still hardly believe it. *Husband.*

Our elopement may have been fast and reactive, born from the need to express how much I love him, but there are no regrets. Instead, peace settles within me. That's what Bentley does—shares his quiet calmness and makes me feel like I'm his and I belong.

More than that, I can be myself with him.

I lean back in my seat, watching the rush of pre-Thanksgiving traffic already around us, stealing glances at Bentley beside me. It feels surreal, the fact that we're married. I suspect it will for a long time.

A smile plays on the corner of his lips, mirroring my own. I squeeze his hand gently, wanting the physical contact for as long as possible. We'll be jumping off the freeway in a couple of minutes. Not much farther and Mom will be on the front steps, my stepdad by her side, ready and waiting to get the Thanksgiving festivities started.

I'm trying to swallow down my frustration that we've had to pass motel after motel. It's unfair on my folks to delay much longer, and it's not like I haven't missed them or my siblings.

"You doing okay?"

"Yeah. Just thinking I could fake a breakdown and we could show up at home tomorrow instead so you can fuck me like you mean it tonight."

"Fuck, Sammy." A whimper merges with his low groan. When he squeezes his cock, I shift in my seat, my own dick thickening. "You can't say shit like that to me and expect me to say hi to your folks with a raging hard-on."

"My cock's just as needy," I complain. Do I stick my bottom lip out in a pout? Damn straight I do. "And hell if I don't feel empty." I'm not even exaggerating. Even before we exchanged vows, need rode me hard. Now, with our combined "I dos" floating around in my brain, I'm desperate to consummate our marriage.

The exit appears up ahead, and with a huff, I flick on the blinker. Fifteen minutes till I have to keep my hands off Bentley.

"No way am I going to survive not touching you how I want." My voice is tight as I pull off the freeway.

"New plan."

My brows shoot high. It's not just the gravel in Bentley's voice that has my dick throbbing. It's absolutely the firmness, as though he knows what the hell he's talking about. He also hasn't let go of his dick, so I know he's as desperate as I am.

That may also be a contributing factor to the discomfort in my pants.

"Which is?" I'm at the traffic light at the corner of Broadbank and Fifth Street. Once I'm through this intersection, I'll be on the main drag home, with just a couple of turns before we're on the street we moved to when my mom remarried when I was six.

There's plenty of traffic around, and if I look hard enough, I suspect I'll see a few faces I know. It's a big small town, if that makes any sense, with a few thousand people living here. And with my high school just five miles away and my reputation for being a loudmouth, it stands to reason that I didn't exactly blend in.

"You got any spots off the beaten track around here that you used to sneak off to when on a date?"

I glance over and catch his smirk and cocked eyebrow. None of that hides the heat in his gaze. He's deadly serious.

"It's daytime," I say, racking my brains about where we could hide to get each other off.

"So?"

I snort. "So, our first time as a married couple is going to be giving each other hand jobs in the back of my Buick, hoping Deputy Dimples doesn't stumble on us. Is that what you're saying?" I grin wide. "Sounds hella romantic to me."

His laughter is loud, the pink in his cheeks the perfect color of sexy as he releases my hand to settle his palm on my thigh. Just an inch over and he'll make me go cross-eyed. That or I'll come in my pants. Both are likely, since I'm so worked up.

"So, you got somewhere in mind?"

I nod as the light turns green. "Yeah, there's somewhere we can go."

I see him smile and relax back in the seat. His gaze is on me when he says, "And Deputy Dimples?"

My lips twitch as I turn off the main road and head out toward the small industrial district. "Deputy Dallas Walmsley. The hottest cop in the state of Tennessee."

"Hottest, huh?" There's not a lick of jealousy in his tone. And rightly so. Bentley is all I can see. All I ever want to see. We have the rings to prove it.

I flick my gaze to him as I turn right. "Cop… not man. You're the hottest in whatever state you happen to be in."

He snorts. "Smooth."

"I like to think so. If you end up seeing the deputy's dimples, you'll understand why he gets everyone in town gossiping and swooning or some shit over him."

My smile falls when I think about the confrontation he had with Trevin.

"What's wrong?" Concern laces Bentley's question, and he squeezes my thigh as I slow at the intersection. There are fewer cars around now, as I'm drawing closer to the older side of the industrial area.

"Deputy Walmsley's gay. Had a run-in a time or two with my old man. He was actually the arresting officer, you know...."

From my periphery, I see Bentley wince. "I bet that was a shit show."

A humorless snort shoots out of me. "And some." I crack my neck.

"So, where's this secluded spot you're going to get me hot and bothered in?"

And this right here is reason 4,635,248 why I love Bentley Sandford. Thinking about my sperm donor, let alone talking about him and all the ways he fucked up, always gets me down. I have no room for my old man at the best of times, and I absolutely don't want him anywhere near what Bentley and I have.

Bentley knows this, and that he's distracting me and giving me an out is everything.

My dick gives a valiant twinge. Hell yes, the mood hasn't been completely destroyed.

"Just up ahead," I answer.

Tension holds us both tight. This need is out of control. If I don't find the spot in the next couple of minutes, maybe I'll just hit the brakes and say screw it.

I turn right, and my relief is immediate. A couple of buildings here still appear boarded up, and at the end of the road, there's a turn into a "community walk" parking lot that has trees and a pathway, but I'm pretty sure not a single resident has used it before.

Well, unless it's because they're up to no good.

"Romantic, huh?" Despite the lightness of my words, discomfort unfurls in my stomach. Bentley deserves better than a quick hand job in my car.

"Hey, don't do that."

I snap my attention his way, the firmness of his voice a pull I can't ignore.

His eyebrows are drawn low, and his gaze roams my features. My shoulders sag. There's no point in bullshitting him. He called me out for a reason.

"You deserve more than this," I admit.

"I deserve you," he says pointedly. "I'll take you however and whenever I can. The where doesn't matter."

He releases my thigh as I come to a stop and turn off the engine. He's quick to undo both of our seat belts.

"This is what we both signed up for, yeah?" He cups my cheek, and I instantly lean into his warm touch. He searches my gaze before saying, "And the secrecy won't be forever." While his tone is tentative, I appreciate that he's not asking a question or for confirmation.

"It won't," I promise, responding even though he doesn't need me to. "I love you."

Heat flushes my cheeks. Is it really just today that I told him that for the first time? What the fuck was I thinking?

I should have told him every damn day.

"I love you too." An uplift of his lips follows as he says, "I'll love you even more if you climb in the back seat with me and celebrate you being my husband with us blowing our loads."

A loud laugh escapes me, free and light. "Get your ass in the back seat," I say with a grin just as my phone starts to ring. "Fuck." I take a look as Bentley pauses from exiting the car. "Nuh-uh. Nothing's going to stop me from fucking your hand."

He smirks as he slips from the car and reenters it to sit in the back. I turn my phone to Silent. It's Mom again. One day she'll understand why we're running so late.

I'm out of the car in the time it takes my heart to beat, and then I all but launch myself at Bentley. We kiss and fumble our way into each other's jeans. Firm hands, spit-slick palms, and messy kisses, and then we're grunting and groaning and working each other at a punishing pace.

It takes barely five minutes for my balls to tighten and for Bentley to be enclosing my cock in his lips to swallow me down. A minute later, I'm savoring his taste, licking his glans, and when I come up for air, I kiss him like I mean it.

Kiss him like he's my husband and the one person made for me.

After we return to the front and fasten our seat belts, our breathing still choppy, faces flushed and clothes wrinkled, I blow a bubble with the spearmint gum I popped into my mouth and sigh happily.

"Feeling pretty pleased with yourself over there?" Bentley arches his brow at me as I pull away from the quiet parking lot.

"Hell yes. A stomach full of cum and a foggy brain. Life's pretty damn perfect." I throw him a wink before placing both hands on the wheel as I maneuver around the parked cars on the busy street we're heading down. My heart stumbles when a sliver of sunlight catches my ring.

I turn it around with my thumb and press my lips together.

"We'll leave them in the car," Bentley says softly. "I thought maybe we could get necklaces or something, but I wasn't sure how that would work in the locker room. But it's not like we can wear jewelry at training or during games or anything."

I glance at him as he shrugs. A shy smile plays on his lips as he casts a look my way.

"Necklaces sound good. We can just take them off before practice." I want to wear it close to my skin. It's cheesy as hell, but the ring makes me feel closer to him. It's a reminder of the commitment I made to him and to myself.

"Yeah?"

"Definitely. I have a couple of old chains at Mom's we can use." The words help me to remove my ring and hand it over to Bentley. It's only been on my finger for a few hours, but it already feels comfortable there.

I watch as he pulls his off before returning my attention to the road ahead. He places the rings in the glove box, and fuck if my heart doesn't stutter when he closes the door, hiding them away.

Without a word, Bentley squeezes my thigh. I know he's feeling this ache too.

But it's only for a while that we need to keep up the ruse.

Seeing my childhood home in the distance, I smile. There's barely enough space for a lawn outside, but Leroy, my stepdad, is house and garden proud. The patch of grass is immaculate. I swear, if I pulled out a ruler, each blade would be the exact same length.

A border of plants surrounds it. I have no idea what they're called, but they're hardy enough to grow at this time of the year.

"You ready?" I ask as I park outside the house. Making eye contact with Bentley, I smile and release a soft sigh.

"Yeah." He trails his finger over my hand before he pulls back.

"Come on, then, before the masses descend."

I'm only half kidding.

My two younger brothers are in high school. Unbelievably, that makes me the oldest child. The one with the smarts and wisdom to share. Yeah, most people call bullshit too.

But in a couple of days, my aunts, uncles, and cousins will be here. Plus, my two grandmas and my grandpop. It's going to be a full house.

After grabbing our bags and locking up, we walk along the short path as Bentley says, "Leroy's done a great job with the yard. There've been changes since the last time I visited."

I glance over and smile, but Bentley's gaze is soaking up the yard. Doing the same, I take in the few changes since the summer. Honestly, everything looks a bit dead and bland to me. With the temperatures dropping and considering the season, I think that's normal. Not that I know shit about flowers or anything.

Bentley's chuckle catches my attention. It takes me a beat to realize he's laughing at me.

"What?" I quirk my brow, and my smile comes easily.

"You just think it all looks dead, don't you?"

"Am I that easy to read?"

"You get two small lines between your brows"—he gently brushes his thumb over the location—"when you're studying something and are confused." He drops his hand.

"Do I now?" He nods, and I snort, saying, "In that case, it must be a pretty permanent fixture, then."

The door swings open, and we turn and see my mom. Her smile is bright and instant.

"Get your butts in here, the pair of you, and give me some sugar."

In a couple of steps, I wrap her up in a giant hug. Her hold is strong as she squeezes me. I soak in her warmth and inhale the same brand of flowery perfume she's worn since I was a kid.

"Let me look at you." Firm hands squeeze my arms with affection as I lean away, and she peers up at me. Mom's tall for a woman at five nine, so she doesn't need to crane her neck. "Hey, baby." She cups my cheek. "You doing okay?"

I nod before she finishes. "I'm good."

Studying my face, she nods back, a soft smile forming. "I can see that. You have a good drive?" she asks as she releases me and focuses on Bentley.

"We did, considering. Obviously, traffic was a nightmare. It's why we pulled over and are so late. It didn't help that we had to get that flat tire fixed." What I'm saying is a load of bull, but I need to say something about why we're so late.

"You're here now. That's all that matters."

She hugs Bentley, and hummingbirds take flight in my stomach when he wraps his arms around her. When we tell her about our marriage, there's no doubt she's going to be pissed, but eventually she'll understand. She adores Bentley.

Mom pulls away, and just like with me, she cups his cheek. "Have you been taking good care of yourself?"

"Yes, ma'am."

As always, Mom rolls her eyes. "What have I told you, Bentley, about calling me Nova and not ma'am?"

A deep chuckle escapes. "That you're too young to be anyone's ma'am."

"That's right. I already have gray hairs I need to

cover up. Keep calling me ma'am and wrinkles are going to appear."

She finally steps back enough that we can file into the house and close the door.

"You don't have a single wrinkle, Mom. Stop cruising for compliments," I tease, though I'm not exaggerating. Mom turns forty in March next year. A couple of times she's been carded at a bar. She lapped that shit up.

"What, me? How else am I meant to get compliments when I'm surrounded by teenagers whose heads are stuck in their screens every moment of every day." Her tone is light, but I also know my brothers, and I don't suspect she's exaggerating too much.

"And I don't count?" My stepdad's at the stove, stirring the contents of a huge pan. He glances over his shoulder, winks at me, and shoots Mom an amused smirk.

"Let's see how you do on our next anniversary, and I'll let you know." She punctuates her words with a kiss on his cheek.

When she steps back, Dad snags her by the waist, refusing to let her go. He plants a loud kiss on her lips before easing away, saying, "Honey, you don't look any different from the day I met you. Well, maybe more beautiful."

He means it too. He worships Mom. Loves her the way a husband should.

With a smile, I relax into my surroundings. It's always good to be home. The warmth of the house greets me, as does the scent of chili, one of Dad's favorite dishes to cook. "Smells good."

Dad releases Mom, who heads to the sink, and greets me with a hug. "I knew you'd been in need of a good feed." He pats my back. "I made sure I used lean meat too. I know you've got some big games coming up."

I chuckle and stroke my hand over my flat stomach. "I appreciate it. I'm already worried about the workout when we get back to school after Thanksgiving's feast."

Dad laughs and shakes Bentley's hand. "Hey, Bentley. Good to see you. Your folks doing okay?"

"Yes…" He hesitates the barest of seconds before settling on "Leroy. They're doing well." My lips twitch. "They're with my mom's parents this Thanksgiving."

"That's great." He eyes our backpacks. "Why don't you guys go drop your bags in your room and wash up?"

Room? As in singular?

Mom switches off the faucet. "About that," she starts. "We've done a reshuffle, as Leroy's finally finished the office space out back. We bought a new futon for the room, so we thought you guys could go out there. Your brother has a friend staying over, so this way you guys aren't inundated by teenagers."

My grin is immediate, and not for the reason my mom thinks. For the time I'm here, I get to be alone with Bentley at night. Fuck yes.

"That's great, Mom, thanks." I peer over at Dad, saying, "I can't wait to see what you've done with your office." Last year, he started to work from home almost full-time. Our backyard's a decent size, and he's been working on the shed out there over the past couple of years, making it more watertight, even going as far as fitting drywall.

"I have zero plans to work this holiday, so I won't be bugging you guys. Feel free to make use of that lock so Malik doesn't harass you. The kid keeps getting up at six in the morning."

"Really?" Over the summer, I rarely saw my thirteen-year-old brother before eleven. "What's he up to so early?"

"He's all about streaming and making videos while he's gaming. He's made a gaming friend overseas, in New Zealand, I think. Apparently, it's a great time for them to play online together."

"And he keeps going to your office because…?"

Mom chuckles as she pours herself a glass of

wine. "Malik keeps trying to claim your dad's office as his own space. We have to keep kicking him out."

"Does the turd not know how lucky he is to have his own bedroom all these years?" I scoff. Denzel and I ended up sharing the bigger room rather than him and Malik despite them being closer in years. My youngest brother has obstructive sleep apnea.

It was freaking terrifying when he was younger and we had no idea what was happening. Since then, he wears a device at night to help keep his airways open. It also means he gets his own bedroom.

"Come on, now, get moving. Food's almost ready to dish up. I'll wrangle your brothers." Mom shoos us off, and I leave willingly, catching Bentley's eye and indicating for him to follow me. "Be back here in twenty minutes."

"You got it," I call out, opening the back door and stepping out into the chilly air. At least there's no wind. The yard is too enclosed for that. "You okay?" I side-eye Bentley as I reach the new office space and tug open the door.

"Yeah, good." He nods and smiles as we step inside, taking in the room. "Leroy's done a good job." He smooths his hand over the freshly painted walls. They're a pale gray and work really well with the white furnishings.

This may be Dad's workspace, but Mom's definitely decorated.

Someone's already set up the futon too. It's bigger than I expected. Big enough for the two of us but doesn't leave much room on either side. "Looks like you'll need to snuggle up so I don't fall off the mattress." With the door closed, I step into Bentley's space, relishing his warmth and the very fact that I can do this.

He places his hands on my waist as we stand toe to toe. "You know how hard it is not to hold your hand or kiss you whenever I want?"

I nod. "I do. It's a fucking nightmare."

A gentle smile forms as he presses his lips to mine. The kiss is tender, a reminder of our feelings.

"We'll be fine. Being out here alone is a bonus we weren't expecting."

My dick twinges, because of course it does. The barest thought about Bentley and being alone with him gets me going.

"Beats being on the blow-up mattress." Which is where I've slept in the past when Bentley's visited. I've always insisted he have my bed, while I take the floor.

"Come on, we need to wash up."

"Let's check out the en suite." I drop my bag and indicate the closed door.

"There's a bathroom in here?"

"Yeah, it was just halfway done when I left at the end of summer. It's small, but it has a shower, sink, and toilet."

"This visit is getting better and better." He chuckles, his gaze meeting mine. The heat there has me swallowing hard. "You want me to flick the lock on the door?"

"Fuck yes."

He snorts as I start stripping, dumping my clothes on the way to the small shower room. Once I'm inside, I turn the tap on and step inside as soon as it's warm enough.

"You seriously think we're both going to fit in there?"

I arch my brow at him as I step under the warm water. "As long as we get real close, I think we'll be just fine." I rake my gaze over him as he ditches his jeans and boxers. The rest of his clothing, I'm assuming, is on the floor in the office.

There's a smattering of hair on his chest that I love rubbing my fingertips over, but it's the trail starting just below his belly button that I love the most. "Fuck, you have a pretty cock."

His dick twitches at my words, and I grin, snapping my attention to his face and his flushed skin.

"Tonight, I'm going to fall asleep with it buried in my ass."

"Fuck, Sammy." He grabs hold of his cock and squeezes. "We've got exactly fifteen minutes to be back in the house with your family. You can't say shit like that unless you want to do something about this problem I have."

I trail my gaze down his body and settle it on his dick as he lazily strokes himself. I wet my bottom lip, more than up to the challenge of getting him off quickly. At this point, I don't even care if I don't get off again until after. To see him release—watch him give up control and shiver in ecstasy—is pretty fucking amazing.

Just tasting him before hanging out and having to keep my hands off him is enough. For now.

So I do exactly that.

CHAPTER 16
BENTLEY

While being with my in-laws isn't how I envisioned spending my secret non-honeymoon, there are definitely worse ways.

Every time we're alone, we're practically glued to each other, and while it's not often, I commit every touch to memory. And our actual first night as a married couple? Well, needless to say, I'm in awe of Sammy's ass.

That man is the most persistent SOB I've ever known, because yes, he totally had his way and fell asleep with my cock snug inside him.

Was the night full of passion and loud monkey sex? That's a definite no considering his family's close proximity, but it was sweet and gentle and perfect all the same.

Today, though, I've barely managed a second alone with him.

But that's okay, since his extended family are entertaining as hell.

Laughter, loud and genuine, fills the table as we stuff our faces with our Thanksgiving meal. There are at least four conversations going on, and I love every moment.

This is the second Thanksgiving I've spent with Sammy. It makes me hopeful that this is what all our future Thanksgivings will look like. Hopefully with my folks joining us too. Not that I know where we're going to live after college.

We'll be together no matter what. A subject we haven't broached, but there's time for that.

"That was incredible. Thanks, Mom, Dad." Sammy pats his stomach as he places his cutlery on his empty plate. "I'm stuffed. I totally wore the right pants."

He's wearing gray sweats because he's an asshole who likes to torture me. When he moves his leg just so, it shows the perfect outline of his dick. Admittedly, his tee is long enough to cover his crotch, but we've already established that my husband is an asshole who lifts his T-shirt whenever I'm looking.

"You too stuffed for dessert? We have pumpkin pie and a pecan pie too," his dad asks.

My stomach aches at the thought of any more food. And tomorrow's morning run is going to kick my ass.

"Maybe later for me. That means I can have a slice of each," Sammy answers.

There's agreement around the table from his family. There are a lot of folks here. We're spread over three tables, and I'm loving every minute.

Thanksgiving at home is always quiet, just me and my parents. The rest of my relatives live in California, so it's rare that we all get together. It makes the volume in the Hardy house crazy loud, and honestly, I've never felt more at ease.

The whole family is so accepting.

Sammy leans in close, whispering, "You stuffed too?"

My lips twitch. He's as subtle as a sledgehammer. "I can wait for dessert. It'll make me appreciate it more," I answer with an arched brow.

He snorts and stands. "We're on kitchen duty."

I join him and start gathering plates as he tells his brothers to get off their asses to help. They do so, grumbling, but we clear everything away as the rest of his family—his cousins excluded, as they help us in the kitchen—move to the sitting room. A moment later, the TV is turned on for the football game.

While his brothers load the dishwasher and his

cousins tidy away the leftovers, I wash up the pots that can't fit into the dishwasher. I pass Sammy a saucepan for him to hand dry.

"What time do you need to call your parents?"

"After football." Dad will be glued to the TV.

He bobs his head before asking, "Are they still heading over for the game next month after Christmas?"

"Yeah." I shoot him a smile, one which he mirrors. "It's the easiest time for them to travel with their work schedules." I study Sammy when he focuses a little too hard on the tray he's drying. "What's up?"

His single-shouldered shrug is not as nonchalant as he's likely aiming for. He casts a look around the kitchen, and I do the same. Everyone's getting on with their tasks, so they aren't paying attention to us.

"Seriously, you okay?" I keep my voice low and just for him.

"Just thinking, is all." What he doesn't say with his words, he says with his eyes.

Realization hits me, and I don't know whether to smile because he's being adorable even though he doesn't mean to be or throw him a bone and tell him he's got nothing to worry about.

While I don't really know how my folks will react to our news when we finally tell them, I'm confident they'll support me. Will they be surprised? Not any more than I was when my feelings for Sammy grew in a way I never predicted. But they love me without strings, without barriers or restrictions, of that I am certain.

I'm so lucky. I feel that acutely, especially since learning the truth from Sammy. Hell, even now, my gut aches and my heart legit hurts at all he's been through. The last thing I want to do is put pressure on him, but we do need to sit down and talk for real.

"You've gone quiet on me."

I startle at his words and quickly reassure him. "Shit, no. Nothing bad. I was just thinking about my folks." My smile is fast to form. "They'll always be supportive." I raise my brows for emphasis, obviously unable to say more.

When he leans in close, I inhale his cologne. There's a warmth to the scent, reminding me of sun-kissed woods and smoky fires. But it's more than that. It's balanced with a touch of freshness, like a cool breeze cutting through the humidity of a forest.

How fucking odd does that sound? But hell if I don't love how it smells on Sammy.

"You think when we've finished up here, we can go to our room and have a talk?"

Surprise has my heart lurching. I search his gaze,

his expression, and see nothing that makes me worry. "Yeah, of course."

"Good, yeah." He nods and pulls away, out of my space. "Thanks."

Nerves weave through his voice, and a faint blush sits high on his cheeks.

I have no idea what it is he wants to talk about, but I pick up the pace washing the dishes. While I don't think it's anything bad, I don't think he's making an excuse to steal me away to get hot and heavy with me.

"Done," Denzel says with flourish, closing the dishwasher and turning it on.

"Are you going to watch the game?" Sammy peers over at his brother.

"Yeah. Family tradition and all that." Denzel rolls his eyes, but he doesn't look put out.

The rest of the younger members of his family—Sammy is by far the eldest—take that as their cue to abandon their posts and race to the sitting room. No doubt to claim some floorspace for good viewing.

"Don't mind us," Sammy hollers after them. "We'll finish up."

I chuckle and shake my head. "Never a quiet moment, huh?"

"Or a job that gets finished." He grins.

"It's almost done." The abandoned tasks aren't

too bad. There are some unwrapped leftovers, and the kitchen counters are a mess and need wiping down. The bin's also overflowing and needs taking out.

After unplugging the sink, I set about cleaning it out and then start wiping down the countertops with some disinfectant spray.

"Thanks for this." Sammy's at the trash can across the room from me, pulling out the bag.

"You don't need to thank me for pulling my weight. You know I enjoy being here."

His nod is slow, his gaze assessing. He finally settles on "I know you do. Sometimes it's like wrangling hyenas when the whole family's here, yet you take it in stride."

Heat blooms in my chest at the compliment. With no idea what to say, I simply smile and shrug. He bobs his head, then makes quick work of tying a knot in the trash bag before he crams the leftovers into the refrigerator.

"I'm going to head outside to dump this. You good here?"

A low chuckle escapes. "Yeah, I'm good here."

I don't know what it is about my answer that warrants his beaming smile, but I'll take it.

The back door opens, then closes behind him as I rinse the cloth.

"Hey, Bentley."

I peer over my shoulder at Nova. "Hey. We're almost done."

Stepping farther into the quiet kitchen, she smiles and heads my way. "Thanks for tidying up. I saw the kids make a run for it, so I wanted to make sure they hadn't abandoned you with too much mess."

"It's all good. Sammy's taking the trash out, and I just have this surface to do."

"I appreciate it."

I return her smile, feeling fresh heat in my chest, which races up my neck and touches my cheeks. Nova's awesome, but she's also my mother-in-law and doesn't have a clue. Between that and me never really being alone with her before, I feel super awkward and guilty.

"You mind if I talk to you about Sammy?"

My muscles turn rigid at her request, though I nod. It's hardly like I can say no.

"It's really about Trevin. Sammy didn't say much after his last visit."

Wide-eyed, I stare at her.

Fuck, doesn't she know that he was successful at getting a parole hearing? Christ knows how that happened, but it's happening soon.

"I know Trevin's hearing is coming up," she's quick to say, and my breath whooshes out of me. Her chuckle is light. "I figured that's what the look on your face was. He told me that and let me know Trevin has a date for his hearing."

"Okay." Relieved, I nod. "Yeah, that's good. Well, not good." My brows shoot high. "You know what I mean."

The smile she sends me is soft, kind. "I do. And I agree, it's not good that he's got a hearing date. I have to be honest, with this being Sammy's senior year, I'm worried how he's going to handle everything if Trevin's successful."

A lead weight forms in my gut, feeling heavy and uncomfortable. I'm concerned too. Aware Sammy's been gone a while and not wanting him to walk in with us talking about him—even though I'll tell him everything about this conversation later—I peer out the window.

It's still light out. Even though the sky is blue overhead, it looks cold. We're at the back of the house, so if I can't see Sammy, then it means he's still out front.

Turning back to Nova, I promise her, "He'll be fine, whatever happens. I'll make sure he is. Sammy's shaken up about Trevin possibly being released early, but he's also not exactly eager for it to happen three years from now either. But he's got me, and I won't let Trevin hurt Sammy again."

Panic grips my chest when tears well in Nova's eyes. Fuck. I've made her cry.

"Thank you, Bentley. He was hurt so badly when it happened, and not just physically." She sniffs, and thank God, a tear hasn't spilled yet.

"I know."

She steps closer to me, right into my space, and cups my cheek. "I know you do. I suspect you keep all his secrets."

Fuck, fuck, fuck.

The panic's turned into a tsunami of fear as my flight instincts kick in.

"Thank you for being there for him. For loving him."

Retreat. Retreat.

I'm struck mute, which is probably a good thing. What I can't do is deny how much I love him. I can't lie to Sammy's mom.

"Will you promise to call me if you need anything? If Sammy needs anything?"

My nod is slow, almost wooden. "Yeah," I croak. After clearing my throat, I try again. "Of course I will."

A soft smile remains on her face, and while her eyes are watery, she still hasn't cried. Dropping her hand, she rests it on my forearm and squeezes lightly.

"Right." She steps back. "I best grab the drinks I promised everyone."

I work hard at controlling the rush of relieved breath. "Let me help."

She shakes her head. "Why don't you go see if Sammy needs saving from one of the neighbors? They all watch your games anytime they're aired. They like to talk about every play. And if it's Tomas, he'll keep Sammy talking for hours if he's not rescued."

I cling to her offer of escape immediately. Throwing the cloth on the draining board, I get the hell out of there. The cool air is a relief on my heated skin.

Fuck it all to hell. I inhale deeply before exhaling.

What on earth was that?

Does Nova know? Suspect? When she said I love him, did she mean as a friend? Everyone who knows us is aware of how close we are. That's always been the case.

Have we behaved differently this visit compared to last year?

The questions buzz around my mind as I head down the short path and open the gate that leads me to the front yard. Sammy's back is to me. He's just wearing a T-shirt, so he must be cold. Goose bumps broke free on my arms the moment I stepped outside, so given the five or so minutes he's been out here, I suspect he's feeling it.

The scrape of my sneakers on a small pebble on the concrete footpath alerts Sammy. He angles my way, his grin quick to form as his eyes drink me in. It's impossible to not return his smile. The flutter of wings in my stomach, the speed of my pulse—every damn time I lay eyes on the man, my whole body comes alive. So does my soul.

Fucking hell.

My smile slips, as does his when he tracks my expression.

Of course his mom's figured something out. How could she not when every time I'm with her son, all I see are love hearts and a future that makes me giddy.

"They ready for me?" Sammy asks pointedly.

"Yep, I was sent out to get you."

He bobs his head and turns back to the old man he's been talking to. "Good to see you, Tomas. You have a great Thanksgiving, you hear?"

"Will do, Sammy."

They shake hands before they head their separate ways.

"You good?" Sammy asks as soon as he's at my side.

"Yeah, but you want to head out back now?" I have to tell him about his mom. There's a chance I'm reading into the conversation, but he still needs to know.

"Sure. Let's go through the gate rather than the front door."

We veer off the footpath and go straight to the converted shed. Once inside, I sigh at the blast of heating.

Rubbing his hands together, Sammy does a whole-body shudder.

"You need help warming up over there?" While I might be freaking out a little about his mom, I've had to go all day without touching him. It's harder than I expected.

"If you're offering, I won't say no." The right side of his lips quirks, and I step into his space, wrapping my arms around him.

At the contact, my shoulders relax as I exhale. His skin is cold, and his hands trigger goose bumps as his palms settle on my back.

"Hmm, you're warm and toasty." His hold on me tightens.

"That's me, a walking, talking heater."

His chuckle is quiet next to my ear. "Just another reason why I married the right guy."

My heart flips before pounding heavily. It does every time he mentions our marriage. I angle away, wanting to see his face. "I don't think I'll ever get tired of hearing that."

His smile is soft. "I won't get tired of saying it either."

This man, he seriously is the sweetest. I swear no one would believe it. Between his off-topic chats, his loud conversations, and his ridiculous jokes, there's a whole other version of Sammy that no one gets to witness.

No one but me.

The knowledge is heady, as is his trust in me.

The thought is sobering. His mom's words are loud in my head.

A small frown appears between his brows. I've gone quiet, my own smile slipping, so I understand why.

"Let's talk on the bed." Usually, that would not be the safe option. But there's nowhere else for us to sit together, and standing in the middle of the room while talking this out isn't ideal.

When he nods, I kick off my shoes, and he does the same. Once we're on the bed—my back to the headboard and Sammy in front of me—the furrow between his brows has deepened.

"You're kinda freaking me out."

"Shit, sorry, I don't mean to," I say. "When you were out front, your mom talked to me."

He tilts his head and studies my face. "Saying what?"

Heat flushes my skin. His eyes dip, following its path before he makes eye contact.

"She's worried about you. Spoke a little about Trevin."

Sammy clenches his jaw. Every single time Trevin's name is mentioned, he always does. I'm not even sure he's aware of it.

I swallow hard, a little embarrassed by what I'm about to share. "When I told her that I have your back, that I'll never let Trevin hurt you, she seemed happy, grateful even." Sammy's gaze softens, his jaw unclenching. "She then thanked me for being there for you." *Fuck, here it goes.* "Thanked me for loving you."

His eyes go comically wide, and in any other situation, I'd laugh. Silently, he stares at me. Honestly, his eyes glaze over a little, and I'm not convinced he's really seeing me.

When he asks, "And what did you say?" I almost jump, having lost myself in the silence.

I shrug, the movement awkward and far from nonchalant as I admit, "I, uhm… I didn't actually say anything. I didn't want to lie to your mom outright. I just promised to call her if we needed her when she asked me to. Then I came to you."

Try as I might, I can't keep the heat out of my cheeks. That and my pulse races through me so fast, it's likely I'll pass out if I don't sort my shit out.

I kind of want to go back in time and kick my fourteen-year-old self. What a fool I'd been, so desperate to grow up and be an adult.

But fuck if loving Sammy isn't worth all this adulting bullshit.

"Okay." He nods… and nods some more, repeating "Okay" enough times that I'm starting to get worried.

"Okay?" I don't hold back my concern or my confusion.

"Tomorrow morning, when everyone's gone and it's just my folks, I think we should tell them."

My body has a mind of its own as it does this jerking thing. From surprise or excitement, perhaps a little "holy shit" anxiety, I struggle to catch my breath.

"Shit, we don't have to." Sammy reaches for me. Panic flares in his gaze, his expression filling with concern. "It's a lot. Fuck, there's your parents, too, and I don't even know if you want to tell them about us. And if you do, like…." He trails off and shakes his head, his brows shooting high. "Shit, forget it. It's too much pressure. I don't want you to feel like you have to come out. Fuck, this whole time, I'm the one who's said we have to keep this secret because of…" He hesitates but continues with "Trevin and what happened."

Even though he winces, he's on a roll, his words tumbling out as all his thoughts seem to be spilling out in whatever order they wish.

"No, you're right. We shouldn't. I don't know what I was thinking. Nothing's actually changed. When he's released, he'll cause shit if we're together and out. And if he tries to hurt you—" He blanches, effectively cutting himself off as his expression morphs from fear to anger to whatever other emotion he's juggling.

I need to speak, need to calm him down, but I have no idea what to say or do. What's the best thing in this situation? There's no "right" thing, or at least I don't think so. So it has to be about us and what we're happy and comfortable with.

"But I also hate this. We've been married for less than forty-eight hours, and I fucking hate not touching you, loving you the way I want to."

My heart squeezes, and I'm lost in his desperation and confusion. "Which is how?" The question falls out unplanned, but I need to know. Maybe this will be the answer to cut through all the noise. Maybe this will help me decide what I want to do.

He takes a deep breath, his eyes searching mine

for reassurance before he speaks. "I want to hold you until the stars grow jealous of how much brighter you shine in my arms. I want to kiss every inch of your skin until it knows the taste of my love by heart. I want to whisper promises into your soul until it sings with the certainty of our forever. I want to cherish you in a way that makes every moment feel like an eternity, because, Bentley, eternity isn't long enough to spend with you."

Holy. Fucking. Shit.

Speechless, I stare at him, taking in this man before me. Sammy, my husband who, sure, talks a good talk, but a poet he's not.

Until he is. And apparently, it's this very second that I barely recognize him.

Any moment now, my heart's going to explode. It's filling too fast. How much can one heart handle before it expires from loving someone so completely, irrevocably?

"Fuck." It's all I can manage and is the only warning I give Sammy before I launch at him. I need his mouth, his heat, his body, his goddamn soul. I need it all more than I need to draw another breath.

Our lips collide in a desperate, hungry kiss, igniting a fire that threatens to consume us. I wrap my arms around him, pulling him closer, trying to merge our bodies into one. He can't say things like that to me, blow me away with promises and words that addle my brain, and not know how much he rocks my world.

The sighs between us are soft as the kiss slows. A few feet away, there's a houseful of people. Somehow the knowledge wedges itself into my brain, and with one, two, and a final gentle kiss, I pull away. Our breaths mingle as we peer at each other.

Certainty, warm and reassuring, rolls through me. "I can't tell my parents about us over the phone." Technically, I know I can, but I don't want to. This news is big and life-changing. Not telling them in person doesn't feel right.

While he nods, his gaze dances over mine. "I get it. We can wait."

He's not as good as he thinks he is at keeping his emotions under wraps. My heart squeezes as I think about what else he needs to tell his parents. Since he shared with me—and I'm so grateful that he trusts me so implicitly—I can only imagine how the secret still eats at him.

"Let's figure this out," I say. "Together."

He tilts his head to the right, brow furrowing. "As in?"

I don't hold back. "If we talk to your parents tomorrow and tell them everything, I'll want my parents to know ASAP. It doesn't feel right not sharing this news with them."

His eyes flare wide, and a small, tentative smile forms. "Yeah?"

"Yeah," I say softly. "We need to think of how to get my folks over without me freaking them out. And we need to decide if they're the only people we tell." Nerves flutter in my chest.

We're really doing this.

My skin heats. How will people react? I shouldn't care, and in some ways, I don't. No single reaction from anyone will change how I feel about Sammy, but still, potentially dealing with bullshit on a daily basis is a battle I need to prepare for.

That I know that's par for the course sucks. That I accept it so easily says so much about my expectations of society in general. Unsurprisingly, it doesn't give me warm fuzzies.

"Are you thinking about our housemates? The team?" he asks.

Honestly, at this point, I have no idea.

Everything has happened at breakneck speed, especially after giving in to the slow buildup of us hooking up while burying our heads in the sand.

I twist my mouth in thought while shrugging. "These are decisions I never in my life thought I'd have to make."

Worry furrows his brow. "We don't have to decide anything yet. Tomorrow with my parents doesn't even have to happen. Hell, I'm freaking the fuck out about Trevin."

I know it takes a lot for him to admit as much, so I wait patiently for him to finish.

"I just want to know what's happening with his early parole. He'll obviously get out at some point, but maybe I'm a fool thinking that three years from now, I won't give a flying fuck and this… concern I have now won't even be on my radar."

My heart hurts for him, and I want to offer him all the reassurance in the world. Is that even the right thing to do? The last thing I want is to discount his fears.

"What?"

"Huh?" My eyebrows shoot high, and I release my top lip, not having realized I'd latched on.

"You want to say something." He gives me an up-nod. "Tell me what you're thinking."

Words flutter around my mind, and I try to grasp on to the right ones to share. I snatch hold of those I think are the truest. To me, anyway.

"There's no way I can understand or even relate to your worry, Sammy. What you went through makes me so goddamn mad. If I think too hard, I could lose my shit. Hell, I'm so close to calling Ty and making sure Trevin is on his shit list when he becomes a fed."

Sammy's lips twitch, and I relax a little, reaching out and resting my palm on his thigh.

"Honestly, I've thought about it and haven't completely disregarded the idea. It has serious merit."

God, I love him. Even now, Sammy's found a reason to smile.

"Well, maybe we should stick a pin in that and circle back to it." I'm not completely joking.

There's little doubt in my mind that Tyron will be successful in joining the FBI and will be a kick-ass agent. Once he finds out about Trevin and his history with Sammy, I suspect we won't even need to ask him to add Trevin's name to his shit list.

"What I don't want is for you to stop living and us from having a life together," I say, barely managing to keep the tremble from my voice.

This here is some serious grown-up, married-couple shit we're diving into. I am so unprepared for it. Knowing Sammy feels the same way is the only reason I'm not freaking out.

"Fuck, Sammy, I have no idea if I'm gay, or bi, or pan, or another letter of the rainbow. Maybe one day I'll get my head around it, but at the moment, all I am is your husband."

His gaze softens. "That's not all you are," he corrects immediately. "You're a kick-ass college basketball player, and a man who's going to make an incredible landscaper sometime soon."

My smile is instant, and my heart is full. "Obviously, all that goes without saying." I release a soft exhale and a snicker. "But do you get what I'm saying? My sexuality status currently sits in the married-to-Sammy-Hardy category, and I'm more than okay with that."

As I say the words, rightness settles somewhere deep inside me. I really am okay with that. For now, at least.

"I'm ready to tell people whenever you are. If that's now or in a week, a month, or a year, whenever it is, we'll make it work." Even if it's difficult, we'll figure it out. "As for Trevin, who knows if he's going to say or do anything, but at the moment—I hate to say this, Sammy—you're giving him power that he doesn't really have, and he certainly doesn't deserve it."

It's minuscule, but I don't miss the way his jaw clenches.

"Whenever he's released, we take out a restraining order if we have to. We make sure he doesn't know where we live, and you don't see him again." The latter may be impossible, but at least if

Sammy doesn't visit him again, it's a start. "Even if we tell our families and our friends, we never have to tell anyone else. Next year, no one's going to care anyway. It's not like we're Kieran with League plans. At the end of college, we'll just be us. Married and happy. Hopefully not too broke and pissing each other off about whose turn it is to take the trash out."

A glimmer of emotion crosses his gaze. This time I keep my mouth shut. I've spent a long time talking at him. Hell, my voice is a little scratchy, unused to monologuing. I've had my chance to share my piece. It's now up to Sammy to decide how he wants to handle everything.

I've already made it clear: I'll follow his lead.

CHAPTER 17

SAMMY

Power.

Fuck. Is that what I've been giving Trevin all this time?

The thought pulls me up short. My already aching stomach goes haywire, much like my brain as I struggle to process. Jesus, am I really so dim? I know I'm not acing classes, but I'm passing. It's not like I'm even trying to be a brain surgeon. Lofty plans and I have no relationship whatsoever.

"I have no idea why the hell you married me." Insecurities not buried too far beneath the surface spill free. My tone is low, ashamed. I'm not even looking for an ego boost.

"The hell are you talking about?" Bentley's voice is riddled with confusion. "Why on earth wouldn't I want to marry you?"

Is this what I've become? A self-pitying dipshit who seems to spend his life screwing up and making one bad decision after another? Not that marrying Bentley fits into that category, but maybe I put too much pressure on him. Forced his hand.

Nausea swirls in my stomach. I can't look at him.

"Sammy, whatever the hell you're thinking, stop." Soft fingers touch my chin and gently tilt my head. "Please look at me."

My eyes snap to his. I'm not that much of an asshole to not do as he asks.

"Now it's your turn. Tell me what you're thinking."

A heavy throb of my heart takes my breath away, and my body tenses. If I tell him what's going on in my mind, what if he agrees and I lose him? Or worse, what if he stays because he feels sorry for me?

"Please, baby."

I close my eyes. I can't deny him anything. I respect him too much to even contemplate trying.

"I feel like a fool."

Bentley clamps his jaw together, a fierceness forming in his gaze as he stares at me, but he doesn't say a thing, giving me space to talk.

"It's a lot, you know?"

This time, he bobs his head and says, "I know,"

before lifting my knuckles to his lips and pressing a kiss against them.

The gesture, so insignificant in the grand scheme of things, soothes me. My eyes sting, but I don't hide away from Bentley.

"I'm not sure why or even how you can love me after everything I've done and put you through. The last thing I want is to put ideas in your head that'll have you running...." I trickle off with a humorless laugh.

Waiting patiently for me, Bentley strokes his thumb over my skin. I focus on his touch, his calm assurance. I don't think there's been a time when I've been so serious or so lost for words. The whole situation feels alien, as though I'm losing myself.

"Can we tell the guys? Just them," I clarify. He knows I'm referring to our housemates. It goes without saying that includes their boyfriends.

The thought pulls me up short.

"You think there's something in the water at the house?" I'm totally teasing, but I latch on to it like a lifeline. The fact that I even feel like joking is an emotion I want to cling to.

"What are you talking about?"

"The whole fucking household is riding the queer train." A smile pulls up my lips, feeling so fucking good. "How epic is that?" My brows shoot high when I think about what Tyron said in the car. Fuck, was that seriously just a couple of mornings ago? "Tyron's got that statistic he spouted about so damn wrong. Five of us on the team." I snicker, falling into the familiar sensation of ease. "He's going to lose his shit and compile his own study or something."

Bentley's smiling, his gaze searching, but he lets me have this.

We share a laugh, enjoying the momentary reprieve from the weighty discussion. It's moments like these that make it crystal clear why I fell in love with him.

When our laughter settles, I release a steadying exhale. "Telling the guys means we can be ourselves at home. Not quite sure how I'll cope if I'm unable to kiss you whenever I want."

"Yeah, I feel the same."

My heart turns into a pile of goo.

"And, Sammy."

His tone garners my attention. It's a little sterner than I'm used to. Gotta say, I'm not hating it.

"Nothing will make me run. Ever. Okay?"

Whatever is meltier than goo, that's so me. Now. Right this second.

"We take this a day at a time. Perhaps see what your folks have to say about Trevin."

I wince, but he's also right.

I may be twenty-two, but I'll absolutely always be my parents' kid.

"Mom's going to be pissed."

"Probably, but only because she'll hate that you went through all this by yourself."

True.

"And coming out to anyone else, we can do on our terms, but know I'm ready, okay?" He tilts his head, a slow grin forming. "If ever you decide you wanna hold my hand or smother me in kisses, doing the whole PDA thing, you have at it. This is me giving you all the permission you need."

My mouth stretches wide, happiness blooming in my chest. PDA with Bentley is absolutely something I want. Desperately. When I'm ready.

"You know I'm faster than you, right?"

"Uhm… barely," he challenges, glee lightening his eyes.

"Uh-huh, whatever you need to tell yourself, sweetheart, but for the record, I am." I arch my brow at him, and he chuckles. "It means if ever I piss you off enough *to* run"—he parts his lips, no doubt to argue with me, but I carry on before he gets the chance—"I'll catch you."

Bentley launches at me with a low laugh, smothering me with kisses.

All too soon, we stop. My family, I'm sure, is waiting for us. Plus, there's dessert to be had.

In unspoken agreement, we stand and straighten out our clothes.

Gripping the door handle, Bentley turns to me. "Earlier, you said you wanted to talk. Was there something more?"

A soft huff of breath escapes with a smile. "It was exactly this. I wanted to talk to you about telling our parents."

"No shit?"

"Right!"

He presses a gentle kiss to my mouth. When he pulls away, it's hard to remember to breathe.

How it's possible Bentley loves me in such a way that it's impossible for me not to see and feel will probably always blow my mind. While I don't quite understand it, there's not a chance I'm going to fight it.

Loving snuggling in Bentley's arms is the only explanation for me being able to sleep last night. Usually, even a hint of nerves jab at me like annoying gremlins with tiny little spears. And yes, I've visualized them a lot, especially when it's four in the morning.

They're ugly fuckers.

But not last night.

Despite my bouncing knee as I become the worst big brother, wishing my siblings would hurry up and go out with their friends, I slept so well. Hell, I didn't even have a hangover.

I wouldn't have drunk much anyway, since we'll be heading back on the road to college after lunch, but also, me and booze and Bentley is a combination that's just asking for trouble.

"What's wrong with you?" Malik studies me intently, his frown letting me know he thinks I'm odd.

"Nothing. What's wrong with you?"

Bentley snorts at my side, and I flip him off, admittedly only because Mom's back is turned.

Malik, apparently the most mature of us all despite me being nine years older, shakes his head at me.

"Don't you have somewhere to be?" I swear I'm usually nicer to my brothers, but neither of them will leave and give me space to talk to Mom and Dad.

Narrowing his gaze at me, Malik twists his lips. Immediately, I realize my mistake.

"Why do you want me to leave? What's going

on?" He quirks his brow. "Just *how* badly do you need me gone?"

I swear, this kid's going to be a gazillionaire, likely from extortion. Okay, more likely from smarts, though I'm sure to be successful at extortion, you need a brain. Either way, now that I've pretty much told him I want him to take a hike, there's no way he's going anywhere—not without an incentive, at least.

Mom's making coffee while talking on the phone to her best friend. Dad is somewhere, probably enjoying a moment of peace after yesterday's full house. I just hope he's not in his office. There's no guarantee it doesn't smell like sex.

I absolutely need to strip the futon and shove the linen in the washing machine before Bentley and I leave.

"Depends on what it's going to take," I answer.

An assessing smile forms as he eases back, spoon still in hand from his second bowl of cereal. As we know, he's smart. He's not going to ask for cash. My folks work their asses off, but there's not a lot of cash floating around. I managed to score a basketball scholarship, the lucky duck I am. It's the only reason I didn't have to go to the local community college.

While I work over the summers, that cash helps me avoid piling on too much student debt.

Malik's gaze flicks to Bentley. I follow suit. Bentley sits a little straighter, eyebrows high.

After a beat, my brother drops his spoon in his empty bowl and sits forward, urging us to do the same. Confused and amused, I do so with ease, wondering exactly what this kid is going to say.

"After you graduate, wherever you guys are living, I want to stay for the summer and work with Bentley, earn some cash to buy an Alienware Aurora."

Shock reverberates through me, making my ears ring. Not because he wants a new gaming PC or that he's willing to work hard for it.

At my side, Bentley's still. He's waiting for my response, maybe even my reaction.

I clear my throat. "We'll finish a month before your school breaks for the summer. Why do you think I'm not going to be home?" In truth, we still have no idea what we're doing. Bentley is the only one with a realistic job offer. It makes sense to take that, and I'll find something close by.

Malik rolls his eyes at me, legit disappointment pouring out of him as he shakes his head. "Seriously?" he huffs, and damn if I don't want to fidget under his gaze.

"What?" My question is weak.

"All I want is a yes or a no. Can I stay the summer

with you guys?" He focuses on Bentley. "And pick up a laboring gig with you?"

Bentley doesn't hesitate. "Yeah, of course."

"Great." He stands up, gives us an up-nod, and clears his bowl away. He nudges an oblivious Denzel, who's at the table with his earphones on and staring at his phone.

"What?" he grunts, tearing out one of his pods.

"Butt up. We need to clear out," Malik instructs.

Fascinated, I look on as Denzel gets up without resistance and clears his bowl before leaving the room, Malik hot on his heels.

"The fuck?" I hiss and glance at Bentley. His lips are pinched, his eyes lit with amusement. "He knows something, right?"

Bentley bobs his head, finding it hard not to react. And I get it. He wants to know my thoughts.

"It's fine. That he didn't come right out and say anything means he's respecting that we're keeping this quiet." At least, that's what I figure. We may have different bio dads, but we were all brought up by the same father. We know the importance of family and protecting and respecting each other.

Movement at the doorway draws my attention. Dad with a coffee mug in hand. His gaze drifts to me, and he smiles.

"All good? Malik said it was time I topped off my coffee and you wanted to talk to me and your mom."

Lips parting in surprise, I drag in a breath.

Malik did what?

Bentley's attempt at covering his snort of amusement is weak at best. I flash him a wide-eyed look, and any brewing panic dissipates immediately. His smile is soft, but it's the way he's staring at me—all love and understanding—that reassures me.

I've got this.

Before I can respond to Dad, who's yet to drift to the coffee machine, Mom's conversation ends.

"Gemma has more leftovers for you to take back to school with you. She's going to drop them over before lunch," she says, stepping to the table with the coffee pot. "You'll need to put them straight in the freezer when you get back." After filling up Dad's mug, she turns to us with a smile. It freezes on her face. "What's going on?"

The pot wobbles in her hand, and Dad is quick to take it off her and place it on the table.

Speaking directly to Mom, Dad says, "The boys want to talk to us about something."

They share a look, and my pulse picks up speed.

We're doing this. Now.

Have I rehearsed this conversation a million times? Absolutely. It doesn't make this any easier.

"So…." That's all I've got until Bentley moves his hand onto the table. It's subtle, barely a flex of his fingers, but I latch on to his offer—and his hand—like the lifeline it is.

Mom's the first to react. Eyes wet with tears, she sniffs, a smile blooming. Like the incredible father and husband he is, Dad loops his arm around her, his gaze never straying from me.

"So, yeah, I'm gay, and we're married."

A gasp and a whole-body jerk from Mom, and perhaps I could have slipped in the second piece of information a little more delicately. I have no doubt—especially after what she said to Bentley yesterday—that's what this reaction is about.

Her "You're married?" complete with what I'm sure is hurt cement it.

There's no backtracking. Not that I want to, but I don't want her to feel like shit either.

"Officially day four. It wasn't exactly planned." When Bentley squeezes my hand, I immediately glance at him. My pounding heart settles a little, and I turn back to my parents. "But it's the best decision I've ever made. I love Bentley."

When Mom's whole face softens, I know I've said the right thing. Is she still pissed and likely upset that she couldn't share our wedding day with us? That's a given. She'll forgive me, though. Our marriage, our wedding, is all about me and Bentley and what's right for us.

The moment Mom fully recovers, she's practically dragging me out of my chair to hold me tightly, wrapping me up in one of her impossibly strong hugs.

"I love you so much, Sammy. I'm so proud of you. Thank you."

Unable to speak from the tickle in my nose and the emotion clogging my throat, I hug her back and nod. What she's thanking me for, I'm not sure. But what she's not doing is lecturing me. I'll take it as a win.

She pulls away, her palms cupping my cheeks. I peer down at her. Love shines up at me. It settles into my chest, warm and happy. I latch on to the feeling, aware I have more to share with her.

"I have a feeling this is also you officially moving out." A tear trickles down her cheek, but she's smiling. "I'm not sure when you grew up so quickly and to be such a good man, but I really am so proud of you." She casts a glance at Bentley, who's standing at my side. Dad's next to him, having given him a hug while I'd been close to losing my cool with Mom. "I'm so happy for the both of you."

A whoosh of air escapes my lungs. "Thanks, Mom."

She steps out of my arms and hugs Bentley as Dad gives me a giant hug. He may not be as tall as I am, but he still manages to make me feel safe and protected.

"You happy, son?" he whispers as he pats my back.

"So goddamn happy."

Pulling away, he nods. "Then this is wonderful news."

It's hard to swallow as a fresh wave of emotion threatens to unravel me. I suspect Dad knows it, as he squeezes my arms and steps away. Bentley's then at my side, but I need him to hold me.

Turning into him, I sigh at the comfort of his warm embrace. A shuddery breath later, I whisper, "I'm good."

His grip softens, and we make eye contact. "You ready?"

I bob my head before turning back to my folks. "You might want to sit down for this."

Confusion transforms both of their features as they do as I ask, surprising the hell out of me, truthfully. It's rare that Mom's not firing questions my way.

Whatever she sees in my expression is enough to have her staring at me in wide-eyed expectation.

With a deep breath, I settle as close to Bentley as I

can without sitting on his lap. His presence helps soothe some of my fear. My discomfort.

And I tell them. Everything. Even the parts that have my tears spilling and Mom sobbing. Dad's fists clench as I share each word, his emotions playing out like a building storm.

Their disbelief and anguish are palpable as I recount every harrowing detail of that night. And my shame. My guilt.

While they knew Trevin had hurt me, all they'd been told was it was in the process of me trying to stop him from killing Jamaal. I'd been in the way. The hero they thought I'd been was all bullshit, a pile of ash washing away with our mutual tears.

Not that that wasn't exactly what I'd been trying to do. But the first punches that night were Trevin's on my face as he kicked Jamaal off his knees so he could get to me first.

Mom's gentle hands reach out to comfort me despite the way her jaw tightens with restrained fury. At her side, Dad remains a silent sentinel, his struggle almost tangible.

As I finish speaking, there's a heavy silence in the room, broken only by the echoes of our shared pain. Their love presses into me, their support enveloping me. But fuck if I don't feel the weight of their anger.

Not at me. That I know with certainty, with a

conviction that's been forged out of love and protection.

Dad's the first to speak. "Sammy, we love you." His swallow is loud in the otherwise silent room. "You mind if you boys head out to the store to get some milk while we process everything?"

I'm out of my seat immediately, Bentley joining me. "Yeah, sure."

Before we can leave, Mom bounds out of her chair and is in my space, hugging me with a fierceness that takes my breath away. This is why Dad wants them to have a moment. Mom is likely to storm out, jump in the car, and drive at breakneck speed to get to the prison. If given the chance, she'll do damage to Trevin.

That he managed to hurt me… yeah, that's not something I'm sure Mom will be able to come to terms with easily.

Nor should she, I suppose.

All this time, she thought she'd kept me safe. That shit is likely going to mess with her head. I hate to disappoint her.

Since Mom's never so much as raised a hand or a wooden spoon to me, her disappearing in a fit of rage hurts my gut. I kiss the top of her head and whisper, "Love you, Mom." Like a fire's been lit under me, I latch on to Bentley's hand, and we make our escape.

Apparently, I need the space as much as my parents do.

The cool air makes my teeth ache as I drag in a breath once we're outside.

"Here."

I startle when Bentley thrusts my jacket into my hands, and I take it gratefully.

"Let's walk."

We don't hold hands, but our shoulders brush, the soft sound of fabric creating a soothing rhythm.

For a few minutes, we walk in silence. While my head's buzzing and I'm emotionally drained, I feel better.

"You think my mom's losing her shit and Dad's having to hide the car keys?" The humor I attempt doesn't quite catch, but Bentley shoots me a gentle smile.

"Possibly." We cross the street before he asks, "Did that pan out like you expected?"

I tuck my hands in my coat pockets to stop from holding his hand and shrug. "Not sure. Yes and no."

He remains silent and nods, giving me the space to try to center myself. It's going to take more than a walk to the store to buy a bottle of milk we don't need, but it helps.

"They took our marriage better than expected. Mom didn't launch into wanting to throw us a party." An uncomfortable ache settles in my chest, knowing we'll never have that. "It's a good thing, I suppose, since we haven't told them we're keeping our relationship on the down-low."

Though, based on everything I told my folks about Trevin and how I've felt, I don't think it's technically necessary. My eight years of silence is telling enough.

"And how do you feel?"

We slow down when the store comes into view. There aren't many people around, since it's still early and this is our local store, not one of the big chains.

How do I feel? This one is easy.

"Relieved." I turn and face him. We're so close, the white puffs of our warm breaths collide. "Maybe uncertain. Not sure what comes next, you know?" He nods. "I've been keeping this a secret for so damn long, letting it eat at me."

"We can work that out together."

Bentley's so earnest, I'm tempted to lean in. I hate that I'm not ready. That there's this big barrier I've allowed to form roots standing in my way.

"Thanks, Bentley. Not sure how I'd be getting through any of this without you." The amount of shit I've put us through is hard to make peace with, even though he's asked me to do just that.

"Always." As he presses his top teeth into his bottom lip, he searches my gaze.

"You okay?"

"Yeah, I suppose I'm just thinking about what Malik and your mom said, about you no longer living at home."

A bubble of amusement breaks free as I shake my head. "It all seems a bit warped when a thirteen-year-old knows more about me than I do."

Bentley's lips twitch. "So, they're right?" Hope caresses his words.

"I just want to be wherever you are." I reach out and tug at the sleeve of his coat. "If you take a job with Grady, I'll be with you. If you find a position elsewhere, then I'm with you."

Tenderness fills his gaze. "Yeah?"

"Yeah."

I'll miss my family, but leaving Tennessee is not a hardship. There are too many ghosts lurking here.

"Let's go grab the milk and maybe snacks for the drive back." What I also want is to be in the privacy of my home so I can lean in and kiss my husband.

By the time we get back, Mom's baking.

The woman is an expert with a paintbrush and a screwdriver, but a baker she is not. Unless it's from a premixed packet, she tends to stay well clear. Everyone in the house is grateful that's the way it is.

Honestly, people think my food combinations are strange, but Mom's baking skills aren't even about that.

So this—flour on the counter, chocolate chips sprawled right next to the bag, and her stirring fiercely—is majorly disconcerting.

How long were we gone?

"Mom?" My tone is all caution.

Dad's sitting at the kitchen table, worry in his gaze, but when we make eye contact, he smiles.

"The first batch of cookies will be ready in five minutes."

"Okay," I say tentatively to her, putting the milk in the fridge.

"You need a hand with anything?" Bentley steps past the table and close to the kitchen counter.

At his question, Mom lifts her gaze, almost like she's surprised to see him there. Her shoulders sag as she gives a slow shake of her head. "You're a good boy, Bentley."

There's no lip twitching that she's calling Bentley, who towers over her, a boy.

"Have you told your parents?" The way she peers at him is like she already knows the answer. Not a surprise, since we've been married a total of four days.

"Not yet. I'm going to ask them to come to the

game before Christmas. We'll tell them then. I don't want to speak with them over the phone."

"I know they'll appreciate that." Mom reaches out and squeezes his arm before casting her attention my way. Fresh emotion appears in her eyes. "I'm so sorry you didn't feel able to come to me." I quickly move over to her. "If I'd have known—"

I tug her into my arms, cutting her off. "You didn't do anything wrong, Mom."

While she doesn't argue with me, I'm not sure she believes me either.

At the sound of the oven timer, we pull away. Bentley's there, though, opening the door and pulling out the tray with an oven glove. The look on his face tells me everything.

My lips twitch, a bubble of laughter trapping in my throat. A strangled sound escapes as Mom's brows jump high, but I'm focused on the tray.

The "cookies" don't look like any type of cookie I've ever seen before.

A laugh bursts free, high and a little hysterical.

Making eye contact with me, Bentley winks, a wide smile forming, making him look more hand-some than ever.

Dad's laughter joins in. It's closer than I expected.

Mom turns. "What the hell?" A snorting laugh

follows, the room soon loud with unhinged guffaws as we stare down at her baking attempt.

"They look like mini UFOs crash-landed on the baking tray," Bentley quips, trying to stifle his laughter.

"I was thinking more like the moon's surface after a meteor shower," Dad adds, wiping tears from his eyes.

Mom shakes her head, still chuckling. "Okay, so not the prettiest cookies, but they have character, right?"

"Uh-huh. That's one way to put it." I swipe one of the misshapen treats. "Let's hope they taste better than they look."

Am I nervous to actually eat one? Absolutely. But how can I not?

We need this. This break. This snap of tension.

As I shove the cookie in my mouth, wincing at the bitterness, my heart fills completely.

I did the right thing, finally telling my parents and trusting them with the truth. Not only that, but sharing Bentley with them is everything.

He leans over and accepts a bite, despite the grimace on my face. A loud crunch and a dry swallow later, he pulls me close, pressing a kiss to my neck.

Yeah, we're definitely going to be okay.

CHAPTER 18
BENTLEY

WE'RE NOT THE ONLY ONES WHO SEEM TO HAVE GONE through it this Thanksgiving.

When we arrive back at our shared house, it's to an unexpected scene. Tyron's dads and siblings are here. Their bags are packed and waiting by the door, and while everyone is full of smiley greetings, the fact that they're here means something's gone down.

I greet Tyron with a hug and a questioning gaze. In response, he shrugs. I suspect he'll let us know what's happened when he's ready.

Helping put the pile of leftovers into the fridge and freezer, Tyron asks, "How was your Thanksgiving?"

The best ever. The words are on the tip of my tongue, but I hold them back. Sammy and I plan to tell the whole house tonight when everyone's home. I can keep myself contained until then.

"Yeah, good," I offer. "I'm still stuffed. It was great to get away, but honestly, the thought of practice tomorrow is already making me regret the desserts."

"It's always hard to get back into it after a few days off. Coach is going to kick our asses," he says, the words a little echoey since he's rearranging the contents of the refrigerator.

It's hard not to ask him why his family is here, but I don't. He's smiling, so I figure everything is okay.

Looking around, I spot Sammy laughing at something Tyron's pops is saying. Warmth fills my chest. I'm loving his contentment. Our morning was obviously full-on. We talked, legit cried. But I think it was cathartic for everyone.

The drive back, just the two of us, was surprisingly quiet, but there wasn't a lick of discomfort. We just held hands, Sammy driving and keeping to the speed limit while I fed us snacks even though we didn't need them.

"Is he okay?"

Tyron's question has me dragging my attention back to him. He's on his knees, a mountain of containers around him, but his gaze is on Sammy. When I don't answer immediately, he looks at me.

"Yeah." There's nothing more I can say, not right now. Sammy isn't ready to tell them about Trevin. He may choose to never share that part of his life. Whatever he decides, I'll support him.

"Good." A single up-nod, and Tyron turns to organize the refrigerator. I attempt to help, but I'm sure I'm just getting in the way of his system.

It's my cue to leave when the front door opens and Leon enters.

"Oh, wow, a full house." He closes the door behind him. With Tiller living locally, it makes sense that he headed home to see his folks. "Good to see you all." He shakes hands with Tyron's parents, hugs Sammy, then heads my way when he spots me.

"Hey, Leon. Good trip home?" I ask.

"Yeah. It was good to head back."

That's a relief. He had plans for big conversations with his parents as well this Thanksgiving. I barely stifle a snort when Sammy's suggestion about something being in the water drifts into my brain.

"That's great." I clap him on his back, happy his smile is genuine. "All good with Tiller?"

It was *the* big introduction, something I can now relate to.

For a moment he's distracted as he eyes Tyron to

see what he's doing. "From Sammy's folks?" When I nod, he answers, "Sweet. And yeah, Tiller's awesome. Mom and Dad took everything in stride. A little confused. Thought my heart was going to explode a time or two, but it all worked out."

As he talks, I wonder about my own parents. The idea is to call them later to check on plans next month. They're flying this way for Christmas to spend some time with me around games, but I don't think I can wait that long. They have a heap of vacation days stacked, so I'm hoping I can talk them into coming out even earlier.

If they don't, I either wait it out or we do a video call. The latter I want to avoid.

"Done." Tyron stands, and Leon and I move to his side to stare into the fridge.

"Sammy's folks are the best at leftovers." Leon nods in approval, and hell if a shot of pride doesn't buzz around me. My in-laws are pretty awesome.

"Does anyone know what time Kieran's heading over, or is he staying with Dean tonight?" I ask, trying to figure out tonight's plan. It's late afternoon, and the sun will soon be setting.

"Not sure," Leon answers. "I've only received the texts in our group chat on Thanksgiving."

As Tyron closes the door, I peer back to search for Sammy. I don't need to look far. He's still standing and talking with Tyron's pops. Before I look away, he glances over, our gazes catching and holding.

There's a slight upturn of his lips, and then I lose his eyes, but I gain his laughter. It's just as satisfying.

"What time is your family heading out?" I ask Tyron. Since their bags are already at the door, I'm assuming soon.

"They've got a car booked. It should be here in fifteen minutes."

"Now Sammy's back with his car, you want me to drive them to the airport?" It seems right to ask, and I honestly don't mind. Since Sammy drove us back, I definitely don't want to say he'll take them.

"No, man, that's cool. You've already been on the road for a few hours. The last thing you want is to be heading to the airport." Tyron claps me on the shoulder and passes me a beer. "Drink this, and it means you officially can't."

I snort as I accept the beer. "Thanks, Ty, but dropping them off for their flight's no hardship."

Tyron arches his brow at me before hollering, "Dad."

His dad, who's sitting at the table talking to Tyron's younger brother, glances over. "Yeah?"

"Bentley's offered to drive you to the airport."

Tyron's dad waves me off. "Nonsense, you just got back. That's good of you to ask, though, Bentley."

His gaze drops to the beer in my hand. "You crack open that beer and rest up. Practice starts tomorrow, right?"

"Yes, sir, it does."

His dad chuckles. "In that case, you best enjoy it. I can't imagine Coach Maple is going to take it easy on you all. You've got some big games coming up."

I lift my beer to him in thanks and open it. But rather than taking a swig, I head over to Sammy. Tyron's pops leaves a few seconds before I reach him, leaving Sammy standing in the open kitchen doorway.

"Here." I pass him the open beer when he looks up.

"Thanks."

"Are you tired after the drive?"

At my question, his lips curl up. "Nah, I'm good."

I roll my eyes, knowing exactly what he's thinking. But I can't help looking out for him. It's always been instinctive for me to have his back. And now, everything has changed. This need to take care of him is stronger than ever.

My text alert pings. As do each of ours.

Since Kieran's the only person missing, it's obviously from him.

Sammy's already pulling his cell out. I shift so I

can see his screen. Is it an excuse to get close to him? There's no point denying it.

A stab of disappointment hits me when Kieran says he won't be heading back tonight. He'll see us at training bright and early.

Sammy angles his head so we can make eye contact. His frustration mirrors my own. We have a whole conversation without words.

Are we going to tell the rest of the guys tonight?

It doesn't seem right.

We'll wait. It doesn't mean we can't be stealthy and still stay together.

"Car's here," Tyron's dad hollers, and the house gets moving.

We all join them outside, saying goodbye. The air's cooled considerably in the hour we've been home. The sun's just dipping over the houses. When Sammy shivers, I'm quick to tug him close from behind and wrap my arm around him.

Tyron catches the movement and my gaze. A chin lift later, his focus is back on the road and watching his family leave.

I still have no idea where Logan is, and honestly, it's odd for him not to be here. These days, they're always together—he and Tyron. They're not quite as attached at the hip as me and Sammy, but in fairness, we've been at this a lot longer.

"It's colder than a witch's tit out here." Sammy shivers again.

He's not wrong. The air is the coolest it's been all fall and nips at my nose.

Tyron, always ready with a tidbit of historical knowledge, chimes in, "You know, that saying actually has roots dating back to the medieval era. Folks believed witches possessed cold, lifeless bodies. It's the reason for the comparison."

I grin while Sammy says, "Huh, medieval witches and their chilly anatomy, who knew?" He shivers again, and I rub his arms for warmth. "But seriously, this cold is no joke. I can feel my bones turning into icicles."

Surprising me, Tyron chuckles rather than explaining how cold it would need to be for that to happen. "Drama queen much?"

Well, he's not wrong. I snort and receive a gentle elbow jab for the trouble.

"Embrace the chill, Sammy. Think of it as an opportunity to wear all those cozy sweaters Bentley's been hoarding."

"Me? Don't bring me into this." Shit, I need to go hide the sweaters or else Sammy really will steal them all.

I pause. *Hmm…* Sammy wearing my clothes does have merit.

Sammy snorts, probably at where he suspects my thoughts have gone as well as at Tyron calling me out on my penchant for hoarding. I'm surprised neither of them is breaking into dragon jokes.

"Easy for you to say, Mr. 'I'm wearing three layers under my jacket.' I'm seriously contemplating building a blanket fort just to survive."

Tyron's eyes light up at Sammy's taunt. "A blanket fort sounds fucking epic. We could make s'mores and tell ghost stories and stay up all night."

"Just in time for Coach to run us into the ground at seven thirty," Leon cuts in.

"Seven thirty?" Sammy sounds as disgusted as I feel. "I thought it was eight thirty."

"Check your email. It was sent out a couple of hours ago," Leon says.

"Urgh. Thanks for pissing in my Cheerios."

A petulant Sammy is always fun. I squeeze him a little, wishing I could bury my face in the juncture of his neck and shoulder and inhale deeply.

In silent agreement, we head back inside, all going our separate ways to our rooms—except for Sammy and me. After Sammy dumps his bag in his bedroom, I lead him to mine.

The moment the door closes, I have him backed against the wall. Our mouths meet with a fierceness that's kinda crazy, considering it hasn't been that long since his mouth was on mine. But fuck, I've missed him. In the short hour we've been back, all I've wanted is to hold him close and whisper sweet nothings into his ear.

With our tongues tangling, our lips brushing, we grind against each other. I'm hard enough to punch nails. Horny enough to not care one bit if anyone hears us from the other side of the door.

But that's not what we agreed.

Slowing down, I whisper against his lips, "Get on the bed and undo your pants." Feeling him on my tongue will help me get through the rest of the evening. As long as he's in my arms tonight, it'll tide me over till tomorrow.

There's no need to ask twice. Not with Sammy.

His pants are below his ass before he's next to my bed. I stalk toward him, my breath hitching when he kicks his shoes and jeans off, then strips completely naked. By the time he's on the bed, I'm tearing at my clothes, my gaze latching on to the way he strokes himself.

"You're so hot." Gravel fills my words, earning me a satisfied smirk.

"You want a taste?"

Without answering, I'm on him, slamming my mouth against his. I kiss him eagerly, breathing him in as I snake my hand around his cock.

Sammy grunts into my mouth, and when I swipe the pearl of precum away, rubbing it into his skin and following with a long stroke, a deep moan bursts free from him. "Fuck yeah."

I smile as I pull away, loving the way his eyes glaze over as he ruts into my hand.

It wouldn't take long to get him off like this, but I want to drink him down. Want him to fuck my mouth until all I know is that I'm his.

With urgency guiding me, I make fast work kissing down his body and settling between his spread legs. When I peer up, this time I'm the one groaning. He's so desperate to come—eyes wild, pupils blown, and panting heavily—it's tempting to take my time.

Having him empty his load down my throat is more appealing, though.

I lick along his shaft, working my way around until I reach his balls. I suck one into my mouth, rolling my tongue around it.

Sammy's whimper urges me on.

"That feels so good." His groan is loud as I suck on his other ball.

I pull off with a satisfying pop. "Shh." I grin as he shoots me the stink eye, and when I finally wrap my lips around the head of his cock, it's hard not to laugh when he grabs hold of the pillow and presses it against his face.

Watching and feeling him come undone like this is the best thing ever. His limbs are tight, his cock hard and smooth in my mouth. I bob and suck, lick and swallow, drawing out his muffled moans.

The heaviness in my balls has me repositioning. Just a few drags of my cock across my sheets is all it will take.

"I'm gonna…."

I work faster, my hand joining in to jerk him off. We both need this after the intense day we've had. We need the closeness, the release, the giant escape after the turmoil of this morning and all the serious conversation afterward.

I dry hump the bed as tingling starts at the base of my spine. My cock swells as I dive back onto his cock. I fit him so far down my throat, my vision blurs from lack of oxygen. And I swallow.

"Nnghhh…." Spurts of his cum release into my throat, and I ease off, swallowing properly and inhaling through my nose. Another shot, and my vision whitens as I rub against the sheets, my whole body tensing as ecstasy, pure and fucking magnificent, zips its way through my body.

Only Sammy's cock in my mouth stops me from calling out.

A shudder rakes through my limbs as I come down from the stratosphere, and I keep breathing heavily through my nose. I'm not ready to release him yet.

Gentle fingers comb through my hair. It's time to pull away. I do so, and Sammy gasps. Goose bumps break out across his thighs, and I press a kiss to one and take a moment to rest my head and close my eyes.

"You alive, sweetheart?"

A smile tugs at me, just like every time he calls me that. "Yeah." I don't even wince at the scratch in my voice, too content.

"Five minutes and we need to show our faces."

Is it bad that I hate that Sammy's right? It's probably worse that I'm resentful that our friends are expecting us downstairs, since we agreed to eat together.

"Kieran's not even here."

His chuckle shakes me around, so I snap my eyes open. "What?"

"Suck it up, buttercup. Well, if you can suck up anything else after the way you sucked out my soul."

I smack at his leg and snort. "Asshole."

"Nah, keep it up. I like you all petulant and needy." He tugs on the strands of my hair, and I angle to look up at him. "Don't ever change."

Whatever sound a giant puddle of love makes, that's exactly what's ringing in my ears.

"But what we do need to change is the bedsheets, as no fucking way am I sleeping on cummy sheets tonight."

And there he goes, keeping it real.

On Jell-O legs, we drag ourselves up and get to work on stripping my bed. The whole time, a goofy grin sits on my face. Legit sits there like it's its own entity or something.

I don't even mind that Sammy keeps smirking and rolling his eyes at me. How can I when I know he feels the exact same way?

COACH SPLITS US INTO TWO TEAMS, AND LIKE THE PAST couple of years, I'm in the starting five. As I step back onto the court, the exhaustion from our intense training session lingers, but I push it aside.

Coach can smell weakness from a mile away. If he notices any of us flagging, he's likely to add time to our session.

Sammy's a few feet ahead to my right. Sweat saturates his jersey. That shouldn't be so hot, but it is. It's difficult not to track the bead of sweat that trickles down his temple and travels down his neck.

We've been stealing glances the whole session. Something I've absolutely done in the past, but now, watching him is a distraction I can't resist.

We're in position, and at the sound of the whistle, we're moving.

Kieran, the powerhouse that he is, dominates the court. I'm determined to support him. I'm there and making sure he gets his hands on the ball whenever there's a chance. Lifting him up and helping him prepare to go pro next year has become our whole team's mission. Our household's especially.

I spring into action, racing across the court when Leon takes possession. I'm there in a heartbeat, ready and open. The ball lands in my hands, and I quickly pass it to Sammy, setting the play in motion.

Kieran makes himself available, moving effortlessly down the court, but Davey tries to intercept his layup. It's a quick move, impressive even.

Hell, maybe Coach really did do the right thing keeping him on. This is our last season. It'll be good to know there's some talent on the team when we move on.

But while Davey may be showing some skill, no way will I let him intercept. I block Davey, leaving Kieran free. Acting swiftly, he sinks a layup. I grin, Sammy whoops, and Tyron's shouting at us to get our asses moving.

We don't let up, keeping the pressure on, stealing the ball whenever we can. After three years together, I swear our communication is almost instinctual. Just a glance or a gesture, and we're moving. Understanding.

Fuck, I'm going to miss these guys.

But not Sammy. Him I get to keep forever.

"*Oof.*" My face slams to the right as the ball makes contact with my left cheek.

The whistle blows, and Coach yells, "What the hell, Sandford! You're standing there grinning like you're already holding a damn trophy. Head in the game, and I'm sure your team will appreciate that you've earned them all an extra minute on the clock."

Shit.

My whole team is gaping at me, their disbelief front and center. Except for Sammy. The fucker is vibrating with amusement.

"Sorry, Coach. On it," I holler, sending a wince of apology to Kieran. Our captain's staring at me like I've got two heads. I get it. I don't get distracted. Ever. Sure, I can mess up like the best of them, but being caught unawares as I'm busy grinning and totally oblivious is so not my MO.

How the hell am I going to explain this one away?

For now, I focus on the ball and my team, working hard to ignore the way Sammy makes my heart race and just how impressive he is when on his game—even in training.

Fuck, I need to pay attention.

I get moving, making sure I'm where the ball is.

We play for another ten minutes before Coach stops us.

"Better." He bobs his head, glances at his notes, and eyes the team. Classes don't start until tomorrow, so in theory we can stick around longer. Not that he's a tyrant.

But he does like to win. More than that, he expects us to be game-ready.

"When we take on the Buccaneers tomorrow evening, I expect you to be well rested. That means a good night's sleep. We don't have practice, but keep up your usual routines. Pumpkin pie seems to have made some of your feet a little leaden."

He's not wrong. I'm relieved Sammy and I went on a couple of runs while we were away. If we hadn't, we'd be screwed.

"Sandford."

My head snaps up to discover Coach's gaze firmly on me. "Yes, Coach?"

"Put one on the clock."

I know better than to grumble even though I'm exhausted. "Absolutely, Coach." I stand from my squat and jog over to the beep clock. One minute on this thing isn't too bad. What is a killer is that it's only one, which means Coach wasn't planning on making us run at the end of training.

It means this one's on me.

With the clock set to a five-second countdown, I make my way to my teammates already standing at the line. No one grouses at me, and no one even subtly flips me off.

Sammy does throw me a wink, though.

I settle at his side, and two seconds later, the first beep sounds. We race to the line, all of us making it and turning before the first beep. With my pulse thundering in my ears, I draw in air through my nose, exhaling raggedly through my mouth. We're on our fourth turn when the beep sounds barely a second after we turn.

What I don't do is look at the clock.

My lungs burn as I pump my arms.

Get to the line. Get to the line.

Another beep, just as I touch it with my foot and turn.

Sweat blurs my vision, but I push on, not daring to swipe it away in case it burns precious seconds.

This time I barely make it, but I turn quickly, pushing myself hard. Three glorious beeps have me screeching to a halt and bending over, drawing in breath.

"Hydrate and shower." It's Assistant Coach Tiller this time.

There's a collective groan of relief as we drag our feet to the locker room. Exhausted, I don't speak. Neither does anyone else. We're too busy chugging bottles of Gatorade.

The showers are already on with some of my teammates rinsing off by the time I've finished. Sammy's still at my side. Hell, he barely took his eyes off me as I gulped down my drink.

"Thirty seconds longer and I would have thrown up." He chuckles, swiping a hand towel over his face before he's back to studying me. "You okay? A little distracted today?"

The asshole looks at me with a cat-that-ate-the-canary smile.

I flip him off, my lips twitching once before I contain my grin. "Go cool yourself off."

He snorts, strips down, and takes his sweet time before wrapping a towel around his waist, leaving his ass on display for an indecent number of seconds.

What I don't do is glance around to see if anyone is watching. It's best to play ignorant.

As Sammy walks away, I strip and secure my own towel, pausing when Kieran says my name. Turning his way, I smile. "Yeah?"

There are only a couple of other people in the

main changing area. Everyone else is taking a shower, which is absolutely where I need to be heading, as I stink.

Stepping closer, Kieran studies me, and I instantly go on alert.

Shit.

I should have known he would approach me. Truth is, me getting a ball in my face would usually put me at the center of Sammy's attention, and I'd receive a whole heap of good-natured teasing. For obvious reasons, that didn't happen.

Which, I see now, is likely suspicious as fuck. If Kieran had come home last night, we wouldn't be in this position. Not that it's his fault. I know that, but still….

"You good, man? I know I wasn't back last night, so we didn't get the chance to catch up."

I'm nodding before he finishes speaking. "Yeah. Good. Fine." Immediately, I stop myself from saying anything else. How I kept my shit together all the months Sammy and I were hooking up is beyond me. It seems since we got married, I've been spiraling.

At my stellar response, his eyebrows shoot high.

There's only one thing for it. I huff out a breath and roll my eyes at myself. "Honestly, I'm good. That ball in my face was the wake-up call I needed."

"Who's throwing balls in your face?" A snicker follows, and I shoot my gaze to Sammy.

Why he's here after he stepped away less than five minutes ago—

"Hey, I'm just here, innocently getting my tweezers. You're the ones talking about sucking balls." Twinkling eyes stare at me, and fuck if my lips don't twitch.

"Jesus, Sammy." Kieran shakes his head. "I don't even want to begin to figure out what goes on in that brain of yours." Nothing but teasing affection laces his tone. Not that Kieran doesn't appear baffled, as he totally does.

But this is my Sammy, and I completely understand him. And I absolutely know he headed out to rescue me.

"It's probably safer that way." A cheesy wink follows, and my heart flips over when his intense green gaze connects with mine. "Anyhow, losers, I wanna get out of here. You both stink, and I say that with nothing but affection and a petition from the campus board."

When he turns on his heel and walks away, Kieran rubs his hand over his face before glancing over me. "You chose him as your friend."

Best day of my life. "Yup. I imagine that decision will follow me around forever." My gaze follows

Sammy as he continues to walk away until I finally lose sight.

"Didn't he want tweezers or something?" Kieran asks, taking a step away and toward the showers.

"Best not to question it."

He snorts. "Truth."

We go our separate ways to shower quickly. There's an assignment at home I desperately need to put some effort into. It's not just basketball that I need to focus on. Now more than ever, I'm determined to ace my final months at school.

If Sammy and I are ever going to be able to afford a place together, I need all the help I can get. My degree is the start of all that.

CHAPTER 19

SAMMY

Eight nights have gone by, and I'm going stir-crazy.

How freaking difficult is it to have everyone in the house at once? Just one night for everyone to sit their asses down so we can tell them the news—that's all we need.

Everyone having boyfriends is putting major dents in my plans. I'm at the point of saying fuck it and simply acting like the married couple we are. Everyone will eventually catch up.

Bentley's not a fan of this plan, but I actually think I'm winning him over.

Whoever said sneaking around is fun was full of shit.

Okay, I may have said that myself in the past, which I suppose proves my point.

Tomorrow, we have an away game, which means if this doesn't happen tonight, we're going to have to wait longer—obviously, since that's how time works —but I'm spiraling.

"If you huff again, I'm going to think you need an inhaler."

My gaze cuts to Bentley. Any other time, I'd appreciate his wit, but not right now.

"Sammy, it's fine."

Fine? Seriously?

Whatever expression Bentley reads on my face has him slamming his mouth shut.

A wise decision for sure. Am I acting way over the top? I plead the Fifth, though I'm not sure if that's the right amendment, but since Tyron isn't here, I really hope I *am* wrong, just to stir him up.

We're squirreled away in Bentley's room. His bedroom's a little bigger than mine; his mattress is better too.

"You need help?"

I almost huff out a heavy breath but stop myself. "No, I'm good. Thanks, though." Because working on my assignment is actually what I should be doing rather than fixating on still not having told our housemates.

But it's December, and before we know it, Bentley's parents are going to be here, which was easier to organize than we thought. And honestly, I just want some semblance of peace before Trevin's hearing mid-January.

"You want to come over here and suck my cock?"

I snap my hand out and grab onto Bentley's desk to stop from slipping back off the chair. When I'm upright and no longer in danger of landing on my ass, I peer over at where he's lounging on the bed, a textbook on his lap.

Bentley's lips twitch. His gaze snags mine. Yeah, there's challenge there, all right.

He drops his heavy textbook on the bed with a soft thud, his brows lifting in amusement.

"You think you can distract me or something?" He totally can. Hell, he already has, since my dick's hard and I'm keen for his mouth to be on any part of my body.

Some of his amusement melts away, eagerness and heat replacing it. "Doesn't sound like much of a challenge, baby. Maybe more like a treat for the two of us."

I drift forward, all but launching at Bentley. Falling onto him, I press against his warm body, instantly feeling a million times more settled than ten seconds ago.

His "Oomph" is all humor as he holds me close.

The sound turns into a groan as I burrow my face into his neck and pepper him with kisses.

A slam of the front door startles me. Muscles turning rigid, I pause and listen carefully.

Deep voices, a chuckle that's definitely Logan's, and I shove off Bentley. "Tyron's here."

Wide-eyed, Bentley stares up at me. "You mean I'm not getting my cock in your mouth?"

I flick my eyes to his mouth. His tongue darts out and swipes over his bottom lip, reminding me that I'm rock solid for him.

This feels like a *Sophie's Choice* situation. Maybe. I'm not quite sure what that is, but it sounds like a really, really hard decision I have to make right now.

Suck my husband off and obviously come my brains out (it's impossible not to, as it's hot as fuck when he shoots down my throat), or bolt all the doors to stop anyone from leaving so we no longer have to sneak around.

A soft chuckle escapes Bentley. "Come on. Ass up. Let's go downstairs." Warmth and understanding color his tone.

My smile is immediate, relieved. "Yeah?"

"Yeah, let's do this."

I smack a loud kiss against his lips before I move. Once on my feet, I adjust myself, tucking my dick away so I don't put on a show for anyone other than Bentley.

A flutter of nerves springs to life, churning my stomach. The reaction is at complete odds with the bubble of excitement in my chest. I *want* to do this: tell our friends about our relationship. I love him so fucking much, and that's something to be celebrated.

"You good?" With his strong hand cupping the back of my neck, Bentley swipes his thumb along the skin.

Goose bumps skitter in the same direction, and I draw in a shaky breath. "Yeah." I turn to him. "You?"

There's no uncertainty in sight. Nothing but gentle determination and a whole lot of love.

"I am. It'll be good to share this."

For a second, guilt tries to break free and claw its way back to the surface. But at the reassuring squeeze of Bentley's fingers, I stop the emotion in its tracks.

Yeah, it's something I've been working on with my new therapist—something my mom kinda gently insisted on. I had my second session yesterday—remotely, as my schedule is a nightmare. And grudgingly, I can admit it's something I should have started a long time ago. Hell, maybe even before I was fifteen.

But I'm doing it now—something I promised my folks I'd do—and I'm grateful for it.

I reach out and take Bentley's left hand. Just the feel of the metal against his finger shoots tingles around my body. I love seeing it there, feeling it warm against our skin.

In the safety of our bedrooms is the only time we put them on. After this, the whole house will be a safe haven. My smile stretches wide before I lean in and kiss him gently. It's a soft press of our lips, just enough to center me.

Then we're moving, not hand in hand like I'd like, but we need to make sure no strays have come home with any of our housemates first.

I'm first down the staircase. Energy buzzes through my body, tingling my skin and causing my pulse to pick up speed. We follow the noise to the large sitting area and stop in the open doorway.

Numerous pairs of eyes settle on us. There are chin lifts and smiles as the conversation continues between Tyron, who's cradling a large pizza box, and Kieran, who appears to be lecturing him about saturated fat.

Bentley moves to stand at my side, and my breath hitches like a hiccup in a helium factory. I mean, seriously, it's like a cartoon bubble is forming over my head, complete with sound effects—*pop, pop, pop!* I can practically hear the *boing* as love hearts bounce out of my chest. It's like a scene from a cheesy romance flick, except instead of sweeping music, we've got the distant bass thumping from a nearby house and the smell of Ty's extra-cheesy pepperoni. But hey, who needs a Hollywood soundtrack when I've got Bentley?

Everyone is here. Finally. Even Tiller, Dean, and Logan.

Dean stands when he sees us. "You can sit here," he says as he moves to Kieran and settles on his lap.

Kieran doesn't break his stride with the lecture. All he does is wrap an arm around Dean, holding him close.

"Actually…." Nerves ripple over my skin and my voice breaks. Why the hell am I so nervous? These are my closest friends. Even more significant is that they're all queer in some shape or form. I swallow hard, the click of my dry throat making me wince.

I have Leon's attention. Dean and Tiller also snap their heads my way.

Warmth presses against the small of my back. Bentley's touch is gentle, but it provides a strength I absolutely need.

The silence grabs my attention. Ty and Kieran have stopped their discussion about pizza, and six sets of eyes are completely on us.

"Right, so...."

Fuck, this is so not what I practiced.

"What's wrong? Did som—"

Ty cuts Kieran off, saying, "Just give them a second, Key."

My gaze drifts to his, and he sends me an up-nod. Understanding shines in his eyes, and I recall the journey to the airport a couple of weeks ago.

Is that really all it's been?

Bentley strokes his thumb over my back before he drops his hand by his side. He's ready to jump in from a simple look. But I want to do this. I even asked him if I could.

Reaching for his hand, I clasp it. Ty follows the movement, and likely others in the room do, too, but it's easier to look at him for some reason. Maybe because he already suspects. Maybe because he cuts through bull as easily as a swift dribble through a shitty defense.

"We want to share our news with you," I start, flicking my gaze briefly around our group of friends. Kieran's brows are high while Dean's hand covers his mouth. "Bentley and I are married."

A wall of silence presses against us, almost immediately shattering when Dean leaps off Kieran's lap, yelling, "Holy shit. For real?" He latches on to both of us—impressive since he's only chest high. "Congratulations. This is amazing."

As he squeezes us, I release a low chuckle while Bentley says thanks. But my eyes are on my friends, those I've known for over three years. My teammates who I've been keeping a lot of secrets from.

Ty's the first of my housemates to stand. His usual stoic expression is nowhere to be seen as a wide grin is directed our way.

"Married?" he says as Dean steps away. "Admittedly, that's not what I was expecting you to say." He hugs Bentley first, then me. His hold is strong and comforting. "Congrats to you both." He eases back. "When did this happen?"

Everyone is listening. Leon is still gaping at us, disbelief and amusement dancing in his gaze. It's Kieran who's standing back, arms folded, studying us like he has no idea what on earth is happening.

When I don't answer right away, a little wobbly from Kieran's reaction, Bentley reclaims my hand, saying, "Right after we dropped you and Logan at the airport before Thanksgiving."

"Holy shit." Leon's still staring at us with wide-eyed bemusement. "That's just... hell, incredible. Not quite sure if you're pranking us, but yeah...."

At my side, Bentley snorts his amusement. "No pranking. It was sudden, but—" He shrugs and glances my way, stealing a kiss when I look at him. "—it was right."

"What about your parentals? They know?" Leon asks me.

I nod. "Yeah. Surprised but happy for us. That's actually something we want to talk to you all about."

Immediately, our friends back off, giving us a little space.

Bentley speaks first. "I haven't told my parents yet. They're coming a few days earlier than planned before the holidays. We want to tell them in person."

"Good call," Ty responds. He's already returned to the floor between Logan's legs, who's on the couch behind him.

At Ty's words, the room seems to settle, everyone taking a seat, this time leaving the smaller two-seater couch for me and Bentley to settle on.

A weird vibe pulses in the room—not really tense, more like curious anticipation. It vibrates under my skin, making my hands twitch. I go to shake them out, but Bentley's hand captures mine instead.

Immediately, I inhale deeply, drawing air into my lungs. It settles the nervous energy trying to creep over me, and I all but sag against Bentley's side.

His face is already turned my way when I look at him. He's so fucking beautiful.

The question is there in his tender gaze, and I nod, happy for him to take this for now.

"I'm sure this is a bit of a shock for some of you," he starts, and I flick a look at Ty, not surprised that there's not a hint of smugness in his expression—that's not how he rolls. "Sammy and I have been together for a while."

Yeah, "together" and "a while" is what we landed on. Airing our dirty laundry or how much I fucked around isn't something to be shared with anyone.

"Getting married really was unexpected. You probably have Ty to thank a little for the development." Teasing suffuses Bentley's words, and I grin.

Now *this* is something we previously talked about.

As predicted, all our friends spin to look at Ty. He looks completely content with all eyes on him. "Intuitive as fuck, remember?" His lips twitch, and a chorus of groans and snorts flood the room.

It does exactly what I know Bentley intended: cuts through the atmosphere, putting everyone at ease.

"We wanted to tell you as soon as everyone was back after Thanksgiving."

I cut in, "You're worse than herding feral cats. I swear, trying to get you all in the same place is practically impossible." I raise my eyebrows, shooting them all pointed looks. As I make eye contact with Kieran, I swallow. He doesn't look pissed off, but I just can't get a handle on his reaction.

"So, this is us telling you, and this is us asking you to support us, and I suppose making sure you're okay with the living situation."

My heart constricts a little as Bentley speaks. This wasn't something I'd even considered until he mentioned it. Our relationship, us living together, wasn't something any of our friends signed up for.

"What do you mean?" Leon's brows dip low, his gaze flitting between the two of us.

"What I'm asking is, do you want us to move out?"

I have no idea how Bentley keeps his voice so steady, but thank God he's the one speaking. My voice would be pitching all over the place.

"What?" Leon's question is loud. "Why the hell would we want you to move out?"

My gaze darts to Kieran. His piercing eyes are steady under his furrowed brows.

Hitching one of his shoulders into a small shrug, Bentley exhales heavily. His smile is small and a little tight before he says, "We'll be sharing a room every night, living as much like a married couple as possible. It's just…." He hesitates. "We don't want to impose. Don't want anyone to feel uncomfortable, especially as we're also going to ask for you to please not disclose our relationship to anyone outside this room."

Bentley squeezes my hand tighter, his discomfort coming through loud and clear. I push a little closer into his side, trying to give him a boost of strength.

"We still have some things we're figuring out, and we want to wait until we've graduated before we really start living as a couple."

"It's a lot to ask," I say. "Keeping a secret you never asked to know. And I know we didn't give you any choice. We just sort of sprang this on you—"

Kieran standing cuts me off. Fuck, he looks fierce. Seriously, there's an expression on his face I've never seen before. It's kind of freaking me the hell out.

A quick glance at Dean, who somehow didn't go flying from Kieran's lap when he stood, eases some of the tightness in my gut. He's smiling sweetly, glancing up at his boyfriend like he hung the moon.

Admittedly, we all look at Kieran in a similar sort of way. Well, not the "I want to go to pound town" way Dean is, but he's our captain. He's the best player I've been lucky enough to play beside. Hell, if I had life savings, I'd bet every dollar that he'll be the first or second pick in the draft next year.

And that's the thing—I admire and respect him so damn much. We all do. His opinion matters.

"This is what's going to happen," he starts. "We're going to help you move whatever shit needs moving so you guys are officially in a room together while Dean heads out to buy some cheap bubbly wine that we have to pop so we can celebrate properly, and as for us all keeping your confidence… that goes without saying."

Relief, thick and surprisingly heavy, presses down on me. Emotion tries to squeeze its way into my chest because yet again, Kieran, my teammates, our friends have done exactly what I should have always trusted them to do.

Ty and Leon nod in approval as Ty stands, saying, "And I'll order more pizzas."

Leon throws a cushion at Ty as Kieran heads our way. The rest of the guys start to scatter, apparently debating pizza toppings, while Tiller leaves with Dean to go to the store.

Bentley and I stand as Kieran stops before us.

"You both know I'm here for you, yeah?" Emotion spills into his voice, and understanding smacks me in my face.

"We know." I grab him into a hug, saying quietly, "I know you're always there for me… for us." Pulling away, I release a shaky breath. "This is on me."

"Sammy." Bentley's voice is all gravel and disapproval.

The sound caresses my soul, and I smile at him before looking back at Kieran. "I've still got some stuff I'm figuring out. When I'm ready, we'll talk, yeah?" It's all I can offer.

He studies me for a beat before nodding. "Okay. Just… we've got your backs, always. You know that, right?"

"We do," Bentley answers.

I add, "It's why we're all so kick-ass," needing to lighten the moment.

Kieran pounds Bentley's back, hugging him tightly. Stepping away, he shakes his head. "I love you assholes." A soft chuckle follows. "Fucking hell." Another headshake. "Married? It totally makes sense… that's the thing." He doubles down with amusement, a wide grin forming. "It's a shame you're going to wait till graduation. I swear, missing out on Coach's reaction is a pity."

I snort. "Screw you, man. It may be the final queer straw that breaks the coach's back." I'm completely bullshitting. Coach is Tiller's dad, and he's been nothing but supportive—and that's even before Tiller returned to town at the beginning of the school year.

But yeah, his head might just explode if he finds out. Not that I totally wouldn't let him know Bentley's mine if that's what my husband wants.

"Come on, tell us how you want to organize

things to suit your new living arrangement." Kieran leads the way, heading toward the staircase.

The gentle hold on my arm has me staying put.

"'Kay?"

"Yeah." I nod and glide my mouth over Bentley's. It's sweet and soft, and, holy shit, a PDA moment I never dared dream I'd have. "Let's get up there before someone starts rooting around and tries to steal our healthy supply of lube."

A choked snort spills out of Bentley. "Healthy, huh? That's one way of describing it."

A sly smirk forms on my lips as I arch a brow at him. "You ever want to be in a situation where we run out and you can't get access to my ass?"

Bentley's brows shoot high before his lips lower and something oh so sexy appears in his gaze.

"Yeah, thought not," I sass as I leave the room, my grin wide and my heart full.

I feel so much lighter. Like I'm able to take a deeper breath.

And tonight, not having to sneak around… it's going to be the best night ever.

THE PAST FEW DAYS HAVE BEEN AS CLOSE TO BLISS AS discovering your pizza comes with an extra slice for free: it's pleasantly unexpected, a little cheesy, and hell if you're not left feeling pleasantly stuffed.

And let's be clear, I have been so perfectly… filled… every damn night since we came out to our friends.

Not sneaking around at home is awesome. Wearing my shiny ring that's making my finger a little green is the best feeling ever, and the slight moments of PDA whenever the feeling takes me—or Bentley—are making me ridiculously happy.

It's even helping our game.

Sure, it's a challenge not to ogle his ass when we're on the court, but my urges are getting easier to control. As soon as the front door's closed, we're safe. It means less pining—or so Ty tells me, as apparently that's what I'd been doing.

Trust Ty to notice.

And tonight's game? Hell, we're dominating the court. But credit to Westdale. Every now and then, they make a smooth move that takes all of us by surprise. Number 8 especially, a sophomore named Walker.

The guy's grown an extra two inches since last year, and with the way he's playing, he could be a serious contender for the draft when he's a senior.

There are ten minutes left on the clock, and the Westdale coach has called a time-out. We sprint to the sideline, and I take the bottle of water handed to me, my gaze already on Coach Maple.

As we huddle around Coach, Bentley wipes the sweat from his forehead. A quick glance at Ty reveals he's hyper-focused, his eyes blazing with determination. Next to him is Leon, bouncing on the balls of his feet, while Kieran nods along to Coach's words as he finishes saying something just for him, ready to reinforce them when we're on the court.

"All right, boys," Coach begins, his voice firm but encouraging. "We're playing strong out there, but we can't let up now. Westdale might be trailing, but they're not out of the game yet. Walker's proving a handful."

We all nod along.

"We need to keep an eye on him, deny him the ball as much as possible. Defense needs to tighten up. No easy baskets."

He pauses, scanning each of our faces before continuing, "Offensively, keep the pressure on. Move the ball, find the open man. And remember, teamwork makes the dream work."

"Read that on a motivational poster, Coach?" My grin's wide, even though I know I should be keeping my mouth shut. "Nice," I continue, ignoring the "what the fuck are you thinking" looks from the guys. I should quit while I'm ahead, but fuck if I'm not riding a high. "Speaking of dreams, let's turn theirs into a nightmare."

"For the love of God." Leon buries his face in his hand.

Coach Maple shoots me a look, a mixture of exasperation and what I like to think of as amusement crossing his features. "Sammy, focus. We're here to win, not audition for stand-up comedy."

I chuckle sheepishly. "Sorry, Coach."

After a final pointed look my way, he continues, and I nod along with the rest of my team until he finally wraps up. "All right, Bears, let's go show them what we're made of."

Determination is a fierce thrum through my veins.

Fuck, I love this shit.

We break from the huddle and head back to the court. The final ten minutes on the clock are intense, and hell if we don't give it our all.

Bentley drives layups, Leon's precision three-pointers are a thing of beauty, and Ty's ability to lock down defense never fails to impress me. And in the middle of it all is my grinning ass, intercepting and supporting Kieran every chance I can.

As the buzzer sounds, signaling our victory, Bentley's are the first arms I find. I'm wrapped up in them, holding him tight before sharing the love with my team.

Off to the side, I spot the camera crew. Usually, I'm all up in the lights, especially after a win, but I turn my back and happily let Kieran take the lead.

After this, we're going straight onto the bus and heading back to campus. We're only about three hours away, but by the time we crawl into our beds, we'll be lucky if it's before midnight.

Leon nudges my shoulder as we wait on the court, not yet breaking away and heading for the locker room. We'll make sure to stay till the interviews are finished, liking to leave the court as a team.

"Feeling good?" he asks, beaming at me.

"Fucking A. Games like this are the best."

Leon nods, understanding what I mean. We want a challenge, want to be pushed, and need to earn every point, but we should not be shitting a brick and worried the win could turn on a dime.

Those sorts of games get my adrenaline pumping just a little too much.

"What are you getting into tomorrow?" I ask. Tomorrow morning, we have a brief film recap time with the team before we're released for the whole day and evening.

No physical training and no classes, since it's Saturday.

We don't even have any type of charity event.

"Tiller's taking me out on a date." A light blush

appears on his cheeks. "Goofy, huh, since he's my boyfriend, but he wants to take me out for the day. He's booked a hotel room for the night too."

My brain misfires, and an uncomfortable feeling forms in my chest. *A date?*

Shit, have Bentley and I even been on an official date?

"Not goofy," I finally say.

Bentley absolutely deserves all the dates, so many they'll make his head spin and remind him time and time again how our relationship and impromptu wedding were absolutely the right things to do.

"So, what sorts of things have you done on dates, especially when you were keeping things on the down-low?" Tiller is, after all, one of our assistant coaches. It meant their relationship was hush-hush there for a while.

Leon studies me, his head tilted. It takes a couple of beats before his eyes flare wide. "Shit, have you never…?"

I shake my head, not voicing how much of my and Bentley's relationship has been ass-backward.

"Right, yeah, okay." He leans in close, and I angle my head so he can whisper whatever he clearly intends to keep quiet. "Did the two of you actually have a night together, as in a *honeymoon?*"

The last word is so low, I have to strain to hear. The word registers, and it's impossible to not wince.

Fuck me. I didn't even give Bentley a honeymoon.

Whatever he sees in my expression—no doubt panic and horror—has Leon patting me on the shoulder. "Hey, don't sweat it. I'll help you out."

"Yeah, thanks." I huff out a breath, admitting, "It's just, you know, I'm not flush with cash, so…."

He's nodding before I've finished. "I get it, man." He turns away for a second, and when he pauses, his focus clearly settling on Tiller, he glances back at me. "Just leave it with me. I've got your back."

Immediately, a "Thanks, Leon" spills out of me. I'm not too proud to accept any help I can get. Not when it comes to doing the right thing by Bentley.

Thinking of my husband, I search him out, stopping dead in my tracks when I see him standing to the side, Walker—the hotshot—talking to him.

Grudgingly, I recognize that Walker's handsome. You know, if you're into the blond-haired, blue-eyed type of look, which I'm totally not. Bentley's gray eyes will always be the perfect color and shape to capture my attention. His light brown hair, soft and a little unruly, the perfect texture for me to glide my fingers through.

And fuck if his pale skin, so light compared to my

own and dotted with freckles I like to trace with my tongue, isn't the best to run my fingertips over.

Skin, for some fucking reason, that Walker's touching right this second as he reaches out and holds Bentley on his arm, laughing ridiculously at something my husband's saying.

Is Bentley witty, and does he have the best laugh in the world? Obviously. But no other fucker should be appreciating it.

"Where are you—oh…." Leon trails off with a chuckle. But the sound's already in the wind, as I'm several feet away from him, my laser focus on the fingers still on Bentley's skin.

"Sup?"

Startling at my voice—and likely my lame greeting—Bentley jerks his head to face me. In doing so, Walker's hand drops. Lucky for him.

"Hey?" There's a definite uplift of the word as well as a question in Bentley's gaze. "All good?"

"Yup." I pop the *p*, my piss-poor attempt at a smile enough for him to drop his brows in concern. "Just wondering what you were up to." My focus darts to his side and at Walker, who's looking a little perplexed. "Good game." I reach out my hand and shake his. I don't even grip it tightly like a toxic dickhead.

"Thanks, man. You too."

My smile is fixed on my face as I offer him an up-nod before glancing at Bentley. In the time it took for me to act like a weird dick and look back at my husband, it's super obvious he's caught up.

The asshole is smirking at me, right there for anyone to see. I narrow my gaze at him, which apparently is even more entertaining, as he smirks harder.

"You missed me, huh?" He throws his arm around me, just like he would have done at this time last year before there was anything more than friendship between us. Honestly, I'm impressed he can lapse into the role so effortlessly.

I clearly am doing a shit job and need to do better.

Knowing we still have an audience, I roll my eyes. "Yep, missed you like a toothache. Except, you know, a toothache eventually goes away." I flash him a grin, adding a pulse of "you're so going to blow me later" in the whole vibe I'm throwing his way.

This time he contains his smirk, allowing me to see the heat in his gaze before he shutters his reaction.

"So, what are the two of you getting into over here?"

Bentley's not buying my innocence, despite me trying super hard to keep my tone light and breezy.

He presses his lips together. Yeah, he may be

coming across all cute and amused, but did he brush an innocent hand on his arm away? I inwardly scoff. Uhm, no, he did not. And yes, of course it was innocent. Even if this Walker guy was attempting to flirt, I've got nothing to worry about.

The stupid shroud of green that pushed at me when I was with Leon doesn't give a flying fuck, though.

"I just found out Bentley grew up in the same town where I spent most of my summers as a kid." Walker grins over at Bentley's side profile.

I take in this kid's expression, trying to figure out if he was hitting on my man or not.

Jesus. My man. Like hell I'm going to tell Bentley that's the direction of my thoughts.

"It's crazy, right?"

"Uh-huh, *crazy.*"

Bentley, with an arm still around me, squeezes lightly in warning. I'm being an asshole.

"Yeah, that's cool. Small world and all that." I even tack on a smile.

Walker's name is hollered. A glance over his shoulder, and he nods before peering back at us. "That's me. Time to go. We're on the court again in February. See you then." His hand lifts in an awkward wave, his cheeks immediately heating, and my smile settles into something more genuine.

"February," I say. "Keep playing as well as you did tonight, and you'll make me worried."

A bright grin flashes our way before he bounds away, leaving me alone with Bentley. Or as alone as we can be, since we're still on the court with press, players, and spectators all around.

"He's… energetic," I settle on.

Bentley's snort is loud. "Like someone else I know. Well, unless he's being a surly, jealous asshole."

Dammit. I can't even argue with him.

Instead, I elbow him and pretend to scratch my cheek with my middle finger.

His laughter is deep, causing fresh goose bumps to travel along my skin. "Looks like Key's finished. Let's go."

While I lose his arm, our shoulders brush as we head over to our team. Leon catches my eye, and he shoots me a super-obvious wink.

Bentley leans into me. "Do I want to know?"

"Nope." A rush of anticipation fills my chest. I'm grateful to Leon, but I also need to have my own ideas, as tomorrow is going to be my official first date with my husband.

Looks like I've got some research and thinking to do on the bus ride home.

CHAPTER 20
BENTLEY

THIS MORNING I WOKE UP TO A NOTE FROM SAMMY telling me he'd see me at eight thirty. It was weird, him being gone, but I appreciated his note. And that he'd left an "I love you" and drawn a cute heart went a long way to settling any nerves that had attempted to brew over him having gone out to do who knows what.

At the front of the room, Coach is talking to Kieran. It's five minutes till eight thirty, and Sammy's not here yet; neither is Leon. Tiller is, though, also standing in a huddle with his dad and Kieran.

For the millionth time, I tug out my phone. No message notification blinks at me.

"You seriously think they're foolish enough to be late?" Tyron angles a look at me from my right. He's playing *Crossy Road* on his phone, so his attention quickly flips back to the game.

"So, they're together, then?" I ask, his "they're" pretty much confirming my thoughts.

A shrug is my answer as Tyron loses with a heavy sigh.

Another minute passes, and I swear, if Sammy ends up on Coach's shit list for being late, which could eat into our whole day together, I'm going to lose—

The door opens, and Sammy ambles in, Leon a step behind him. Both are out of breath.

Leon quickly collapses on one of the empty chairs while Sammy eases his way over to the one beside me. He's all smiles as he sits, but that "nothing to see here, folks" look on his face is one I'm not buying.

I only have the chance to shoot him a narrow-eyed stare before Coach steps up, a controller in his hand and an expression on his face that means he's all business.

The ninety minutes pass at a snail's pace.

The whole time, I side-eye Sammy, but for the first time I think in the history of ever, he doesn't look my way. Instead, he's staring at the footage and focusing on Coach as though he's a newbie.

As soon as the session wraps up, my knees bounce, and there's a vibration throbbing through my veins. I'm out of my seat a second later, pinning a smirking Sammy with a "get your ass up and outside" stare.

Before he moves, he says something to Leon, who nods enthusiastically before they tap fists and trade back slaps.

Meanwhile, I'm here, impatient as hell.

Whatever's going on, it's nothing bad. That much I can read. Sammy's eyes are bright, excitement shining in them, especially every time he looks at me.

Which he happens to be doing now, gaze raking over me. Not sexually, since we're standing in a room with our teammates, but appraisal gleams in their depths. He bobs his head—which means what? I have no clue—and he finally speaks. "You ready?"

I swipe my tongue over my teeth, completely bemused, but nod anyway.

"Excellent."

Side by side, we head out. The cold bites, and I pull my coat closer. There are a couple of weeks before the holidays, and with how unseasonably cool it's been this year, it really feels like the season's upon us.

Snow here in Georgia isn't all that rare, but we don't get much, and for the winters I've previously lived here, not once have we had snow over the holidays. It would be pretty awesome if we did this year.

However, I don't want the weather to impact our big game on the twenty-sixth.

Rather than turn right out of the facility, which is the way we walk back to the house, Sammy tugs on my sleeve. "This way," he says, leading me toward the parking lot.

"You gonna tell me what's going on?" A puff of white air chases my words.

"Impatient much?" There's nothing but gentle amusement in his tone.

I snort. Out of the two of us, I've never been accused of that before.

The parking lot is practically empty. It means his car is easy to spot. When we reach the passenger door, he opens it for me. Surprise has me tilting my head. My heart flutters even as glee bubbles to life.

I press my lips together, wordlessly settling into the seat as Sammy closes the door behind me quietly. Jogging around the front, he's at his door in no time.

I've yet to buckle in, feeling too many things to function, to be honest.

He enters with a breeze of cool air and immediately starts the engine and turns on the heater. Finally, he peers at me. He absolutely has my full attention, but it's the pink coloring in his cheeks that has me repositioning in my seat to take him in more fully.

"Sammy?" I leave it there, my tone soft, questioning.

"Right, so." Raking his fingers through his hair, he clamps his bottom lip between his teeth.

A nervous Sammy always takes me by surprise. It's also weirdly endearing.

I reach out and hold his hand, giving it a light squeeze.

A wisp of his exhale follows, and he releases his puffy lip. "Are you good with spending the whole day with me?"

I smile, feeling a flutter of excitement mixed with tenderness at the uncertainty in his tone. "Of course, Sammy. Isn't that already the plan?" From his whole disappearing act and his clear discomfort, he has something specific in mind that we haven't discussed. "What are you thinking we do?"

Eyes lighting up with relief, he expels a breathy chuckle. "Okay, a date. I want to take you on a date. Well, for the whole day to be a date," he says, a little flustered and a lot excited as he gains his momentum. "We've never been on an actual date before, and I want us to. I want us to do datey things and, I don't know… woo you."

I want to laugh, swoon, grab hold of him and kiss the hell out of him. I settle on the middle choice, my whole body—and absolutely my brain—

going melty for him. "You want a date with me, baby?"

Yes, I know he's already said that, but fuck if it doesn't mean everything. I definitely want to hear it again.

"Yeah," he responds softly. "And we're staying out overnight. We never had a honeymoon."

As Sammy's words sink in, a wave of surprise washes over me: a warm, comforting sensation that envelops me like a soft blanket on a chilly evening. It catches me off guard in the best possible way.

My heart flutters with excitement even as guilt tries to weasel its way inside.

"We didn't have a honeymoon," I repeat. "Shit, baby, I'm sorry. I didn't think either. I just—"

"No," he cuts me off, squeezing my hand. "There's no need for any of that. This is something I wanted to do for you. For us. Though I may have had some help."

"Leon?"

"Yeah." His smile widens, and my heart tumbles when he says, "They all pitched in, paid for our room tonight. I found a place for, like, seventy bucks, but Leon vetoed the hell out of it last night and went on a mission."

"They did?" The emotion lodging in my throat takes me unawares.

"Yeah." His snort is tender. "Said something about our wedding gift." A light shrug follows. He's downplaying it. There's no doubt in my mind that he struggled with their thoughtfulness last night. It probably overwhelmed the hell out of him.

"That's amazing of them," I settle on, a spark igniting within me. It spreads a gentle warmth from the pit of my stomach to the tips of my fingers and toes. My heart flutters with anticipation, and as soon as a wide smile forms on my face, he mirrors it with his own.

A rush of gratitude for Sammy, for his thoughtfulness and his unwavering love, races through me. Fuck, I'm lucky he's mine.

"So, this date?" I prompt with renewed eagerness. A day and night with my husband, just the two of us…. I can't wait. I'm going to PDA the hell out of every moment.

Sammy's eyes light with relief as he gathers his thoughts. "Well, we're going to take a drive to Panola Mountain State Park. It's about an hour away. They have this kick-ass archery range and a 3D archery trail. I thought it would be fun for us to try something new together."

A swell of excitement fills my chest at the idea. "It does sound pretty badass."

"Right!" He beams at my enthusiasm, the tension

in his shoulders easing. "And after that, we can either go bowling or there's an ice-skating rink close by. We can check into the cabin at one."

It all sounds amazing. Is it wrong to simply want to hide him away in the cabin as soon as it's available and thank him in a way that'll blow both our minds?

Sammy's smirk and arched brow catch my attention.

"What?"

"You've got that look in your eyes."

"What look?"

"Like you're thinking of all the ways you can make me come."

My dick twinges, a throb of desire shooting into my balls.

"Yeah, that look right there."

"Which is completely your fault. All I can think is, at one o'clock, I can have you all to myself. No interruptions. No worrying if someone's going to knock on the door."

"So, at one, we'll go straight there."

"Yeah? You won't mind not bowling or ice-skating?"

He shakes his head, desire swirling in his gaze. "We've got the rest of our lives for more dates, right?"

Happiness, all light and floaty, twirls around inside me. "Yeah, we do."

"So, it's settled. After archery and our picnic."

"We have a picnic?"

"Yeah." A rosy pink floods his cheeks. "It's what Leon and I were organizing this morning. He even borrowed a wicker basket from Tiller's mom. It's in the trunk."

My hands are on him without thought. I drag him close and meet him halfway. Stopping short of kissing him, I press my forehead against his. Ragged breaths, fueled by emotion, saw out of me. "I love you so fucking much."

"Love you, too, sweetheart."

God, I want to kiss him. I'm desperate for his touch.

I swallow hard and reluctantly ease away.

"It won't be like this forever," he promises.

He doesn't need to elaborate. He's not talking about his sweet, thoughtful dates.

Our dream is small—at least in the grand scheme of things. Kissing each other whenever we want is going to happen.

Just five more months.

IT TURNS OUT I'M USELESS AT ARCHERY. SINCE SAMMY is, too, we spend our time giggling like schoolkids while trying to learn the proper form. By the time we're let loose and start our walk and 3D hunt, it's clear we're not taking this seriously.

"What on earth are you doing?"

Sammy's crouching low, coating his fingers in mud. As soon as I figure out what he's going to do, I'm backing away and chuckling.

Two streaks of mud coat each of his cheeks. Grinning maniacally, he wriggles his muddy digits at me. "Your turn."

I scrunch my nose. "Seriously?"

"Hell yes, seriously."

And just like that, I give in.

The mud is cool against my skin, and I try not to think too long and hard about what wild animal's crap I'm wiping on my face.

"There." He nods, his smile so big and happy that I expel a soft sigh.

If the idiot asked me to roll around in the mud, I'd likely do so if it makes him this happy.

"You look hot."

"Uh-huh. Sure I do," I answer, knowing full well we both look like dicks. But there's no one I'd rather look like a fool with than this man.

"You do." He leans into me, not bothering to

glance around. A rush of adrenaline pulses through me, closely followed by a swirl of happiness at how free and safe we feel in this moment, surrounded by sweet gums and red maples and an abundance of other huge trees I have no idea the names of.

The heat of his lips presses against mine, warm and familiar. I sigh into the touch, wrapping my free arm around him. The kiss is soft, gentle, and just right as we stand between the trees and the soft rustling of their leaves from the cool breeze.

Our kiss slows until we pull away, our breaths mingling, blissed-out smiles aimed at each other. This right here is how I want to spend the rest of my life with Sammy.

"What are you thinking right now, other than how sexy I look with my camouflage?"

His question draws a quiet chuckle from me before I answer honestly, "This is already the best date I've ever had. I'm thinking that we should find time to steal more moments like this, especially when we're finished with school."

His blink is slow, a little lazy as he studies me. We're still close and wrapped up in each other. "Are you getting a Robin Hood or a Hawkeye kink?" he teases.

"Maybe more like a Sammy… Hardy addiction." I stumble a little. For the first time, which is kind of ridiculous that I'm only thinking about this now, I tripped over his last name.

"I'm in support of that addiction, but what's with the frown?"

I ease back a little so I can see his whole face more clearly. I drop my arm from around his back and hold his hand instead. "Our last names are different." I shrug, not sure where I'm going with the observation or even what I'm truly suggesting.

What I am sure of is, I don't like that our names are different one bit. The discomfort takes me by surprise, especially as it's not something I've been mulling over. It's not like it's been playing on my mind or anything.

His brows shoot high as he studies me. "Right, yeah." He pauses as he rubs his thumb over my hand. "Is that something you want us to change?"

"Yeah," I admit. "I think so. I haven't put too much thought into it, but I think it kind of bothers me."

His nod is slow and assessing.

"Obviously, we don't have to do anything right now." I tack on, "While we're still at school."

Though, wouldn't it make it easier for our degrees to be in our new names? I have no idea how this shit works, but people do it all the time, right?

Have documents that don't match their married or changed names?

"We can talk about it for sure." The words are measured, his uncertainty ringing loud and clear.

The squeeze in my chest is uncomfortable.

But what did I expect, for him to jump up and down and start googling to figure out how we make it happen? The small internal *Yes* is louder than I'd like. I can be disappointed, though, right?

"Okay," I settle on, trying to shake off my frustration. We have plenty of time to make these decisions together. The last thing I want to do is ruin our date-slash-honeymoon. At that thought, I tug him close and press a kiss to his lips before saying, "The highest points for being on target wins a massage."

The smile beaming back at me is instant. "You don't need to win anything for me to put my hands on you." His tone is all heat and amusement.

He's got a point.

"Okay, how about the loser is responsible for doing laundry for the week?"

His lips twist in contemplation, no doubt calculating his odds. It could honestly go either way. I wasn't exaggerating about us both being lame.

"Fine." He nods. "You've got a deal." He tugs out the park map that labels the areas with the 3D targets. "Come on, Robin. Tug up your tights, and let's go shoot shit." A smirk's aimed my way. "Hopefully."

We chuckle as we follow the map. The tagged-on "hopefully" sounds about right. We'll be lucky if we manage to get within a foot of the targets.

By the time we reach the fifth one—a carved bear that's big enough that we really shouldn't miss—our losses are pretty even.

I grin as we approach the target, its wooden form large in front of us. "All right, time to show this bear who's boss." I nock the arrow onto my bowstring.

At my side, Sammy chuckles, his own bow ready. "Oh, I'll show it, all right," he replies, adopting a mock-heroic pose.

He looks appropriately ridiculous, so it makes sense that warmth settles in my chest. When we're this relaxed, this silly, it feels like we're doing something right.

"Prepare to witness the prowess of Hawkeye the Blind-Eagle Archer."

A guttural snort tears out of me at his antics. "Uh-huh. I'm shaking in my tights," I tease, taking aim at the target. Just as I'm about to release the arrow, his large hand appears on my ass and squeezes.

"Hey, none of that." I thrust back, trying to knock his hand away, my grin stretching wide. "I need to concentrate here."

Sammy smirks mischievously, wagging his eyebrows. "Where's the fun in that?" he retorts, squeezing once more for good measure. "Maybe I should drop to my knees and blow you instead. See if that helps your concentration."

The asshole knows what he's doing. The thickening of my cock doesn't come as a surprise.

"When I hit this target, then you can blow me. I'd say it's your punishment, but we both know that's bullshit."

As soon as the words are out of my mouth, I realize teasing him with a good time is a mistake. The prospect of Sammy's mouth anywhere near me means I'm hard and ready to go.

"Looks like you've got a problem." He leans in close as he trails his fingers to my crotch. When he tightens them around me, a grunt spills past my lips. "A *big* problem from the feel of it."

My lips twitch even as I close my eyes, trying not to sag into his hold and push him to his knees. After a couple of breaths, I stare at him, soaking up the heat in his gaze. "Shall we call it a draw and get the hell out of here?"

He's nodding before I've even finished.

We make quick work of returning the equipment and all but dive into the car. It's tempting to find a secluded spot, the need like fire in my veins, but we have access to a cabin, and we're committed to making good use of it.

"How far does it say?" Tension makes his voice tight.

"Hold on." I'm waiting for the Maps app to give me the route. The details flash up, and I exhale in relief. "Seventeen minutes."

He grunts, letting me know he's heard as he continues down the winding road out of the park.

"You know, we've still got the picnic to eat," I say, trying to distract both of us.

"We'll need the energy after." His lips curve up as he indicates left, following the directions.

So much for trying not to think about getting off. To be fair, all it takes is a look, a touch, a glance, or a taste, and I'm hard for Sammy.

The journey passes with us shooting the shit about movies with archers. By the time the app tells us we've reached our destination, we're in agreement that there's a pitiful number of movies with archery in them.

"The place looks great." I'm already halfway out the door, taking in the rustic charm of the cabin nestled among tall, swaying pine trees. Their branches reach out like welcoming arms, casting dappled shadows on the wooden exterior of the cabin. Neighbors, if there are any, remain out of sight, hidden behind a wall of dense foliage.

Sammy reaches for the coded box and deftly enters the combination to retrieve the keys. With a click, the lock opens, and we step inside. The contrast between the rugged exterior and the surprisingly modern interior is striking. The cabin boasts sleek furnishings, a cozy fireplace, and even a gleaming hot tub on the small deck visible through the french doors.

"This place is awesome." I step behind Sammy, wrapping my arms around his waist. He leans into me, a happy sigh easing out of him. A surge of gratitude expands my chest as I think of how our friends gifted us this getaway. "We owe them big-time."

Nodding, Sammy turns in my arms. "Why don't you go get our bags, and I'll meet you in the shower?"

My dick throbs, liking that idea, knowing exactly why he wants to freshen up. "I can do that." I punctuate my words with a kiss before adding, "But leave the prep to me."

A shudder ripples through him, his gaze heating. "Yeah, okay."

I back away before I lose all sense of control, wanting to give him the chance to shower first like he requested. Before I've left the cabin, the water's running and I'm grinning. With my pulse racing in expectation, I focus on collecting our bags—I'm mildly curious about what my Sammy-packed contents will be—and the picnic basket. I also find a six-pack and a small bag of groceries.

It's amazing how far Sammy went to do all this and make our time together special. Being loved by him is heady and fulfilling in ways I didn't dare imagine. That this is our life now is beyond epic.

I close the cabin door with my hip, backing into it to ensure it shuts properly. A few steps later, I put the beer and groceries in the fridge, then drop our bags in the bedroom. It takes me less than thirty seconds to get naked and be standing in the doorway of the steamy bathroom.

My breath catches, gaze locking on to Sammy. Lather coats his wet skin, which appears a couple of shades darker even as the suds trail down his muscular shoulders. They trickle down the arch of his back, reaching the top of his globes before gathering there and making their way over his glutes.

I'm transfixed, still not breathing. Luck shone so damn brightly on me the day we met. It doesn't matter the humps, the hurdles, the lonely nights. None of that matters.

Dragging in a breath as I watch him turn, his cock hanging thick and long between his legs, I lick my dry lips. The movement catches his attention, his dick bouncing, hardening.

"Is there a reason you're still all the way over there?"

At his words, I tear my gaze away from his erection. It's a challenge, as all I can think about is wrapping my lips around him and drinking his cum.

"Just getting my fill." Smirking, I offer a light shrug.

"Your cock in my ass is the only filling that's needed." He grips his own cock and slowly drags his hand up and down.

"Is that right?" I take a step toward him, grateful there's no glass separating us in the wet-room shower. "You don't want my fingers?" His nostrils flare. "My tongue?" A grunt escapes him.

One more step, and I knock his hand out of the way, moving one of mine in its place. I secure my other hand on his hip, still keeping my hand on his cock. His breath hitches before a moan breaks free.

"So, is it just my cock you want filling you?" I glide my grip over him, working us both up to a frenzy.

"I want it all."

"Yeah? Right now?" Trailing kisses over his shoulder, I loosen my hold on his waist and drag my fingers to the crack of his ass.

A stuttering breath escapes him as I ease them between his cheeks. When I gently stroke his hole, his limbs shake.

"I just want you to fuck me."

"With…?" This teasing is going to be my undoing. My balls tighten in preparation.

"Your cock. I just want you to fuck me. Everything else later."

Sammy captures my mouth, taking control and simply owning me. His kisses are fierce, desperate as he grabs clumsily for a towel.

"What—"

"I want you to fuck me on that giant bed."

From the way my cock throbs, I'm more than okay with that. It's barely lunchtime. That means we have twenty hours in this cabin. Twenty hours to see how many times I can make him come. Twenty hours to worship every inch of his skin.

Sammy pats himself dry before throwing the towel at me and escaping from the bathroom.

"Hey." I laugh. "You're not waiting for me?"

"Getting the lube. Fuck, Bentley, I'm so horny, I'm going to bust a nut as soon as you get inside me."

I chuckle as I drop the towel and follow the sound of rustling. As I enter the bedroom, Sammy stands upright, triumphantly holding the bottle of lube. His smile is all smug satisfaction until his gaze dips, taking me in.

When he swallows hard, the click loud in the otherwise quiet room, my chest expands. Having Sammy's gaze on me, appreciation easy to read in his eyes, is a high I'll never tire of.

Anticipation surges through my veins like a live wire, sending shivers down my spine as I gaze at Sammy, my heart racing with barely contained need. "God," I moan, unable to contain the arousal coursing through me. "Get on the bed and lift yourself up."

Sammy's breath catches in his throat, his eyes darkening with desire. "Like this?"

Fuck, I love his confidence. His certainty as he opens himself to me, thighs up, revealing his puckered hole. The temptation to get my mouth on him has me stepping forward.

"Nuh-uh." Despite the way his body trembles, amusement crosses his features. "Playtime's later. Right now, minimum prep, then fuck me like you mean it."

Jesus H. Christ. What this man does to me.

Easing forward and swiping the lube off the mattress where Sammy dropped it, I pour the cool liquid on my palm. "Are you that desperate for my cock?"

His gaze meets mine, filled with longing as I stroke myself. He clamps down on his bottom lip and nods. "Fuck yes. Always," he breathes, his lips parting slightly as he watches me slick my dick.

With a teasing grin, I press my fingertip against him, feeling him yield to my touch. "Open up for me," I murmur, my own desire surging forward as his pupils dilate.

As he eagerly complies, I'm struck by his beauty, his arousal evident in every trembling breath and flushed inch of skin. I can't remember ever feeling this consumed, this desperate for someone's touch.

I circle his entrance before gently sliding a slick finger inside. His gasp ignites something primal within me, fueling my need to possess him completely.

"More," he pleads, his hips moving in rhythm with my touch, his body welcoming me with an urgency that leaves me breathless.

I oblige, adding another finger and relishing the way he stretches around me. "You feel incredible," I murmur, unable to tear my gaze away from him.

With each thrust of my fingers, I feel him unraveling beneath me, his cries of pleasure driving me to push further, to give him everything he craves.

But I need more. I need to be inside him, to feel

him completely, to lose myself in the ecstasy of being buried so deep that it's like we're really one.

"Please," Sammy begs, his desperation mirroring my own as I prepare to enter him.

With trembling hands, I add more lube as I press against him, ready to fuck him so completely that his voice will be raw from screaming my name.

His legs wrap around me, pulling me closer, and as I breach him, a wave of emotion washes over his face, leaving me awestruck by the depth of feelings in his eyes.

I don't want to remember a time before him. Before us.

I sink deeper into him, savoring the sensation of being enveloped by his warmth, his acceptance feeling so perfect, so right. "You…." My voice trembles. "Fuck, Sammy, you're fucking everything."

He shudders, cupping my face and tugging me down for a kiss. He explores my mouth, and I open willingly, accepting his tongue, committing his touch to memory.

As I begin to move in earnest, my shallow thrusts become deeper. Tearing himself away from my mouth, his cries fill the air, urging me on, pushing me to lose myself and make him lose his mind.

With every thrust, I draw him closer to the edge,

his body responding to mine with a fervor that leaves me dizzy.

"Harder," he demands, his voice raw with need, and I comply, losing myself in the rhythm, canting my hips just so until his cries die off and he parts his lips in a silent scream.

I'm relentless, pressing against his prostate with strained control. My balls tighten, limbs tingling. Moving faster, I work my hand between us, gripping his cock and jacking him off.

"Nnngh...." Sammy's hips stutter just as he clamps around me. As his body tightens, his grip on my arms intensifies. He calls out my name, his cock swelling until he releases in my hand.

I don't stop, so close to release. My hold on Sammy is the only thing stopping me from leaving the ground.

"Fuck, fuck, Sammy...." My words are garbled as my vision whitens, balls drawing high before I come hard. Ecstasy pulses through me as I jerk and release inside him.

He groans, tightening around me again. Our oversensitive bodies are on the verge of too much.

Spent and breathless, I collapse against him. Even as he grunts at my weight, he wraps his arms around me, peppering my shoulder and neck with kisses.

"Wow. Fuck, baby," I whisper, my heart overflowing with love for the man who has given me everything. I rise up a couple of inches so I can see his face and check he's okay.

He smiles up at me, his eyes shining with affection. "That was… incredible," he murmurs, his fingers tracing patterns on my skin.

I lean in to kiss him, savoring the taste of him on my lips.

His smile against my mouth has me drawing back. "You fucked me like you meant it." He follows up with a half-assed pat on my shoulder. "Epic effort."

"Asshole." I snort with amusement, immediately wincing as his body contracts around my cock. The vise grip is worth it.

"Let's try for a real shower, and then we'll eat," I suggest.

He nods. "Then you can fuck me with your tongue for dessert."

My lips twitch, as does my spent cock.

It's definitely time to ease out and wash up. If not, he's going to be too sore for me to get anywhere near his ass again. That would be a tragedy, especially when we're finally on our honeymoon.

CHAPTER 21

SAMMY

THE LAST DAY OF FALL TERM COINCIDES WITH OUR FINAL game before Christmas. It means we have a full house. What better way to start the winter break than taking in a Bears game, followed by multiple parties tonight?

Tomorrow, campus will be a ghost town. Only our team, those students who, for whatever reason, don't plan to go home, and locals will be sticking around. Fortunately, local residents tend to fill out the crowd when we have a game during the winter break. This year, though, we won't be playing at home on the twenty-sixth.

After midmorning training today, Bentley and I met up with his folks for a light lunch. Honestly, I'm still pinching myself, struggling to get my head around how incredible they've been.

Once Bentley told them he's now a married man —with the bombshell that I'm his husband—they started talking about home renos and adding on an extension to make life easier should we move in with them next year after college.

Not only that, Lauren—my mother-in-law—has been in touch with my mom, and we're all playing big happy families on Christmas Eve and heading to my folks' place to celebrate our first holidays together.

"Your head in the game?" Bentley's nudge at my side has me snapping my attention from my phone to him.

We're in the locker room, waiting to head onto the court. What I should be doing is getting in the zone. What I am doing is looking at house prices and rentals close by his parents' place and figuring out what kind of cash I need to be earning to eventually get a place of our own.

Not that their offer isn't incredible. But no way do I want them to do work on their house and spend money on it for us. It's all just a little too much.

"Yeah." My nod is weak, and Bentley knows it.

He leans into me a little, saying, "I explained that their offer is incredible, but I've told them no. It'll all be okay. For now"—his knee knocks into mine—

"let's focus on giving everyone out there a reason to celebrate tonight, yeah?"

There's no denying him. His smile is wide, his gaze steady.

At the upturn of my lips, he squeezes my knee and stands. "Now, listen to your music. We're heading out in two minutes."

I jam my EarPods in, hitting Play on my music app. "Lemon Pepper Freestyle" fills my ears, and I bend my head forward and close my eyes. I focus on the beat more than the lyrics. My pulse settles as I draw in a breath.

It's gonna be a kick-ass game.

I crack my neck side to side and rub my hand over the back of my head, focusing on the texture of coarse hair from the fresh fade. Feet appear before me, just like they do every single game since playing for Brixham.

One more deep breath and a steady exhale, and I'm ready. My gaze connects with Bentley's. The slight curve of his lips is the same one I've spent almost four years focusing on for just a beat before I stand.

"Ready?" His voice is steady, familiar.

"Fucking A."

And then we're moving, making our way onto the court as Dean, fully decked out in his mascot gear, is dancing his giant, furry bear butt off, getting the crowd revved up. The room is electric tonight. Our colors span the majority of the crowd, chants and cheers already blowing the roof off.

This game is being televised. Several cameras are set up. With this being my fourth season in, they're no longer a distraction. Most of the time, I forget they're there.

We warm up, shooting hoops, practicing passes, our team surrounding each other, working as a unit. The usual five of us are starting tonight, just the way I like it.

I wonder what it'll be like next year, switching on the game and watching the Bears, a new starting five taking the mantle. It's wild. A year from now, our lives are going to be so different, which is absolutely not what I should be thinking about right now.

Kieran calls us over, and we huddle close. "Bears, listen up. Bentley, Leon, I need you both locked in from the get-go. Bentley, I want you driving that offense. Ty, you're our defensive anchor—shut down anything that comes your way. Let's set the tone early and show them what we're made of. Break!"

We take our positions, anticipation filling the air, and the adrenaline kicks in. The ref blows the whistle, and the game begins with a lightning-fast pass from Bentley to Kieran, who sinks a three-pointer.

The crowd erupts in cheers, electrifying the atmosphere twofold.

And we keep moving, not stopping.

With each possession, we execute our passes and shots with practiced precision, feeding off the energy of the crowd and dominating the court.

The game is fast. I barely have time to wipe sweat from my eyes as the Pythons push hard.

"Sammy."

The moment I hear Kieran, I'm moving to center court. The Pythons have possession. We're winning by nineteen, and their mistakes are piling up. Dodging left, then right, I intercept, immediately passing to Bentley. More points, and the crowd goes wild.

As the game intensifies, Leon's relentless. His presence on the court is a sharp-as-hell thorn in the side of the opposition's forward. The guy's red in the face, getting pissed. I hang back, holding my line, ready to intercept when I get the chance.

A second later, Leon captures the ball. I move, ready to make myself available just as the forward lunges at Leon, his arms flailing in an attempt to dislodge the ball.

That or the guy's taking up some dickish dance move I've never seen before.

The ref's whistle pierces the air, signaling the foul.

Again. Immediately, the forward, a guy with short dreads, scowls, muttering a curse.

I snort, raising my brow and shaking my head. The dude seriously doesn't want to piss off this ref. Donnie isn't known for suffering fools.

We move immediately as soon as play continues. Undeterred by the occasional shoves and frequent whistle blows, we press on relentlessly.

"Time-out."

It's from Coach.

"You think we're going to be entering a scene from *Fight Club* or something soon?" I chuckle, side-eyeing the dark expressions the Pythons are shooting our way.

Leon's at my side. "They weren't this bad before, right?"

Ty shakes his head. "It's their new captain. The guy's a prick."

I angle a look over my shoulder, realizing it's number 2, the forward who fouled Leon earlier. Well, one of the countless fouls made against him, and that's just in fifteen minutes of play. "You know him?" I peer back at Ty.

"He's a prick on social media."

My brows shoot high. His school lets him get away with that? "A prick how?"

"Team, gather around," Coach instructs,

preventing Ty from answering. "Bentley, I want you supporting Leon."

Glancing around with a frown, I wonder what Coach's play is. I go to look back at him but pause when I notice Tiller's face of thunder. He's pissed.

"Yes, Coach." Bentley's tone is grave, and fuck if understanding doesn't slam into me, probably ten minutes too late.

The fuckers are targeting Leon. The hell?

"All of you, keep the ball moving, keep driving forward. With us moving Bentley, I need you to shift positions and fill in that gap, Sammy."

"Absolutely, Coach." Conviction, hot and bitter, races through my veins. How the fuck I missed the focus on Leon, I don't know, but I'll do everything in my power to make sure it doesn't happen again.

"Leon, a word."

Leon nods and steps to the side with Coach Maple. Their heads are close, their conversation low.

"Did you hear what he called Leon?" Bentley's voice startles me from trying to lip-read whatever Coach is saying to Leon.

My pulse thumps heavily as I make eye contact with Bentley. Intensity burns brightly in his gray eyes. The tic in his jaw takes me by surprise, immediately putting me on high alert. "Fuck no. What?"

"Talking shit about him and Tiller. Spouted words

that need to have him pulled off the court, fined, and given a broken nose."

My brows dart high just as Bentley blanches. "Shit, I didn't mean that. You know I'd nev—"

My gut twists even as I squeeze his arm. "It sounds like he'd deserve a broken nose, and I know you wouldn't." I loathe violence, but I understand the draw in situations like these.

Relief softens his gaze, and he expels a breath.

"Come on, hotshot," I say. We need to get back on the court. Now isn't the time for us to lose our focus. "We've got a game to win and pricks to put in their place."

We get moving, the teams taking the court and getting right back into the thick of things.

Time seems to slow down as the Pythons keep pushing, just shy of fouls or away from the ref's focus.

The forward is talking shit again, this time out of earshot of the ref. Donnie's dealing with a foul several feet away.

It's when number 2 sneers at Leon as he walks on past that I open my mouth, unable to keep a lid on it. "Man, if you have enough energy to keep spouting the crap you are, it's no wonder you're losing so spectacularly." I shake my head at him, not holding back my disgust. "If you threw that energy into playing a clean game, just maybe you wouldn't all suck."

The narrowed glance he shoots my way is full of loathing. I bounce my brows at him and follow up with a wink, focusing on Ty and the ref.

The game continues, and one thing's clear—Bentley sticking to Leon, ensuring he isn't fouled, is pissing the Pythons off. Another layup from Leon, and the crowd cheers. Bentley jogs past me, and we high-five. The sound of the ball hitting the polished floor refocuses me a hundred percent.

I get moving, looking to intercept, but number 36 manages to pass the ball to one of their players. My gaze snaps to the left, following its projection. Bentley's close by, between the basket and number 19.

One thing to know about my husband, he's like a shield, all broad shoulders and strong arms. He jumps high to block just as the forward appears out of nowhere. He's under him, his shoulder hitting Bentley's gut as he seems to balance in the air.

Blood drains from my face as the hit changes Bentley's trajectory. He spins and flips. I can't blink. Can't look away. I can't even move as he crashes to the floor.

I have no idea what hits first, his head or his hand, but the bang reverberates around my brain like I've been hit in the head by a heavy plank.

"The fuck!" I holler, already moving, fucking charging.

I don't know where to look, where to go. Acid burns my stomach, anger red-hot and turning to fire in my veins when the forward simply glances down, a sneer of indifference on his face.

I'm going to fucking kill him.

"You piece of shit." I slam into him with my arm, shoving him away. He staggers back, his gaze snapping to mine. "You—"

"Sammy." Kieran wraps an arm around me, his voice at my ear somehow cutting through my pulse that's pummeling my brain and the uproar from the crowd. I go to shrug him off. His "It's Bentley" stops me in my tracks.

The blood drains from my face as I spin on my heels. My knees weaken, the acid already swirling in my stomach intensifying.

"Bentley."

Kieran lets me go, and I'm moving.

The ref and Ty are by Bentley's side. Lacey, the athletic trainer, red bag in hand, reaches Bentley before I do.

I slam to my knees, wide-eyed and with ice in my veins. Bentley's prone form is at a slightly awkward angle.

"Bentley." My voice trembles. My hands itch to

reach out and touch him, but I'm too terrified. "Bentley." I lift my head, looking at the assistant coach. "What's wrong with him?"

Ignoring me, Lacey's checking his pulse, head low and staring at his chest while listening for Bentley's breaths.

The hell…? Is he checking if he's breathing? Why the fuck wouldn't he be—

His "Shit" shoots fresh panic like a bullet to my heart. His fingers move to Bentley's mouth, and I watch on, dizzy, as he pries Bentley's mouth open, shoving his fingers inside.

"What are you doing? What's—"

"Got it."

What the hell has Lacey got? I want to shove his hands away, but even in my panic, I know something is seriously wrong, and whatever Lacey is doing, he's helping Bentley.

"We need to move him onto his back. Where's the backboard?" Lacey whips a look over his shoulder. I follow the movement. Two EMTs are racing this way.

I jerk at the touch on my arm, my whole body trembling.

"We need to give them room," Ty says, his words barely managing to penetrate the thick fog of fear shrouding my mind.

"Room for what? To do what? Why the fuck

aren't his eyes open?" I demand, my words choked with fear and frustration.

My gaze darts back to Bentley, lying so still on the backboard, his chest rising and falling with the rhythm of the handheld respirator they've put over his nose and mouth. The sight of his unmoving form sends another wave of nausea crashing over me, and I stagger backward, barely able to stand.

"Please," I beg, turning to Ty with desperate eyes. "Please tell me he's going to be okay." But even as the words leave my lips, I fear the answer. The uncertainty, the helplessness, threatens to suffocate me as I cling to the thin thread of hope that he'll open his eyes. That he'll be okay.

The EMTs start moving. I'm close on their heels.

Coach Maple appears out of nowhere, and I go to dodge around him, refusing to let Bentley out of my sight. "We can meet them at the hospital."

I shake my head. "Not a fucking chance. I'm going in the ambulance."

"His parents are here. His mom or—"

I don't stop moving as we reach the exit, shouting, "No."

"Sammy, I know—"

The doors of the ambulance open.

"Why aren't they giving him oxygen?" Panic

surges forward as I wonder why they aren't squeezing the bag.

One of the paramedics looks my way. "He's breathing on his own now. He'd bitten his tongue and it started to swell, blocking his breathing." He focuses on the gurney, turning his back to me.

"I can come in the ambulance, right?" Everything's hazy through my damp eyes, but I see the second EMT shoot a look over her shoulder.

"We can allow one person. You say his parents are here?"

"That's right. They're just coming now," Coach confirms.

"Not a fucking chance he's going anywhere without—"

Coach Maple moves to my side. "We'll be right behind the ambulance."

I'm already shaking my head.

"Sammy needs to go."

I sag at the sound of Bentley's mom's voice. When I glance her way, her red-rimmed gaze connects with mine, and I nod.

Coach grunts at my side. I coax my attention to his, finally making eye contact. He doesn't look pissed, maybe a little frustrated at my stubbornness. When he looks at me, his features soften.

I part my lips to say thanks, maybe to ask what's

happening with the game—even though I don't actually care. Instead, the words "Bentley's my husband" spill out. "Wherever he goes, I go, Coach."

Coach's eyebrows shoot up, his mouth slightly agape. For a moment, he seems at a loss for words. His gaze shifts from me to Bentley, who's being loaded into the ambulance by the EMTs.

Finally, Coach clears his throat, his expression softening further. "I had no idea," he murmurs, his tone carrying a mix of sympathy and understanding. "Of course you should go with him."

He gives me a reassuring pat on the shoulder before turning to Bentley's parents, his voice firm as he assures them, "I'll make sure you get there safely."

As the female EMT beckons me toward the ambulance, I steal one last glance at Coach, grateful he's rolling with this. Then my eyes are on the man I love. The beeping heart monitor settles my mind.

The rhythm is steady.

The paramedics also said he's breathing. The oxygen mask must just be making it a little easier on him.

They're all good signs. It's what I focus on as the sirens wail and we race down the street.

"Why isn't he awake?" The question catches on the lump in my throat.

The EMT in the back with me doesn't glance my

way as she continues strapping Bentley's wrist. "It looks like he took a knock to his head. Either a possible concussion or being without oxygen for a little while is the likely reason."

"But he'll wake up?" The click as I swallow is loud.

This time, she looks at me, compassion in her gaze. "He's in good hands, and once we're at the hospital, we'll know more."

So that's a "no fucking idea," then?

A shaky breath tears from me as I watch her work. As she's finishing up, I ask, "What's wrong with his wrist?"

"A possible break. Maybe a bad sprain. It's swollen."

I wince. Bentley's going to be so frustrated. At least it's his right hand, so he'll still be able to sketch away at his designs.

"It was a tough game out there tonight," she says.

A humorless snort escapes. "That's one way of putting it." The whole team needs kicking out of the association for the shit they pulled tonight.

Jesus. I lean over, arms on my knees as I hang my head low. I drag in a shaky breath, trying to stop the dizziness from encroaching.

"You doing okay there?"

I manage a "Yeah" before sucking in another

lungful of air. I know what this is: an adrenaline crash. After a few seconds of deep breaths, I manage to center myself. Now is not the time for a meltdown.

Bentley needs me.

Lifting my head and straightening my back, I peer over at Bentley's motionless form. He's wearing an oxygen mask, his chest rising and falling every few seconds. The EMT monitors him carefully. Bentley's wrist has been strapped, and he's still unconscious.

I rest my palm on his bare leg. Warmth seeps into my cold, clammy skin. It's reassuring, calming me a fraction more. "How much longer?" I ask.

She peers out the front window before saying, "Three minutes." Her gaze stays on me for a beat, a gentle smile forming. "When we get there, you'll need to go to the emergency desk and give details."

I part my lips, ready to argue, but she pushes on.

"They won't let you back there while they're checking him over. Plus, he'll likely go straight for a CT scan."

CT scan? The thought stops any complaint close to escaping.

"Your coach said he'd make sure your husband's parents arrive safely, so you won't be by yourself for long. As soon as the doctors have information, they'll speak to you, okay?"

Numbly, I nod. "Thanks," I croak as the vehicle slows.

Before the doors open, she squeezes my arm. "Listen, his vitals are good, yeah?"

An unsteady breath rushes out of me. "Okay, yeah."

And then we're moving.

It's hard not to follow the gurney, almost impossible to let Bentley out of my sight. The ache in my chest threatens to cut off my breathing, but I can't let it.

Fuck.

Sucking in a lungful of air, I head to the emergency desk and give the receptionist as much information as I can. By the time she asks for his medical insurance, I sag in relief when Bentley's dad reaches my side, taking over.

"Let's go sit." Lauren wraps her arm around me. This dot of a woman holds me up, and Christ, I'm grateful. Before we sit, I wrap my arms around her. Her small frame shudders in my embrace.

"The EMT said his vitals are good." Conviction coats my tone. "He'd stopped breathing because he'd swallowed a tooth on top of his tongue swelling up." I clench my jaw, blinking away the tears of what could have happened.

I swear, Coach Lacey saved not only Bentley's life on the court but mine too. I'll be forever in his debt.

"But he's going to be okay." I press a kiss on the top of her head, then release her into Fred's arms when he joins us, Coach Maple at his side.

Coach sits next to me and angles to look my way. "You doing okay, kid?"

"Yeah." I clear my throat. "Just need him to wake up and be okay."

His large palm squeezes my shoulder.

Tears are close to strangling me. I refuse to break, not now. Distracting myself, I ask, "The game…?"

"Canceled."

Shock has me sitting upright and looking more fully at him. Sure, Coach is here, but the assistant coaches remained. Plus, canceling midplay…? "Seriously?" I've only seen that done twice in college basketball in the time I've been playing.

Obviously, Bentley's injuries are serious and will have shaken the team, but—

"They had to get that forward, Carlisle, off the court, and the rest of the team too. The Bears fans kind of lost their shit."

"For real?" It's likely I should be horrified, but fuck if I'm not proud. Carlisle's foul was the most deliberate attack I've ever seen in my years on the court and as a fan.

"Coach Lacey texted, letting me know security and the police had to be called. Everything seems to have calmed down, but the team required an escort off the campus. The footage is being reviewed by the College Athletics Board. I suspect the consequences are going to be pretty major, for the team as well as Carlisle."

I take in his words. While anger still sits heavily in my gut, it appeases some of the need to scream and lose my shit.

"The rest of the team are almost here."

I nod, grateful my friends will be by my side.

"I need to warn you, Sammy," Coach starts, his hand moving back to my shoulder, capturing my attention completely. "You know the game was live. The footage is going to be everywhere, so do not look at it, okay?"

"Yeah, okay." I swallow bile. Just the thought of seeing Bentley crashing to the ground is enough to have my vision blurring. The memory is already seared into my mind. I don't want another reminder.

"There's more." His voice drops lower, quieter, putting me on high alert. "When we were all outside and the EMTs were getting Bentley ready for transport, one of the camera crews was there, recording."

My nose twitches in distaste. Again, that's nothing I want to watch. "Yeah, okay, thanks." I frown when he doesn't let go, his gaze completely focused on me.

I'm missing something.

"What is it?"

Coach's lips stretch thin and tight. Discomfort settles on his face. "You told me you and Bentley were married, and the camera was pointed directly at you."

Oh shit. Yeah, I definitely missed something.

Cameras were the last thing on my mind at the time. Sure, I knew there were multiple bodies around us, but I didn't pay a lick of attention.

"It's fine." My attempt at being blasé falls flat. The sympathy in Coach's expression confirms it.

Immediately, thoughts of Trevin lodge in my brain, but it's not like he has free and easy access to any media inside. My pulse hammers loudly in my head.

There's nothing to be done now. My fear, what's kept me rooted in the need to keep our relationship quiet, is still there, but at the moment, I have to focus on Bentley being well. Once I know he's going to be okay, then I can freak the fuck out and figure out what I need to do to keep Trevin as far away from Bentley as fucking possible.

CHAPTER 22

BENTLEY

For two days, Sammy hasn't left my side. The only time he's stopped touching me is when he has to go to the bathroom. While it's endearing, my worry for him keeps escalating.

What I'm hoping is, the doctor will finally agree to release me. At least then we'll both be somewhere more comfortable, and, hopefully, Sammy will finally rest.

Mom and Dad just left to get fresh coffee. Not that I can have any.

Severe concussions suck. Like majorly blow.

It's still a struggle to remember what exactly happened. Apparently, there's footage, but the thought of watching it makes my stomach churn and my constant headache pound even harder.

"What about this one?" Sammy's voice is whisper

soft; anything louder pierces my brain with the force of a thousand blades.

"Hmm?" Even speaking is a struggle, but I could listen to Sammy's comforting voice forever.

"Document control analyst." He turns his gaze to me. "It says it's working with a project team and is about ensuring proper document management. Lots of admin and project support."

A swear, a little piece of my soul shrivels up as he speaks. It sounds boring as hell, but this is Sammy's new mission since I woke up after a couple of hours of unconsciousness. He's planning ahead and looking for steady, mostly entry-level positions he can apply for next year before we graduate.

How my landing on my head has Sammy turning into Mr. Responsible is… honestly, it's disconcerting. I just don't have the words to tell him all that just yet. Not while everything hurts so much.

"Working with a team's good. I could handle that." His voice lacks conviction, but I love him for trying.

"You're great in a team," I say softly, squeezing his hand.

His grunt is low as he continues looking through job ads or one of those "what the fuck do graduates do with a business degree" websites. I suspect it's the latter.

His phone vibrates. He immediately winces, mouthing, "Sorry."

I simply smile. As long as the phone's not on my person, shaking my body, it's all good.

"It's Mom."

A smile settles on his lips, easing some of the tightness in my chest that sits there every time I see him pushing himself to potentially do something that I'm sure will make him miserable.

His chuckle is light, so very aware of my pain levels. "Mom wants to know if you've tried candied yams."

"No, but if she's making it, I'll definitely try it."

He shoots me a soft smile as he types on his phone. Another vibration, and he shakes his head with another gentle smirk. "She wants to know ham or turkey."

"I think that's a decision for someone else."

"Turkey it is." Sammy bounces his brows, and amusement blossoms in my chest.

"Your folks don't need to go to all this trouble." It's touching, but it feels like I've sort of taken over festive plans.

With a roll of his eyes, Sammy waves me off. "Puh-lease," he says with sweet exasperation, "Christmas Eve dinner was always going to happen. Mom and Dad just want to make a bit more of a fuss.

I think she's excited about spending time with your parents, getting to know them better."

Admittedly, the whole thing is a little surreal, but I'm all for this plan. Our parents have met before. We all had dinner together last year when my folks were in town for a game. But this time is so much more significant.

The door opens, and I wince at the light. It sucks that just a sliver of brightness from the corridor shoots fresh pain into my brain. As it is, the room blinds are closed. A single light—thankfully with a soft yellow glow—is on in the corner of the room.

Vampires have a really sucky deal with the whole daylight thing.

Dr. Patel enters the room, shutting the door quietly behind her. "How's the patient?" Her volume is considerate and low.

"Ready to get out of here." If I could win her over with a full, charming smile, I'd do so. The problem is, even a grin is out of my comfort zone.

"In that case, I have good news. Your new CT scans from this morning are great. No changes," she begins.

"So, no bleeds or swelling?" Sammy clarifies, his hand tight on mine.

"No. The scans remain clear. I'm happy to sign your discharge papers and let you head home. Give me an hour, and you should be good to go." From the end of the bed, she peers over at me, her gaze assessing and kind. "A reminder that severe concussions can cause issues for an undetermined amount of time. It means you need to listen to your body and do what it wants and needs."

"And his wrist?"

A heavy thud in my heart makes me wince. With so much pain in my head, it's so easy to forget about my wrist.

"Sprains can be tricky." The doctor moves to the side of my bed and gently picks up my right arm. She carefully removes the brace and assesses my weak wrist. "There's virtually no swelling, which is incredible, especially as your body's already working overtime with your concussion."

She turns my wrist. It's sore and tender but not agonizing.

"You need to keep it strapped for at least a week. After that, work with your team's trainer. They'll give you strengthening exercises. The positive news is, it's not a bad sprain. There's limited bruising. We don't think any tears. But ligaments sometimes don't like to behave."

"Thanks, Doctor."

She smiles back at me. "Any more questions?"

Shaking his head, Sammy softens his hold on my hand. "No, thanks, Doctor."

"Okay. One of the nurses will be by soon. They'll give you some literature about your concussion. Be sure to have lots of downtime these holidays."

Even though I smile, my heart plummets. It's still a few days away, but with how I'm feeling, there's no chance I'll be able to get on a bus with the team to watch their game.

As the doctor leaves, Sammy stands. I glance his way when I realize he's staring at me intently.

"Great news, huh? We can get you out of here."

My smile is half-hearted at best.

The expression he's directing my way transforms into worry, and he carefully wedges his ass on the bed so he can get close. I melt into his touch. Gentle fingers stroke my head. It's the best feeling ever, soothing the ache in my temples and the frustration settling like lead in my heart.

"Just look at how quickly your wrist is healing. Before you know it, the headaches will fade, and you'll bounce right back." He presses a kiss on my forehead. "We'll just take each day as it comes."

My lips twitch, and I want to tease him. Want to call him out and question when he started to be all wise and sensible. Instead, I turn my head into him, capturing his scent. The hospital soap isn't the most pleasant, but underneath that is Sammy's familiar fragrance.

I close my eyes, tiredness hitting me.

In an hour, we get to leave, but until then, I just want to sleep.

THE PAIN JOLTS THROUGH MY SKULL LIKE LIGHTNING, splitting my head in two. It's a relentless assault, throbbing, pulsing, refusing to let me retreat into the oblivion of sleep. With a stifled groan, I clutch my head, trying to contain the agony.

Beside me, I feel Sammy stir, his concern palpable even in the darkness of the room. "Are you okay?" he asks, his voice laced with worry, his hand finding my cheek in the pitch-black.

I try to form words, but they evaporate in the haze of pain engulfing my mind. All I manage is a weak nod, hoping it will suffice to reassure him.

The painkillers I took earlier seem futile against this onslaught, as if my brain has decided to rebel against any attempts to subdue it. I'm caught in a vicious cycle of agony and exhaustion, unable to find respite.

I fucking hate it.

The asshole who's responsible may have been

kicked from his team, but resentment is a vicious, twisted emotion. It's hard not to drift into frustration and despair.

How Sammy's putting up with my mood swings and borderline petulant behavior, I have no clue, but I'm grateful he does. I don't mean to be a grump or complain, so most of the time, I keep my mouth shut.

It's easier that way. Plus, it hurts less when I stay quiet.

In the distance, I hear the faint sounds of Christmas preparations—laughter, music, the clanging of pans. It feels like a world away, separated from me by an impenetrable barrier of pain.

Desperation claws at me, urging me to find relief, but there's no escape from the torment within my skull. I feel trapped, isolated, a prisoner in my own body.

Sammy's hand finds mine, offering a silent anchor amid the storm raging within me. His touch is a lifeline, grounding me in the midst of chaos.

With every ounce of strength I can muster, I whisper, "I'll be okay. I'll shower and get up."

I have no idea how early it is. My in-laws fitted blackout curtains in the office where we're staying because that's how incredible they are.

"You don't have to."

Warmth spreads over me, a comforting blanket.

He's so damn thoughtful, but I want to do this for him, join in the festivities, celebrate with my family and his. Sammy's love for the holidays is no small thing.

Our college house is plastered with decorations. It looks like a Christmas elf vomited over every square inch of the communal spaces. Sammy's smile, his genuine joy, is worth the brain overload of color and light.

"I'll be fine. More painkillers and sunglasses, and I'm ready for you to open your gift."

He presses against my side, his naked body flush with mine and sending delicious heat over my skin. When he buries his face carefully in the juncture of my neck and shoulder, I feel his smile. "Thanks, sweetheart, but if it's too much, just say, and we'll come back here."

I expel a hum of agreement. There's no point trying to argue with him about his leaving the cele-bration to be by my side.

"Let me get you some fresh water and your meds. I'll turn the fairy lights on."

As Sammy sets about making me comfortable, I stretch carefully and wiggle my fingers and toes. It's going to be a full-on day, and I want to make the most of it.

We got here yesterday after Sammy's training

with the team. He arrived home still damp from the shower but had snuggled up with me before he'd packed a few things for us and settled me in the car to collect my parents from their hotel so we could all head to his hometown.

After dropping my folks at an Airbnb just a block away, we headed here before Sammy squirreled me away to hide in the darkness of his dad's office. But with tomorrow being Christmas Day, we'll be celebrating today before staying the night and heading back to college midmorning for basketball training.

Both my folks and Sammy's have tried to convince me to stay here, and while I know I can't handle the trip to watch Sammy play, I want to be waiting in our bed for him as soon as he gets home.

"Here."

Under the soft glow of the fairy lights, I focus on the white pills in Sammy's palm. I take them gratefully and wash them down with the glass of water he hands me. "Thanks."

After pulling on sweats and hoodies, we stick our feet in the matching slippers we found at the end of the futon yesterday. They're cute and a little cheesy and feel ridiculously comfortable.

When we enter, the kitchen is bright. Immediately, Nova hugs me gently and ushers me into the sitting room. The main lights are off again, and the twinkling lights of the Christmas tree give just enough glow to help us see, since the curtains are closed, keeping out the rays from the rising sun.

Everyone's up and all smiles, their conversation dying down, their voices softening when they see me.

"Merry Christmas," I say, even managing a smile.

Mom and Dad wrap me up in their arms, wishing me the same; Sammy's dad follows with a gentle hug a moment later, and fuck, I'm already exhausted.

"Let me go help Nova. She keeps trying to shoo me away." Mom's all smiles. It's a relief that she and Sammy's mom seem to genuinely like each other, though. The same goes for Dad and Leroy.

"What are you looking at?"

Sammy's nose is buried in his phone. A quick glance my way, and from the grimace he fails to hide, I have my suspicions.

"You should just delete all your apps." While I haven't read any of the comments or the posts about Sammy outing our relationship on live TV, he's shared a few with me. Do I suspect he's not told me everything? Absolutely. While I get that he's trying to protect me, I don't give a shit about anything anyone has to say.

The most important people are in this house with me.

"I swear, Kieran didn't get this much attention." A trickle of exasperation winds its way into his tone. "Which, you know, is great. The only attention he should have is because of his skills on the court." He shakes his head. I'm a little envious of the movement.

There are a few moments in the day when I almost feel human—usually once the pain meds have kicked in. But even then, I'm too scared to do something as simple as shake my head.

"Why are there so many dicks in the world?"

The fact that he doesn't follow up with a lip twitch about actual dicks lets me know just how frustrated he is. I cringe on the inside even as I ask, "What's being said?"

He hesitates, but whatever he sees on my face must tell him I want to know. I suppose I'm morbidly curious. On top of that, I don't want Sammy to take all this on by himself. It's unfair.

I've lived a privileged life in the grand scheme of things.

White, a man, just smart enough to attend college and do a little better than okay. My folks do all right financially. They're not rolling in dough, but they're meticulous savers. Me joining the alphabet mafia is the first time I've left myself open, vulnerable to assholes and bigotry.

Sammy's black skin means our experiences are so

different. I wouldn't even try to imagine or presume anything about the day-to-day systematic racism he experiences. All I know is what he's shared and the times I've witnessed—and tried to shut down—racist bullshit and, more often, implicit bias.

"Sammy," I push.

He releases a sigh before saying, "I'm not reading you anything, but there's stuff about us and the team."

Yeah, I can imagine. Five out players on a single team must be some kind of record. Add in an assistant coach and a generally supportive fan base from what I witnessed before our relationship was shared with the world, and you've got a team that's not just breaking records on the court but also breaking barriers and stereotypes off the court, right?

Maybe that's the drugs that are working their way through my system talking. But surely it's a testament to the progress we've made as a school, if not a society, and a celebration of diversity in basketball.

Sammy saying, "Some idiots are congratulating Carlisle and the Pythons, tagging on their disappointment that they didn't take more of 'us' out" douses my pretty thinking in a gallon of gasoline and throws a match on it.

So, maybe not a celebration of diversity in basketball after all.

"Please delete that shit, Sammy." Exhaustion ripples through me. I haven't even had a decaf coffee or breakfast yet, but my brain needs a break from social media and offensive dickwads.

I suspect Sammy hears the tension and tiredness in my tone, as he closes out whatever app he's been looking at and places his cell on the table. "Done." I witness him shaking off the heavy weight of what he's read, and a couple of beats later, he grins at me. "So, gifts."

And just like that, he transforms. It's not even fake. I know each of Sammy's smiles, and genuine excitement all but vibrates from him.

All I can say is, I'm relieved I already bought and wrapped his gift before the concussion. "Sounds good."

Effortlessly, he jumps up, dots a kiss on my forehead, and bounds into the kitchen. His voice is low as he rushes our moms. Meanwhile, I glance around the room, remembering we weren't alone when that whole conversation was being had.

Concern clouds my dad's usually smiling face, his shoulders tense with the weight of parental worry. He stares at me with furrowed brows before glancing at Leroy, his gaze reflecting a shared understanding. Leroy stands tall beside the fireplace, his indignation palpable as he clenches his fists.

This is the last thing I want. I understand their worry and frustration, but this is my and Sammy's life now. Together, we'll keep moving forward. My injuries are already massively impacting our celebration. I don't want the conversation they heard to bring down everyone's mood even more.

"So, Malik," I say, switching the focus, "what's the plan with those gifts under the tree?"

Putting down his phone, Sammy's youngest brother grins at me. "As soon as Mom's here, I can start passing them out. After that, it's a free-for-all."

"It's pretty cool that we're celebrating a day early. We usually do gifts Christmas morning." Denzel offers an up-nod as though I'm responsible for our basketball schedule and the need to leave early tomorrow.

Carrying a couple of mugs, Sammy heads back into the room. He passes me my decaf coffee, which I try not to sneer at, and sits next to me.

"Thanks." I inhale. It smells pretty real. Maybe I can convince myself it'll give me a caffeine hit if I keep taking a big sniff before every mouthful.

Movement at the door catches my attention. Nova enters, saying, "We're here."

Mom's at her side, a soft smile immediately on me.

"Yes!"

A burst of pain at the noise, and my body flinches.

"Malik," Sammy hisses.

"No, no, it's fine." I focus on Malik. The poor kid looks panicked. "Honestly, Malik, I'm cheering on the inside with you."

It takes a moment for his guilt to clear. As soon as it does, he focuses on the gifts under the tree while I nudge Sammy.

When our gazes connect, I whisper, "It's fine. Please don't make a big deal."

The argument's there, easy for me to read in his expression. I narrow my eyes at him, expecting a throb of pain. When it doesn't come, my frown eases.

"The painkillers are working."

Eventually, he nods as he holds my hand and brings it to his lips.

He is so sweet and attentive, but people walking on eggshells around me is beginning to grate on my nerves. I'm grateful, truly—but I'm counting down the days until life gets back to normal.

CHAPTER 23

SAMMY

The envelope shakes in my trembling hands. Throwing it straight in the trash is the sensible thing to do, but curiosity wins against self-preservation.

Swiping my finger through the gap in the envelope, I wince as the paper slices my finger. "Fuck." I shove the tip in my mouth.

That's got to be an omen, right? A cut and spilled blood, all from what feels like a card stamped by Westhaven Penitentiary, seems like a giant setup.

"All okay?"

Jumping at Bentley's voice, I stare at him wide-eyed, finger still in my mouth. I hum around my finger before murmuring, "Paper cut."

"What from?" He steps farther into our bedroom and drops his laptop on the bed.

I didn't hear him come home, I was so focused on

this damn envelope—which, shamefully, I'd planned to hide from him. In my defense, the last two weeks since leaving my folks' place have been a roller coaster.

There have been severe highs and lows, specifically with Bentley's pain levels.

Not realizing my husband could be so majorly stubborn is completely on me. He refuses to stay at home, insisting on attending classes. I get it; he's worried about falling behind. But this is after his department agreed to give him extensions and additional support should he need it.

Which he obviously hasn't taken, as he's more stubborn than a mule with its hooves superglued to the ground.

That I haven't told him about the phone calls already sits heavily in my gut, but since I didn't accept Trevin's three attempted calls, there's nothing much to say. The truth is, it's unnecessary worry. It's a no-brainer that if Bentley's upset, his head's going to hurt.

Plus, he keeps feeling dizzy.

And *that's* something he's trying unsuccessfully to play down.

But as I'm standing in front of him, Bentley's gaze narrowing by the second and drifting down to the envelope, it's time to fess up.

"It's from Trevin."

Intensity blazes in his eyes as he snaps his attention to the envelope. "Have you opened it yet?"

I shake my head. "Just about to. I think the bastard rigged it to give me a paper cut." My snort is all forced amusement.

"You want me to do it?"

My shoulders sag a little, and like always, he reminds me how amazing he is. "Best not in case there's anthrax or something in here." I'm only half joking.

With twitching lips, Bentley moves to my side, wrapping an arm around my waist. "In that case, I think it's best we go down together."

I feel more centered, and my hands no longer shake as I open the envelope. It's definitely a card.

I tug it out, turning it over. The front of the card displays a cartoon bride and groom, but my gaze can't focus enough to roll my eyes. Instead, they're fixated on the words that fill me with dread: *Congratulations on your wedding.*

With a deep breath, I glance at Bentley, his reassuring presence grounding me.

My heart pounds louder as I carefully unfold the card. Inside, the message is short, but its implications weigh heavily on me.

I missed the big day. Don't worry. I'll catch up with

you soon to give you my congratulations in person and deliver a proper gift.

A wave of nausea hits me, and I clutch the card tighter, as if trying to ward off the unsettling feeling it brings. What does he mean by "catch up"? Is he planning something? My mind races with questions, the uncertainty gnawing at me.

Turning to Bentley, I swallow hard. His steady gaze meets mine, but I'm feeling anything but in control.

"Is that a threat?" I hate the wobble in my voice. That I'm fucking scared shitless seems like just another way Trevin's got a complete hold over me. "It's a threat, right?"

"Hey." Bentley takes the card from my hand and throws it to the floor. Then he's in front of me, forcing me to make eye contact. "Fuck Trevin. When he's released, whenever that may be, he can't cross the state line, and if he does, we'll celebrate, as it means he'll have broken parole and be sent back to prison." He cups my jaw, caressing my cheek with his thumb. "You know this, yeah?"

I do. Rationally, I know he's right.

"What did Matt say about power?"

The mention of my therapist helps me draw in a jagged breath. Bentley's question pierces through the tumult in my mind, bringing me back to the tools I've been given to navigate moments like these.

"He said…." My voice wavers, but I cling to his words like a lifeline. "He said that Trevin doesn't have power over me. That I have all the control, and I always have the option to take his power away." I repeat the mantra like a prayer, trying to anchor myself in the truth of those words. "He said that I'm the one in charge of my life, not Trevin."

Bentley's grip on my face softens, his expression filled with a mix of concern and determination. "That's right. You're in control, always. And we'll do whatever it takes to keep you safe."

I lean into his touch, finding solace in his unwavering support.

Do I find it ironic that Bentley's protecting me from Trevin, even though I've always promised to protect him from the man who hurt me so badly? Yeah, a little, but I'm pretty sure that's how this whole marriage thing works.

Despite the lingering unease sparked by Trevin's message, I take comfort in the reminder that I'm not powerless—that with Bentley by my side, I can face anything. Even Trevin.

"Do you think we need to take this to the cops?" Caution strains his tone.

"And say what, Trevin sent us a card to celebrate

our marriage?" I keep the bite out of my words. I'm not pissed at him.

The reality is that when I chose not to tell the whole truth to the police, it made everything complicated. Sure, I'm still a victim of assault, but the story behind how and why makes it impossible to follow through with any complaints without retracting my story.

That's the last thing I wish or am willing to do.

Hell, I haven't even been contacted by the prison or parole board or whoever it is who contacts victims about the parole hearing. It confirms the story I told the police and that they don't believe Trevin is a threat to me. My injuries were caused by me "being in the way," and I was "not the focus of his malicious attack," or however the police and courts chose to word it.

Remaining silent, Bentley tugs me into his arms. His wrist is no longer wrapped, and I'm assuming he's having a good day, since he hasn't shown signs of being in pain. I hug him back, taking comfort in the heat of his solid body.

"If you keep burrowing your nose into me like that, I'm going to think you're finally ready to get in my pants."

I smirk at his teasing tone, appreciating that he's giving us a moment to think about something else.

However, it doesn't stop me from being serious when I ask, "And what number has your pain been today?"

A deep huff from Bentley teases my hair.

His lack of immediate answer tells me that while he may be okay this second, that hasn't been the case all day. "Yeah, that's what I thought."

"Whoever put you in control of my orgasms sucks." There's zero heat in his complaint, especially as he knows the likelihood that the strain of coming is going to bring on an intense headache.

He's right about it sucking, though.

Saying that…

"No one said I can't have an orgasm sucked out of me… you know, if you go really slow and use a lot of wrist action."

Bentley stills in my arms before angling to look at me with heat in his gaze. I swallow hard as his hand immediately palms my cock.

"Fuck." A guttural moan follows. "No, I can wait."

That's what I have to say, right, being a supportive husband and all that?

I think it's the lack of conviction in my voice that has him snorting. "You want me to stop?"

"If you stop, I think I might die of blue balls."

He licks up my neck as he unbuttons my jeans and pulls down the zipper. "We wouldn't want that," he mumbles as he presses open-mouthed kisses against me.

I should stop this. Me coming is going to make him impossibly hard. If I even side-eye his cock while he's so horny, he's likely to blow untouched.

When his warm hand eases into my boxers, wrapping around my cock, my knees go weak. "Fuck, we should stop."

He's jacking me off in earnest now. "We can if that's what you really want." The thumb against the head of my dick smooths out the precum. "Jesus."

Yeah, my thoughts exactly.

"I need to look."

I don't stop him as he angles away and tugs down my jeans, then kneels. Sure, I have a healthy amount of precum, but I haven't jacked off, not once, which means I haven't come since the morning of Bentley's injuries.

The precum that's leaking from my slit is so much more than normal. Hell, there's enough there that he could scoop it up, lather his own dick, and take me to pound town.

"Nngh…," I grunt, liking that thought far too much. That he's teasing my cock like it's a specimen worth examining, which it totally is, may also have something to do with the involuntary thrusting of my hips.

"F-Fuck," I stutter. Okay, so involuntary is code for me fucking his grip.

I glance down, mesmerized by the expression on his face.

"God, I wish you could fuck my throat." He peers up at me from his knees with so much want in his eyes that I almost nod and tell him that's the best idea ever.

Pulling in the last semblance of my control, I instead say, "Soon."

The way he bites onto his bottom lip lets me know what he's planning. I narrow my gaze at him. Or at least I try to. It's hard—literally—to think of anything when he's jacking me off and looking at me like I'm the hottest man he's ever seen.

That and my balls draw tight, the tingling at the base of my spine shooting bolts of pleasure to every nerve in my body.

"Just a taste." He opens his mouth, tongue out, lapping at my cock like my dick's a lollipop.

"Oh, fuck… sweetheart… fuck…." Ecstasy slams into me with the speed of a flying arrow. It finds its purchase, and I explode, coming in thick spurts, each drop landing on his tongue.

A ripple and a shudder, and I stop thrusting. Bentley immediately latches on to the head of my cock, swirling his tongue, dipping it into my slit before lapping and swallowing with a dirty groan.

It's all I can do to stand upright.

I'm blissed out, a complete blob of contented goo.

As he pulls away with a satisfied pop, I glance at him through half-lidded eyes. His lips are wet, eyes bright, and what I wouldn't do to be able to return the favor.

I want that so desperately.

"I feel like I should be pissed off at you, but my orgasm is telling me I'm an asshole if I am."

He chuckles, and I help him stand. The movement draws my attention to his tented jeans. I wince, imagining how much he must be throbbing. It looks painfully uncomfortable.

"I'll feel shitty that you're left with that as soon as the glow of you sucking my soul out fades." Right now, I can't pretend to feel too badly. I certainly don't regret it.

He presses on his junk and shifts in clear discomfort.

"You know I'm taking no responsibility for this." I'm full of shit as I lean in and lap at his mouth, knowing I'm not helping the situation. The taste of myself on his tongue shouldn't be as hot as it is. It definitely shouldn't be enough to get me hard again, but if I keep this up, that's what's going to happen.

I ease away, tracing the wrinkle from his forehead. It smooths out, his body relaxing.

"Two days with nothing higher than a three, and I promise to do anything you want, okay?"

And wasn't that a fucking hilarious conversation to have with Lacey? It took some work to agree to a pain threshold of three, but it's a much more realistic number than one.

"Fine, I know." He steps away and picks up the card. "You want this?"

I hesitate. Maybe it could be useful for summoning demons or something. "I don't know."

Bobbing his head, Bentley shoves the card back in the envelope and tucks it away under a pile of books on the bookcase. "I'm going to take a cool shower." He arches his brow, daring me to tease him.

I think better of it and shoot him a butter-wouldn't-melt smile.

"Are you going to be okay?"

I don't hesitate. "Yeah."

Trevin has no real power over me. Gut-deep, I know it. The problem is, sometimes, my memories get in the way. That shit is hard to navigate and push aside.

"I will be," I amend.

"Love you." He backs away, heading to the

shower, and unashamedly, I watch his delectable ass go.

***

Tonight, Bentley managed to watch the whole game courtside.

Did I show off a little? Damn straight I did.

One of the awesome things about playing at home is our crowd. With classes back in session, the seats are full. More than that, our fans are hella supportive.

More and more Pride flags and a whole array of rainbow paraphernalia litter the crowd. It's only now, with the game finished and a win in our pockets, that I'm fully able to appreciate it.

Not that I'm naive to the fact that some of our fans wish we'd all stayed firmly in the closet, but as long as they don't share their bigotry, I can let it slide.

Bentley heads my way, beaming at me.

This is now day three of pain levels below two. It's one of the reasons I'm sure my shoes grew wings when we played. It's been almost three weeks since his injuries, and he's showing real signs of improvement.

It's something we're definitely going to celebrate,

and I'm going to make good on my promise to do whatever he likes tonight.

Bentley greets me with a giant hug. I sigh into his hold, loving the PDA, which I admittedly have become needy about—not that he complains.

Fuck, I love being out, being so publicly us.

"Amazing game, baby." The words are whispered close to my ear before he presses his lips to mine in a swift kiss. "You all killed it."

We did. "Thanks. I still can't wait till you're back on the court." Not gonna lie, it's been hard without him, even though Downey has done a decent job of slotting into his spot, and today, he was definitely on form.

I suspect knowing Bentley was attending had something to do with that.

But yeah, we played hard tonight and came away with the win, but Bentley brings a certain finesse to the court that Downey just doesn't have. Next season, he'll have his chance, but for now, Bentley's already had a couple of sit-downs with the coaches.

His wrist is healing fast. The strength is almost at a hundred percent. It's just the pesky headaches that need to disappear. At least now, I finally believe him that his dizziness has gone.

Leon grabs our attention as he bounds over. Like all of us, he studies Bentley's face before hauling him into a hug. Huffing out a grunted laugh, my sexy-as-fuck husband, who is totally rocking my number tonight (much to the team's amusement), hugs Leon.

"Man, it's so great that you're here." Still flushed from the game, Leon's eyes are bright. He's totally riding the high of the win. "Tiller said you were going to start training again with us next week."

My brows shoot high. "He did?"

A shifty expression appears on Bentley's face. "Yeah." He cards his fingers through his hair. "It was going to be a surprise," he says, side-eyeing Leon.

"Shit." Red races up Leon's neck. "Fuck, was Tiller not meant to tell me that? Sorry, I didn't know."

"Didn't know what?" Ty's beefy arm wraps around Bentley. As he squeezes, he looks at us expectantly.

Sighing in defeat but still looking happy as a pig in mud, Bentley answers, "I'm back training next week."

Ty's grin is instant. "Hell yes. Best news ever, man. Are we celebrating tonight?"

Before Bentley or Leon can answer, I jump in. "Yes. Privately, in our bedroom. You'll all need earplugs if you're staying in."

Damn, I love it when Bentley turns that shade of pink. It usually spreads all across his chest. It does mean his freckles disappear, which is a bummer but totally worth it.

"No shit?" Ty gives a nod of approval. "Another day under three?"

"Jesus." Rubbing his hand over his face, Bentley shakes his head and huffs out a heavy breath. "What happened to good old-fashioned everyone keeping their shit to themselves?"

My snicker earns me the stink eye.

To be fair, I made the hardship of going without orgasms no great secret. Maybe a little too vocally at times. But seriously, having blue balls and being frustrated while our housemates were still getting some put me in a pissy mood.

While I got off once, which admittedly was epic, that was still just once in twenty-four days.

And yes, I have been counting.

"I'll take that as a yes. Congrats, man."

I high-five Ty, saying, "Thanks," like somehow I'm totally responsible for Bentley's progress.

Instead of calling me out, Bentley chuckles, but the heat in his gaze remains a steady burn. He is so going to blow in under two minutes. My plan is to do that as soon as possible. That way, we've got plenty of the evening left for him to come at least once more —maybe even a third time, depending on how he's holding up.

From the way he's staring at me and the intensity there, I suspect he's got a good idea of what my plan is—even though I've said he can ask for whatever he wants.

"You coming to the locker room?" Ty asks.

I glance around to see the rest of the team are ready to move. "Yeah. I could do with talking to Coach."

With a smile, I hold Bentley's hand, luxuriating in the contact that I'm sure billions of people take for granted every day.

Once out of the public eye, we shoot the shit while getting undressed. A quick check of my phone, and I smile, seeing the notification from my dad. I send him a *Thanks* and head for a shower.

This is going to be the quickest shower known to man. Actually… if I jump in one of the private showers, I could totally do a bit of prep before I steal Bentley away.

Do I totally whistle on my walk over to the cubicle? Why, yes—yes, I do.

CHAPTER 24

BENTLEY

COACH IS ON THE PHONE WHEN I SEEK HIM OUT, SO I backtrack to the locker room.

A couple of guys are already showered and getting dressed. We're talking about their plans tonight, making bullshit excuses for why I'm not heading out.

Apparently, they're the only players who don't know I plan to fuck my husband tonight.

Which I absolutely plan to do. Several times, if possible.

Not that I've told them that.

Waking up without a headache yesterday confused the hell out of me. It took me longer than it should have to work out what was different. And this morning. I'd almost wept in relief when, while my head was a little foggy, there was no headache in sight.

Best morning ever.

"… next week, yeah," I say, telling them about joining practice. "It finally feels like I have—" The *John Wick* theme tune blasts out, cutting me off. "Let me just see who it is."

I leave the guys to jog over to Sammy's locker. His phone's out, the theme tune still playing. I smile as I pick up. The music always makes me smirk. I get it, though. Keanu Reeves is a total badass.

Unknown.

Frowning, I hit Answer. Before I can speak, there's silence and a quiet click of what I'm sure is about to be a voice recording. I roll my eyes, fed up with scam calls like this. As I go to hit End, the voice recording starts.

"You are receiving a call from Trevin Houston at West-haven Penitentiary. This call is subject to monitoring and recording. To accept this call, please press one. To refuse this call, please hang up now. If you would like to block any future calls from this facility, please press two. Thank you for using Westhaven Penitentiary communications."

Fuck. I pull the phone away and stare at it, my heart pounding. I hit the number one.

Fuck, fuck, fuck. Why the hell did I hit one?

Shit.

Sweat breaks out on my brow. I need to hang up. Sammy's going to lose his shit and—

"Sammy. That you, boy?"

I put the phone back to my ear and take a shaky breath. It's not too late. I can just end the call. "No, it's Bentley."

I squeeze my eyes closed and turn away from the room, facing Sammy's locker.

A raspy chuckle that somehow manages to sound cruel, though that could be my imagination, travels down the line.

It makes my skin crawl. It also makes me stand up straighter.

Sammy might lose his shit, and I suspect I'll have a big apology to make, but Trevin also needs to go fuck himself.

I weave steel into my tone when I ask, "Why are you calling?"

More to the point, why hasn't Sammy blocked his calls? Number two expels all the shits, apparently.

"The infamous son-in-law." I can practically hear his sneer. *"Now, is that any way to speak to your father-in-law?"*

I refuse to buy into what he's attempting, repeating, "Why are you calling?"

At the sound of him sucking his teeth, my eye twitches. Everything inside me is screaming at me to cut him off. I should. But this is the piece of shit who hurt Sammy so badly that eight years later, he continues to struggle to move on with his life.

"Just checking there's a welcome home party planned when I make early parole in a couple of days." A gruff laugh makes me shudder.

My temper is a boiling volcano, red-hot and so close to exploding that my voice shakes as I say, "Whatever you think is going to happen is beyond crazy. You're not coming within ten miles of Sammy."

I take a surreptitious glance around the room, remembering where I am. A couple more guys are back, but there's no one close to me.

"Now, now, son, there's no need to get defensive. I'm just making sure that boy of mine's grateful for what I did for him."

What. The. Fuck? "Did for him?" My voice is too loud, too out of control. I drop it instantly. "You really are fucking insane."

"Mind your words, boy. Sammy's lucky I stopped when I did. Owes me his life. When I get out, he needs to repay that in kind."

I see red. Anger poisons my veins as I recall what Sammy told me about that night. What Trevin did to him. "Let me make myself crystal fucking clear. You're not to come anywhere near Sammy. You don't call. You don't send any cards through the mail. You forget his name and that he ever even existed." I can't stop. I barely take a breath. "You're the biggest piece of shit, and you need to rot in fucking jail."

With a shaky finger, I hit End. I clench my fist, so tempted to throw Sammy's phone, but stop myself before I do anything else foolish.

Fuck, fuck, fu—

"Bentley?"

For the love of fucks….

I turn, facing Sammy, dreading to see his reaction. My eyes widen, realizing that Tyron is next to him, his face a mask of concern. But beneath Tyron's worry, I see the flicker of readiness. He's ready to throw down should I need him to.

Snapping my gaze back to Sammy, who's barely ten feet away, I cringe at his neutral expression. Except his eyes. There's a hell of a lot of emotion swirling in their depths, so much that it's a struggle to figure out exactly what he's thinking.

"I'm so sorry." I flick a glance at a couple of the younger guys on our team, noticing their curious expressions.

Fuck. Just how loud was I?

Shame sits heavily on my shoulders. I loosen my grip on Sammy's phone and stare down at it. It's a surprise to see it, which makes no sense. But that whole conversation feels unreal.

I look up when Sammy's bare feet come into view. A towel is around his waist, and a few waterdrops still glisten on his broad shoulders, and fuck, what have I done?

His hand moving startles me, and I realize he's taking his phone out of my hand. I release it immediately, making eye contact.

"I thought it was a scam call. Then when I realized, I…. I shouldn't have. I'm so sorry." I stop short of blurting out the whole story. This is not the time or the place for this conversation, but it's hard to think through the ringing in my ears. A dull throb starts, and I wince, pressing the heel of my hand against my temple.

Not now.

"Does your head hurt?"

Why does he sound so calm and together?

I remove my hand and manage not to wince. "I'm fine."

The muscle in his cheek tenses, his eyes narrowing.

"A little. Just a two."

The barest flicker of a smile teases his lips, but it disappears before it properly forms. "Let me dress, and then we'll head home."

I have a feeling it's not for the sexy times we planned. God, I'm a dickhead.

But fuck, it felt good to tell Trevin what a piece of shit he is. Let him know there's no way in hell he'll get to Sammy.

It's best I swallow that feeling down. Not sure it's the right time to share that particular reaction with Sammy. One day, maybe.

It feels odd just standing here while the guys are dressing. "I'll… uhm… just wait outside."

Once Sammy nods, I walk out, not daring to look at anyone, especially not Tyron.

I should be talking to Coach, but I don't have it in me. Not right now. I'll do so later when I'm calmer.

While I wait, I take a couple painkillers with a can of Coke I grab from the vending machine. It's the first time I've had caffeine in weeks. Hopefully, it'll give me the energy boost I need for when Sammy and I are back home.

After making quick work of my soda, I throw it in the recycling bin just as Sammy exits. A tentative smile plays on my lips while his own is tight.

Silently, we head out. There are still plenty of people around campus. Several students are already well on their way to partying. Plenty of hollers reach us, calling our names, mainly those telling Sammy, "Good game."

He accepts each one with an up-nod and a barely there smile. The farther we walk away, especially from the on-site accommodation, the quieter it gets. Streetlamps guide our way, giving us enough light that the white clouds from our warm breaths float before us.

"You think it might snow?" The question is lame, and I wince, but the quiet is eating at me. To be fair, it's cold—definitely the coldest night this season.

"Maybe."

My gut drops when that's all he offers.

Seeing our house up ahead, lit up by the single lamp on the porch, my heart stumbles. Not knowing what Sammy's thinking is messing with me. He has every right to be mad, but he's not going to be *mad* mad, right?

When we reach the door, he unlocks it and lets me pass before he closes the door behind us.

And I just stand here, having no clue what to say or do.

"How's your head?" he asks as he unzips his coat.

Right, coat and shoes off. That I can do.

"Okay. I took a painkiller," I admit. "My head's not bad, but I wanted to nip it in the bud before it got worse."

He nods and walks past me into the kitchen. I follow him like a lost lamb, my nerves shot. I'm so not good at dealing with this weird tension thing between us.

Standing in the doorway, I watch as he opens the fridge and grabs an armful of snacks and two bottles of water. Apparently done, he knocks the door closed with his hip, then walks past me again.

The second his foot plants down on the first step, he glances my way. "Coming?"

My nod is fast, my feet swift as I follow him up.

What I could be doing is telling him what happened, apologizing again—because I am legit so sorry, ashamed even, especially doing that, *saying* that in the locker room. In public.

But something keeps me quiet. Maybe a little worry, since I can't read him. But also, there's something about the set of his shoulders, his composure that tells me he needs me to let him take the lead on this.

As soon as we're in our room, Sammy sits on the bed, leaning against the headboard. Fresh nerves spring to life in my stomach. He surprises me by passing me one of the water bottles.

"Drink this and come sit."

I do so, taking a position opposite him, the weird combination of snacks spread out between us. He's always hungry after a game, so the food's not a surprise. What is a surprise is that he's not yet tucking in. Instead, his gaze is on me.

"What happened?"

Taking a deep breath, I launch into telling him as precisely as possible what happened and what was said. Sammy listens attentively, flashes of emotion occasionally appearing before he dons a more neutral expression.

"… I fucked up when I lost it." I shake my head. "Saying all that in the locker room where people can hear…. Sammy, I'm so sorry. The last thing I ever want to do is break your trust."

"Drink some water."

"Huh?" Okay, I'm confused.

"You need to hydrate, so please drink some water."

I have no idea what's going on or why he's so insistent about my H_2O needs, but okay…. I take a healthy swig and gulp the contents. The cool liquid soothes my dry throat. Apparently, I was thirsty, and I have done a lot of talking. A lot more than normal.

When I'm done, I throw the bottle into the trash can. It sinks in, but my usual lip twitch doesn't come. My shoulders sag a little with relief that I've told Sammy the truth and apologized.

I don't recall a time I've ever been so worked up before. So fucking angry.

A shaky breath later, and I peer over at Sammy. His gaze is on me, assessing and still quiet.

"So…." I trail off, not knowing where to go next or what to say. All I'm certain of is that his silence is freaking me out.

One arched eyebrow is the first real reaction I get. It's a total Sammy move.

"Are you still under a three?"

What the…?

He dips his head pointedly, indicating he wants an answer.

"Yeah." I nod, wings taking flight in my stomach and having a grand old time while I'm wondering if he's serious.

"Take off your clothes, sweetheart."

Holy fuck. That's a yes, then.

There's zero finesse as I strip. My cock throbs as I stand naked before him. He eyes me lazily before he moves off the bed, taking the snacks with him and dumping them on the desk.

I jump when he touches my back. Firm, warm fingers travel down my spine. Sweet kisses follow. With a needy whimper, I drop my head back, finding purchase on his shoulder.

"Do you forgive me?" I whisper.

In answer, he steps closer to my body, his covered groin rubbing against my ass, hard and big. Next, he sweeps his hands over my chest, trailing fingers up to my neck. Taking hold of my face, he angles me, lifting it and moving me slightly. His lips descend on mine.

Slow, hot kisses, scorching enough to burn, press against me. We kiss until I struggle for air, still so painfully, deliciously slow as our lips glide, tongues tangling.

It's wet, messy, and so possessive, I feel owned.

The sensation ripples through me with the ferocity of wildfire with a strong wind, thickening my cock and making my knees weak.

It's no good. I need air.

I pull away, gasping for breath. Wrecked. Sammy's wrecking me so completely, and God, I want him to do that so throughly that everything but us… together… at this moment… turns to cinders.

"Get on the bed, on your back."

Holy fuck.

The gravel in his voice gets me moving. In bed, Sammy's never like this. Needy for sure, but I tend to take control, delighting in unraveling and taming his mind from his millions of thoughts.

God, I am so here for this moment.

Once again, he arches that sexy eyebrow at me. It's all a challenge, and I realize I'm still a panting, trembling mess.

"Right, on the bed, on my back. Got it."

His lips twitch. The movement is subtle, but it's all it takes for the stranglehold on my heart to release.

We're going to be okay.

The certainty and relief have me moving. With my back down and cock rigid, my fingers twitch to do… something. Anything. My dick's *right there,* weeping and desperate.

"Don't you dare."

My hand freezes, and a shaky breath punches out of me.

Jesus, Sammy's good at this.

Our eye contact remains steady and intense as he undresses. It continues when he pulls out the lube.

My breath hitches when he climbs on top and straddles me. His skin is warm, dark, fucking beautiful. Gripping his waist, I allow the feel of him to settle over me.

Firm and smooth. Strong and silky soft. I'm so caught up in sensation, his "Give me your hand" startles me.

I hold out my left hand and shiver when he drips lube over my fingers. A drop of the cool liquid falls on my stomach as he rises, saying, "Get me ready, sweetheart."

Oh, fuck.

A pulse of my cock, and I grab the base quickly. My hold's firm, my breaths sawing out of me with a speed that makes my head spin.

Sammy's eyes flare. Yeah, I totally almost blew while getting my fingers slick, ready to fingerfuck my husband. Heat blooms in my chest, catching his attention.

"You good, or do you need me to do it?" Amusement colors his tone, a reassuring balm to my soul.

It's oh so tempting to sit back and watch him prepare himself. Is it more likely that I'll blow with him doing it or me? I don't have time to debate. Instead, I take action.

Still gripping my cock to attempt to keep myself in check, I encourage him to scoot forward and lift up for me. My slick fingers find his hole immediately, one of them sliding in with an ease that has me biting my lip and looking at him in contemplation.

"Did you put fingers in yourself when you showered?" Gravel coats my words, the visual close to fucking me over and making me come.

He bears down on my finger as I work it in and out of him. Clamping down on his bottom lip, he nods before releasing the pink flesh, saying, "Yeah. I think you can slip three right on in there before I fuck your fat dick."

"Jesus." My hips jerk.

My mind pores over his words and the visuals, wondering when he got such a dirty mouth on him, even as I do exactly what he says. Three fingers slip inside, past his ring of muscle. I go slow, continuing to ease inside as he grunts and drops his head, hands pressing against my chest.

"Fuck, okay, quick. I need your cock."

I dip in and out, twisting, reaching out with my middle finger to brush against his prostate. His cock jerks, his eyes closing, and a deep, guttural moan flies free as I do it again and again.

"Fuck, okay, stop."

I freeze immediately and ease out when he pulls away. A second later, he knocks away my hand, takes hold of my cock, positions it at his entrance, and eases down on me.

Fighting to keep my eyes open, I gasp at the sensation of being wrapped in his hot channel. With parted lips, he looks so desperate and hot. A whimper escapes as he bottoms out and stills.

It takes everything not to fuck into him. But we both need to reset. Me especially, as the tingle in my balls is going to be my undoing far too quickly.

We're breathing heavily and remain still until Sammy opens his eyes and stares down at me. When his palms return to my chest, he rises slowly before easing down with a wisp of a moan. He does it again and again.

Fucking me.

Owning me.

"You went to battle for me." The words are choppy as he speaks, sinking down on me, strangling my dick with a perfect grip.

Surprise that he's speaking about this, now of all times, slams into me. But I'm quick to respond. "Yeah. Always."

"That's so fucking hot." A slow lift up, and he gently swirls his hips before his ass touches my balls.

"Fuck," I groan. "It is?"

"Yeah, sweetheart."

I grab hold of his shoulder and drag him close, capturing his lips with a gravelly groan. The kiss is hungry, almost sloppy, with the desperation urging me to fuck him, climb into his body, and never leave.

Unable to take any more, my control snaps, crumbling away like brittle leaves in the grip of an unforgiving wind. I grasp his hips and thrust into him in earnest.

He rasps out my name. "Bentley, fuck… yes. I've needed you so fucking badly."

I'm almost brutal, picking up a punching pace as loud, earth-shattering moans free-fall from his parted lips.

"I need you to come," I demand, so close to losing control completely. I need him to spill. Need the evidence of his passion to soak my skin.

A hoarse cry escapes Sammy when I grip his cock and stroke him. The movements are fast and tight with a small twist at the end. Just how he likes it. Exactly what he needs to fly.

A ribbon of cum flies free, landing in a splash on my stomach. His groan is feral as his body shakes, gripping my cock so tightly, I gasp.

Another strip paints my chest. I slow my hand, milking every last drop, and I follow him over. My orgasm punches out of me, taking me by surprise with its speed and ferocity.

A low growl tears past my lips from deep in my chest.

Tensing, I drive into him, Sammy's soft gasps in sync with each shot of my cum coating his walls.

"Fuck." I push up, wrapping my arms around him, clinging to Sammy as a final shudder ripples through my wrecked body.

Tightening his arms around me, Sammy kisses me. It's sweet and lingering as we struggle to take full breaths, but we don't stop as we mold against each other, each stroke of our tongues drugging.

We slow, easing back in short bursts, not quite ready to part, my cock still nestled inside him.

"Thank you for loving me." The tenderness in Sammy's voice takes me by surprise.

Leaning back to properly see his face, I cup his cheek. "You never need to thank me for that. I'll love you forever."

He swallows hard, emotion playing out on his face.

"Do you forgive me?"

"You never need to ask me to forgive you when you're trying to protect me," he says, turning my words back on me.

Relief unfurls fully in my chest. It settles there like a warm embrace.

"Did you know, when you were knocked uncon-scious, I was this close"—he holds his thumb and pointer finger an inch apart—"to kicking that twat's ass?"

Wide-eyed, I stare at Sammy, my heartbeat quick-ening. "I didn't know that."

My dick twitches, and I drag my lips between my teeth to stop smirking.

That doesn't stop Sammy, though. "You like that, huh?" Amusement twinkles in his eyes, spreading across his face like sunlight breaking through clouds. A soft chuckle escapes his lips, the sound playful, carefree. His grin widens, infectious in its warmth.

"Yeah, it's probably fucked-up that when I heard what you were saying, my dick got hard."

A startled laugh escapes me.

"Don't get me wrong, it threw me for a loop… and Ty was right there."

I wince. "Fuck. I'm sorry." It's what I suspected. Having it confirmed is like a brick dropping in my gut.

"It's okay. It happened." He shifts on my lap, discomfort morphing his features.

I ease back carefully as he lifts up. A groan passes his lips, my already thickening cock not helping at all. Once off me, Sammy all but falls to my side. Unable to resist when he's peering up at me so blissed out, I kiss him. It's soft and lazy, not working up to anything.

After a few tender presses of my lips to his, I ease away. "Let me grab the wet wipes."

I make quick work of pulling them out of the drawer next to our bed, then wipe Sammy's ass and cock carefully. He lets me with a soft smile and heat in his cheeks. Once I clean my dick and stomach, I throw the wipes in the trash can and scoot down beside him, tugging the rumpled covers over us.

"I had all the plans for you tonight," he says.

We're face-to-face, heads on just one pillow.

"I know." I brush my finger over his bottom lip. "I'm more than satisfied."

Tonight's been a lot. Emotionally, I think we're both wrecked.

"How's your head?"

There's no throbbing, but I'm tired. The physical exertion has worn me down. "Okay." A yawn breaks free, and I'm quick to cover my mouth.

"Let me get the light, and we'll sleep."

My eyes have already slipped closed as exhaustion presses down on me. I think I nod and feel him move before sleep takes me.

CHAPTER 25

SAMMY

"WHAT THE FUCK?"

The sun's not up. I may have even only just closed my eyes.

Another round of knocking—a little heavier than the sound that dragged me from sleep.

"What?" I call out. There's light visible under the crack of the door, shadowed feet obvious.

When there's no response, I sigh just as Bentley rustles at my side.

"What's going on? Time is it?"

"Fuck knows," I grumble.

I clamber out of bed and flick on the lamp, since we're both apparently awake at—my eyes widen as I look at my phone—4:27 a.m.

"The building better be on fire." I tug on a pair of sweatpants and unlock our door.

I don't get the chance to open it before Ty's barging in, his eyes almost wild.

"Why don't you come on in?" I don't hold back the snark.

I go to close the door but stop when I see Logan. He looks wrecked, and not in a just-fucked way. He's bleary-eyed. He also winces when we make eye contact.

"I'm so fucking sorry. I tried to get him to wait until the sun came up, but he hasn't slept."

Jesus. "Okay." I glance back in the room. Bentley's up, looking confused as hell. The bedsheets are low at his waist. The trail of hair leading to my happy place is ripe for the viewing. "New plan," I snap, turning to Ty. "Make coffee. We'll be down in two minutes."

Parting his lips, Ty looks ready to argue. Thankfully, Logan steps to my side. "Tyron, come on. Let them get dressed and wake up. They'll be down soon, yeah?"

"Fine." Ty huffs as he stands.

I keep my mouth shut, not wanting to get into anything with him right now. Ty, the genius that he is, can become almost manic when he's fixated on something.

Shit.

What exactly has kept him awake is pretty fucking obvious.

Defeated, I say, "Two minutes," as I make eye contact with him.

His expression softens. "Okay."

I'm quick to close the door. As soon as it's shut, Bentley's out of bed.

"This is all my fault. Fuck, baby, I'm sorry."

I wave him off as I look for my hoodie. The chill in the air pebbles my skin. None of us should be awake at this time to feel this level of cold.

No longer freezing my butt off, I step up to Bentley. "I meant what I said last night, okay?"

Exiting the shower at the same time as Ty, and then stumbling upon Bentley losing his shit on the phone, I'd been confused, then startled. It hadn't taken long to realize he was on my phone and who he was talking to.

The world around me had shifted a little, but what kept me grounded was Bentley. His voice. His words. The absolute conviction in his brutal defense of me.

Getting him home to fuck him, the desperation to show him what his words, his actions meant to me, had kept me silent. Seriously, none of my teammates would have been happy if I'd pushed him onto the bench and fucked him right there.

"Okay," he finally says, a breath huffing out of him.

A featherlight kiss later, and I pass him a hoodie to pull on. Dressed, we head out, tiptoeing down the staircase.

All of the doors are closed. I have no idea if the rest of our housemates are asleep or awake and wondering what's going on. Either way, I don't want a bigger audience for this.

Logan's next to the coffee machine, four mugs out while he waits for it to brew. His smile is soft, apologetic.

He knows.

Ty's at the kitchen table, gaze snapping up as soon as Bentley and I step inside and join him.

"Your dad's parole—"

"Trevin," I cut in. He stopped being my dad a long, long time ago. Something I made as official as possible when I turned eighteen and legally changed my last name to match my parents' and siblings'.

Ty's frown relaxes as he nods. "Trevin's early parole hearing is tomorrow morning."

"That's right." I don't even question how he knows this. This is Ty. He's going to make a kick-ass agent one day, and honestly, the day he gets sworn in, I'll feel safer for it.

The hiss of the coffee dripping into the pot fills the void. Its scent is strong, filling the kitchen.

"You were one of the teenagers he hurt?"

Bentley reaches for my hand, and I take it willingly. "Yeah," I answer. "The other was a friend… another player I was hooking up with," I correct, no longer needing to lie.

"The reports say that the attack on your friend was a hate crime."

The banging of my pulse is loud in my head. "Yeah. Trevin found Jamaal sucking me off."

Two lines appear between Ty's eyebrows.

I clarify, "That wasn't reported. Jamaal was out. The only kid in our school."

He nods his understanding, and I take a deep breath, focusing on the gentle strokes of Bentley's thumb on the back of my hand.

"Okay, I understand better now."

Logan places a mug each before me and Bentley. They're made how we like them. Wrapping my hand around the handle, I smile my thanks.

Another appears before Ty, and Logan gently clears his throat. We look his way, and he smiles a little uneasily. "I can go back upstairs."

"It's fine. I don't mind if you stay."

He already knows, and this shit is heavy. Not only to me but to anyone who knows about it.

"Okay." He settles close to Ty.

"And he's threatening you?" Ty asks.

I huff out a breath. "I haven't spoken to him since this past summer when I visited him." If Ty's surprised by that, he doesn't show it. "He asked me to talk to his brothers and told me about his parole hearing. I didn't reach out to his family. Not that I know where they are, but even if I did, I wouldn't."

When Ty's gaze flicks to Bentley, he tells him word for word what Trevin said.

There's a weird bubble in my chest. It feels like a laugh could spill out, inappropriate and truly not funny. But fuck, it's not even five in the morning, yet Ty's gone into full FBI mode, and we're spilling all our secrets with such ease that I honestly don't know how I kept my mouth closed for eight long years.

When Bentley's finished and Ty's peppered him with questions, he asks, "And you haven't been contacted by the parole board?"

"No." I shake my head and explain my theory of why that may be the case.

"Yeah. That makes sense. You weren't viewed as the primary target. Collateral damage."

"Fuck." A huff of laughter breaks free, and I shake my head. "Collateral damage. The story of my life with Trevin."

Bentley draws my attention to him when he lifts my hand and kisses my knuckles.

"So, back to tomorrow," Ty says after taking a gulp of coffee. "How do you feel about speaking to an attorney about revisiting your previous testimony and providing additional information?"

As Bentley squeezes my hand, a surge of unexpected emotions floods through me.

I glance between Ty and Bentley, surprise, fear, and a glimmer of hope battling it out behind my rib cage. The idea of revisiting my previous testimony, of speaking up about what really happened, feels daunting. For so long, I'd buried the truth, convinced that speaking out would only bring trouble.

But Ty's reassurance and Bentley's unwavering support give me a flicker of courage. Can I do this? Anticipation stirs in my chest.

Taking a deep breath, I meet Ty's gaze, feeling the weight of his words. "I… I think I'm scared," I admit, my voice barely above a whisper. "But I also… I want to do this. I want to speak up, to make things right, if I can."

Above all else, I want Trevin to fuck off from my life and rot in jail. Even if he is released, he doesn't have any power over me.

Not anymore.

Ty's expression softens, his eyes filled with understanding. "You don't have to do this alone," he says, his voice steady and reassuring. "I've already set up a meeting for you with an attorney in Tennessee."

Holy shit. How the fuck did he manage that?

"They're good. They're someone who'll listen to you, who'll fight for you. And whatever happens, we'll be right here beside you, every step of the way."

With my heart close to breaking free, I look at Bentley. He nods, letting me know whatever I decide, he's with me.

A spark of determination ignites within me. "When do we need to leave?"

A grin, all pride and approval, brightens Ty's expression.

"An hour to be safe," Logan answers for him.

"I spoke to my pops last night." Ty shrugs, and I know that's his attempt at an apology for interfering. And for this, I can handle him sticking his nose into my business. "He gave me the name of the attorney. He seems to think there may be a way to get in front of a judge and the parole board."

"Really?" His pops is a detective, but not in Tennessee.

"Yeah. He's going to make calls this morning, see what he can do."

The warmth of Bentley's hand is a steady presence. "Okay, and all this before tomorrow?" It doesn't seem possible.

"Yes."

"Fuck, Ty, you're one determined asshole." The words spill out of me with an emotional laugh. I stand, reaching for him to hug the crap out of him.

His grip is tight, reassuring. "We'll make this happen so you can have your say. And whatever happens, you can know you've done your part."

"And a protection order." Bentley stands close. "We need a protection order too."

I step away from Ty, my smile slipping a little. How the hell am I going to pay for an attorney? Not a chance am I asking my parents. They don't have anything to give. That means they'll either feel awful or they'll threaten to sell their car or something.

"How much is this going to cost me?"

"Us." Bentley loops his arm around me.

I swear, if we weren't already married, I'd drop to one knee this very second.

"Not sure. Ballpark is likely $350 an hour."

"Fuck." Okay, I have maybe nine hundred in my account. Perhaps a little more. It'll make eating a challenge, and I'm not sure what a couple hours will get me, but it's at least worth meeting and seeing what he has to say.

"It's fine." Bentley's arm around me tightens as he speaks.

I turn in his arms. "What's that mean?"

"Uhm… we're just going to go shower and dress." Logan shuffles past us, tugging at Ty's arm.

"It means I have the money." He trails his hand down my arm and loops my fingers with his.

"You have potentially thousands of dollars squirreled away?" I track his expression. What I don't miss is his slight wince. "What is it?"

"My parents put money in savings for me. A nest egg, I suppose. It's money to buy a house, furnish an apartment… whatever I might need it for."

"How much?" I probably should immediately be saying, "Hell no," but color me curious.

"They've been saving money every week since I was born." His lips twist before he pulls them between his teeth and finally says, "I think it's somewhere around $222,000. The interest has gone up over the last few years, so it could be more."

Fuck me.

"You have over $200K sitting in a bank?"

Even though he shrugs, red infuses his cheeks. "Yeah. Well, it's in my name, but it's technically our money now, right?"

"No." I shake my head. "Absolutely not."

A stubborn set forms in his jaw, and I narrow my gaze.

"Sammy, you need to hear me. I love you. We need to do this. I'm not prepared for us not to do this. You going through with this, changing your statement, fighting Trevin… you're honestly telling me if you back out now, you won't live to regret it?"

The asshole is right.

"But the money—"

"Is for us to help our future. This right here is more about our future than a house or furniture." He tugs me close and breathes me in. "Is it so hard to admit I'm right?"

I snort, hearing his light amusement. "You sure about this?" Pressing against him even closer, I absorb his quiet, determined strength.

"Abso-fucking-lutely."

With my heart going haywire, I pull away. "Thank you."

"Always." Bright-eyed—as we're most definitely now wide awake—and smiling, Bentley leads me up the stairs.

I can't believe we're really doing this. I have no idea if we can pull this off, but God, I want to try.

IT'S BEEN A LONG-ASS DAY. WHAT'S WORSE IS THAT WE have a session in the gym tomorrow at 7:30 a.m., and Trevin's parole hearing is at 10:00 a.m.

"What time is it?" Bentley asks as we pull up. He drove back since my nerves are shot and exhaustion licks at my heels.

Also, the clock in my car's broken. But once again, she's made the journey to Tennessee and back, so the little bits that are falling apart don't matter so much.

"Just after nine," Logan answers.

Yeah, definitely a long day.

We made the trip with Ty, who shot a group text to our two housemates we'd left behind, letting them know we were heading out of state and we'd be back tonight. Unsurprisingly, at some point after eight this morning, when we were already over the state line, the notifications had started.

In the end, I fired off a message, letting them know the guys were doing me a favor and that I had some family stuff to deal with. I also told them not to worry and to give me time before I discussed things with them.

Kieran had responded immediately, making it clear that he and Leon were there for me—when and if I was ready to talk.

We ate drive-through food on the way back. I'm

not sure about the rest of the guys, but I feel that crappy deadweight from eating too many carbs and grease. None of it sits well in my stomach.

The engine cuts off, and Bentley unclips his seat belt and stretches. "Everyone good?"

There's a low mumble of agreement as we vacate my car. Tiredness shrouds us all. I glance at Ty, wincing when I take in his exhaustion. He didn't sleep at all last night. He managed a couple of hours on the drive back, but those two hours cramped up in my car won't have given him any real reprieve.

"You heading straight to bed?" I ask.

A jaw-cracking yawn escapes Logan. He quickly covers his mouth and starts nodding, finally saying, "Yeah. You need anything?"

"No, thanks."

The lock of my car engages, and I hang back for Bentley, calling out, "Thanks for today," to both of them. Going through this by myself... hell, that wouldn't have happened. I'd been convinced nothing could change. Believed I'd lost my voice a long time ago.

"All good. See you in the morning." Ty salutes us with a heavy hand before heading inside with Logan.

When Bentley reaches my side, he pauses rather than heading straight for the house.

"You knew I wasn't ready to go in yet, huh?"

A tender smile curves his mouth. "I thought you might need a minute. Today's been a lot."

"I'm glad it's over."

He blinks rapidly as if processing my words. "Over?"

"I've done everything I can, right?"

He nods.

"So tomorrow doesn't matter. As far as I'm concerned, it's over."

Emotion flickers to life in the depths of his gaze. I have a second to appreciate it before he hauls me into his arms. I land with a grunt and a laugh.

"Fuck, I love you, baby. Do you know how amazing you are?"

My huff is light, and I roll my eyes. "You're biased, and I'm fine with that."

I choose to ignore the way my lungs fill, happiness unfurling with pride that he feels that way.

"Uh-huh. Fine, but the words are still true." He searches my gaze. "Have you thought more about talking to your parents?"

"I will after the gym in the morning. Before ten."

Fortunately, I don't have classes after training. My afternoon is slammed, though. It's a relief it's panned out this way. Going to the gym and disappearing in the burn is all I'll be able to handle until I hear from Marcus Allen, the attorney who's somehow made so much magic happen today.

"Let me know if you want me there."

"Will do." I glance down at my wrinkled clothes. My suit needs dry cleaning. The shower is also calling my name. "I need to get out of this getup."

"I happen to think you look delicious in your suit." He fingers the lapel of my jacket.

Heat from his compliment winds its way through me, despite me feeling like at any moment I could drop down and fall asleep where I stand.

"You look pretty hot yourself, Mr. Sandford-Hardy."

The moment his brows shoot high, almost touching his hairline, I shrug. It's casual as hell, even though my pulse is racing.

"What? Just trying it on for size."

"You're thinking a double-barreled name?"

It seems that way. "Yeah. You know my parents' name is important to me."

"I do, and I'm more than okay with joining them like that."

"You think Coach will have a hissy fit if we ask him to change our jerseys?" From Bentley's scrunched nose, I'll take that as a yes. "In that case, I think you should ask."

A laugh bursts out of me as he shoves me lightly

before hitching his shoulder under my stomach and picking me up in a firefighter's lift.

A super-masculine squeal escapes me through my snorts of laughter.

"Your head." I tap his ass. Damn, he has a good ass. His glutes are something to be worshipped.

"Is fine," he shouts, walking toward the house.

"This is the best view I've had all day." I squeeze his cheeks for good measure. His glutes tighten in response.

"If that's the case, you can keep your hands on them when you're sucking me off. My gift to you."

My laughter is loud and infectious. I love it when he's like this. Quick and sassy and ridiculously sexy. And that he's carrying me with such ease is pretty damn hot too. We honestly don't do enough of that— me climbing him like a tree, letting him pick me up while he fucks me against a wall.

We need to fix that.

"Whatever you're thinking, yes." He smacks my ass, and I grunt and jerk against him.

My hardening dick presses against him. Now it makes sense how he knows I'm horny. To be fair, it's not like I ever try to hide how he makes me feel.

We enter the house and head straight up the stairs. Kieran offers me an up-nod and a smile, Dean grinning beside him. Leon's in the kitchen doorway, shooting me a smirk and a wink.

This right here is how I want to end all my days.

Okay, not necessarily exactly like this, but it definitely has merit.

Feeling loved and safe while loving with my whole damn heart.

And my friends…. This may be our last year together—just four more months of living in each other's pockets—but they're family. Even when we're scattered all over the country, they'll never feel that far away because I know with just a call, they'll have my back.

And damn straight I'll always have theirs.

Bentley, this fierce, gorgeous, caring man who I somehow convinced to be mine, drops me on the bed and grins down at me. The heat in his gaze is all for me. It's pure fire and love, and I don't plan to be without it ever.

"You ever wonder why everything's so easy between us?"

His lips curve, fingers nimble on my shirt buttons as he says, "Because, babe, we're easy, schmeasy!" He chuckles, eyes sparkling with mischief as he pops open another button. "We're like peanut butter and jelly, cookies and cream—"

"Sushi and apple pie?" For real, they're an epic combo. Don't knock it till you've tried it.

A fond smile forms. "—or sushi and apple pie… just meant to be together. No need to overthink it."

So I don't. Thinking is the last thing I want to do.

Tomorrow, the only thing that matters is us, our future together.

With a breathy sigh, I lift my ass as he unwraps me like the gift I absolutely am. Once he has, I'll make good on yesterday's promise and let him take me in whatever sinful ways he wants to.

EPILOGUE
BENTLEY

"WHAT DO YOU THINK?"

Why this part always makes me nervous is lost on me. Sammy, the supportive asshole husbutt he is, apparently finds it endearing.

It's not. I don't care how many bjs it earns me because I'm being "cute," the process freaks me out.

"Bentley, it's incredible. Seriously."

"Yeah?" The tightness in my voice is obvious.

"Yes." He loops his arm around me, forcing his hand into my back pocket. "Seriously. The design is incredible. The client's going to fucking salivate and throw their money at us so damn fast, we just might be able to get our car serviced at the dealership." He bounces his brows at me.

I snort. "Now, let's not get carried away. Going to Mike's is just fine and will easily save us a grand."

"Hey, dreams are not meant to be destroyed so swiftly." His pout is half-hearted at best. It also looks kinda ridiculous. Okay, and maybe a little hot. He does have the best bottom lip for nibbling and sucking and general all-around kissing.

And when wrapped around my cock, fuck yes. Best lips ever.

I swallow hard. Sammy has a call with Senator Banks in fifteen minutes, so I need to rein my desire in. Since we already shot our loads before coming into the office this morning, it's doubtful I'll be able to come so quickly again.

Age has that effect. Not that thirty-five is old. Far fucking from it. But when it comes to coming, yeah, at least a five-hour break is needed if the mission is a fast release.

"Dude, why's your dick hard?"

"Hmm, what?"

He shoots me his "don't 'hmm, what' me" look.

"Nothing. It'll go down in a minute. Keep talking."

"About what? About how *tight* I think the space is there, right next to the *rear opening*." A megawatt smile quickly forms as he points at the back door of the house on the half-acre property we're land-scaping.

"I think we'll need to go *slow* with the *insertion* of the pieces they want around the herb garden."

"You're an asshole." A rush of gratitude has me happy sighing and pressing a kiss to his temple. That we're able to do this together is one of the best decisions we ever made.

Not that it was easy to get to this point.

After Trevin was denied early parole, life eased up a bit, but when it was time for Sammy to figure out what to do with his business degree, life became a challenge.

He struggled there for a while—as in almost three torturous years of him being miserable, locked away in offices that slowly sucked out his soul. The only positive is that along the way, he learned and gained genuine experience. We were lucky that his misery at least meant he earned enough money that we could put a deposit—*thanks, Mom and Dad*—on a small condo and afford the monthly repayments.

It was then, almost at the same time as Trevin's release—when I worried for a moment there that Sammy would lose himself a little—that Grady offered him a position. Yeah, I was still working for him back then.

We were just fortunate Grady's such a good guy that he let me venture into design rather than always being on the ground with a tool in my hand.

And Sammy, well, my talented husband found his calling.

Working on pricing jobs, sweet-talking clients, and wrangling outside contractors, the man's skills are limitless. It made sense that four years ago, we bought Grady out.

Again, talk about another poignant moment. Just as Grady announced his retirement, asking if we wanted to buy him out, we also got word of Trevin's death. It was a bittersweet time. But putting that part of Sammy's life completely to rest, I don't know, it kinda made the decision to buy the business crystal clear to us.

Owning our own business can be tricky, but the rewards are worth it, and this particular job is pretty major. It's for a local politician, Senator Banks. We latched on to the whole support-local and celebrate-diversity vibe she has going on. Well, *that* and we need the work.

But this project is going to appear in a national magazine, so yeah, if she loves it, if we pull this off, it's going to be a game-changer for us.

"And you think the veggie garden works?" I worry my bottom lip, taking a look at the plans for the millionth time.

"It's perfect there. Completely uptown-chic-meets-farm-to-table vibe." Even though he's teasing, he's not wrong. "Honestly, sweetheart," he says, turning me into him so we face each other. And yes, all these years later, I still melt every time that endearment slips past his lips.

I think the first time it happened was the moment that changed everything.

There's been no looking back since.

"The design is perfect. The last two modifications have nailed her vision. We'll just walk her through them together, then tomorrow, prepare ourselves for the camera crew coming around."

A camera crew is a good thing. I know it is. There's a whole video documentary paired with the magazine spread. What did I say about Sammy finding his calling? This is it.

As soon as he discovered the senator was in the market for a landscaper, he put together this whole marketing pitch. Talked to the magazine. Even got in with her PR firm. Sure, at college, he'd taken a couple of marketing-esque classes, and from what I remember, he'd enjoyed them, but combined with the business side of things, something just clicked for him.

But still, the two of us together in front of the camera makes me sweat.

"We're going to nail it, yeah?"

I bob my head. There are only a few times he's led me wrong… though usually that was on the way to a good time. But never in business. Never when it impacts our livelihood.

"Yeah, I know." I reluctantly pull away. At least my cock's behaving. "Do you have everything you need for the call?"

Rather than rolling his eyes at my anxiety and pestering, he nods. "I do. Everything's ready."

"Okay."

And that's the thing: everything will always be okay. Even in the lows—the money problems, the bickering about whose turn it is to do laundry—and the highs—spending time together shooting hoops or going to the archery club—we're in this together.

The phone rings, and with a deep breath, I nod at Sammy, letting him know I'm ready.

With a grin, he answers the call: "ES Landscapes, Sammy speaking."

I can't believe the series is over. What a bitter sweet feeling. I've adored writing both the Zone Defense and Fast Break series so much. Be sure to check out the bonus scenes where Bentley Tells His Parents and when Sammy Receives Parole News. See the next page for more.

TWO FUN BONUS SCENE TO CHECK OUT

1. Want to see the emotional scene where Bentley tells his parents about his sexuality and his marriage?

This is a Ream exclusive. The great news is it's available to followers (free to follow) and all tiers.

If you do select one of the subscription tiers on Ream, more great news is there are lots of exclusive bonus scenes to come.

HTTPS://REAMSTORIES.COM/BECCASEYMOUR

2. Do you want to see Sammy's reaction when he receives news about Trevin's parole hearing?

There are two ways to get access. One is via the pinned link in my Facebook group .

HTTPS://WWW.FACEBOOK.COM/GROUPS/ROMMANCEWITHBECCALOUISA/

The other is for newsletter subscribers.

HTTPS://BOOKHIP.COM/NAMZNCM

ABOUT THE AUTHOR

I live and breathe all things book related. Usually with at least three books being read and two WiPs being written at the same time, life is merrily hectic. I tend to do nothing by halves, so I happily seek the craziness and busyness life offers.

Living on my small property in Queensland with my human family as well as my animal family of cows, sheep, chooks, and dogs, I really do appreciate the beauty of the world around me and am a believer that love truly is love.

To check for updates head to my website:
https://beccaseymour.com
Join my newsletter:
https://landing.mailerlite.com/webforms/landing/r9f0i4
Plus, join my Facebook group:
https://www.facebook.com/groups/rommancewithbeccalouisa/

facebook.com / beccaseymourauthor

x.com / beccaseymour_

instagram.com / authorbeccaseymour

bookbub.com / authors / becca-seymour

tiktok.com / @beccaseymourwrites

reamstories.com / beccaseymour

www.ingramcontent.com/pod-product-compliance
Lightning Source LLC
Chambersburg PA
CBHW050956210726
48287CB00004B/1255